A compulsive traveller, occasional scuba diver and incurable beginner saxophonist, Charles Benoit has worked in education and advertising. He and his wife, Rose, currently live in Rochester, New York. *Out of Order* is his second novel, following the highly acclaimed *Relative Danger*.

# OUT OF ORDER

Jason Talley lives in Corning, New York. His friends are Sriram Sundaram and his wife, Vidya. But after Sriram confides he's planning to return to India, the next evening the couple are dead — the cops call it murder-suicide. Jason decides to fulfil Sriram's quest and books himself a trip to India. Travelling, he meets Rachel, and together, they embark on a journey into danger . . . Sriram was a computer genius who had sold out his colleagues, and Jason has sent details of his trip to Sriram's e-mail list, hoping to meet up with Sriram's past. But when he does . . .

*Books by Charles Benoit*
*Published by The House of Ulverscroft:*

RELATIVE DANGER

CHARLES BENOIT

# OUT OF ORDER

*Complete and Unabridged*

# ULVERSCROFT
*Leicester*

First published in Great Britain in 2006 by
Robert Hale Limited
London

First Large Print Edition
published 2007
by arrangement with
Robert Hale Limited
London

British Library CIP Data

Benoit, Charles
  Out of order.—Large print ed.—
  Ulverscroft large print series: adventure & suspense
  1. Mortgage banks—New York (State)—New York—
  Employees—Travel—Fiction 2. Americans—India—
  Fiction 3. India—Fiction 4. Suspense fiction
  5. Large type books
  I. Title
  813.6 [F]

  ISBN 978–1–84617–856–6

Published by
F. A. Thorpe (Publishing)
Anstey, Leicestershire

Set by Words & Graphics Ltd.
Anstey, Leicestershire
Printed and bound in Great Britain by
T. J. International Ltd., Padstow, Cornwall

This book is printed on acid-free paper

To Rose
*Ahcha maahi ve*

# Thanks

To Ed and Jo Benoit for the support, the cheerleading and the wine, to Merle for showing me how to make every day an adventure, to my sisters — Helen, Barb, Anna and Teresa — for the inspiration, to Ike and Lydia Tischler for foolishly letting your daughter marry me and to John and Karen who let her be the middle child, to Rick and Paula (and all the Roths) for knowing me so well and still letting me hang around, to Robert Rosenwald and Barbara Peters and the Poisoned Pen Press Posse for making dreams come true, to Kuwait's Top Floor Tiki Bar regulars for the industrial solvents, to Delicia for being so unpredictable, to Chuck Murrman for being such a mellow traveling companion (sorry about the monkeys), and to Mike 'Let's go Bowling' Schwabl and the entire crew at Dixon Schwabl Advertising — you really do make it happen.

Lots of folks worked to make this a better book — Dr. Lou Boxer, Margaret Watson, Carol 'Mom' Roth, Jyoti and Sridhar Moorthy, and countless members of the India Railways Fan Club. If I got it right it's because of their help, if it's wrong it's all me.

# 1

Jason Talley tightened his fingers on the handle and prodded with the point of the knife, looking for signs of life. He held the blade ready, his nerves tensed to react to any movement. Across the room Vidya Sundaram narrowed her almond-shaped eyes, a thin white smile peeking out between her red lips.

'Go ahead, smart ass,' she said, half whisper, half growl. 'Make fun of my cooking and see if I ever invite you up again.'

Jason continued to poke the pan-seared, gelatinous cube with his knife. 'I'm not making fun,' he said without looking up. 'I'm just curious.'

'The problem with our friend here,' Sriram Sundaram said, waving his fork in Jason's direction, 'is that he is too picky. Look at me. Do you ever see me shy away from any of my wife's cooking? No sir, not one bit. And does it bother me that a good south Indian girl prefers to cook like she's a Rajasthani princess, with all those thick sauces and spiced yogurt? Dig in, Jason. If it doesn't kill you it will make you stronger.'

'And you be careful too, my sweet,' Vidya

1

said as she sat down next to her husband. 'I might decide to try Mexican cooking next.'

Jason pushed the edge of his knife into the top of the cube, which split open to reveal a smooth light tan interior. 'Is it chicken?'

'It's sheep's brain,' Vidya said, smiling as Jason's mouth dropped open. 'It's tofu, you silly ass,' she added. 'You had it last week.'

'You said it was chicken.'

'I tell you everything is chicken.' She closed her eyes for a silent moment of prayer before stabbing into a pile of peas with her fork.

Jason inched a sliver of the sheep's brain/tofu around his plate. 'Next week why don't we plan on dinner at my place. I'll cook for a change.'

Vidya and Sriram concentrated on their food, each trying to outlast the other. Sriram broke first, his loud laugh startling the cat off the sofa in the adjoining room. Vidya clapped her hands together as tears welled up in her large, dark eyes.

'What? I can cook.'

'And you can order pizza, too,' Sriram said, slapping the corner of the table. 'You fill two recycling bins each and every week with those big boxes from Salvador's.'

Vidya dabbed her eyes on a blue cloth napkin. 'We were beginning to think you had a crush on the delivery boy.'

'Very funny.' Jason skewered a larger piece of tofu as he spoke. Like every meal at the Sundarams', one taste led quickly to a second helping. 'I happen to like pizza.'

It was Vidya's turn to laugh, her voice rising and falling with a musical cadence that Jason found both exotic and alluring. 'What you like, my dear, is the fact that all you have to do is pick up the phone. In twenty minutes there it is, right at your door. It's wonderfully predictable and it fits nicely into your schedule.' The way she pronounced *schedule* — dropping the c and d and adding a z — gave an Oxford flair to her Indian lilt.

'You should see his day planner,' Sriram said, opening a can of Odenbach lager with one hand. 'Every moment of every day accounted for. The man is a model of efficiency.' He opened a second can and handed it to Jason.

'Guys, it's not like that,' he said and took a long pull on his beer, the pungent spices having their usual effect on his vanilla-based taste buds. 'I just like to have things planned out. It makes the day a lot easier if you know what's coming next. In my job if you're not organized you can miss one step and if you miss one step then the whole file is messed up and the loan never closes. Besides,' he added after another sip, 'you're a freakin' computer programmer so don't tell me you don't like things orderly.'

'Order has nothing to do with it. What makes us tick is the irrational and disorderly. And the truth is, I am not a programmer. I am a wizard. I make the impossible, possible.'

'Oh god, you had to get him started.' Vidya rolled her eyes.

Sriram ignored the interruption. 'The owner and I, we've been developing a new computer chip, all top-secret stuff. Nothing so revolutionary as the company propaganda would have you believe, but quite helpful for a few key niche markets. Trust me, it's magic.'

'Sure. I finally get a laptop and you're ready to introduce the next generation. I'll be obsolete by the end of spring.'

'It's not the next generation,' Sriram said, waving his fork like he was conducting a tableside orchestra. 'It's just a profitable little second-cousin that will make its mark on the current computer generation. And it all fits in a chip no bigger than a postage stamp.'

'Domestic or air mail?' Vidya said, opening her own beer.

'Well, congratulations, Sriram.' Jason raised his half-empty beer in salute. 'I bet the boss is quite pleased with you.'

Sriram and Vidya exchanged glances, their

smiles leveling for a second but returning twice as wide. 'Oh I think he'll be quite surprised,' Sriram said, returning the beer-can toast.

Like everyone else in Corning, New York, Jason knew the story behind Raj-Tech, how Ravi Murty, an American-born Indian, using funds earmarked to lure computer-based industries to rural parts of the state, had opened shop five years ago. Building a specially designed plant in a tax-free zone, he had convinced the local government to underwrite most of the operating cost, with as yet unrealized promises of jobs and economic windfall. Many in the community had begun to doubt Murty's claims but Jason remained hopeful that the plant would spark a long-overdue local recovery.

'It's amazing,' Jason said, dishing out a tofu-laden second helping. 'You grew up way over in India, I grew up ten miles down the road, and here we are, having dinner at your apartment. And it's all because of your job. You ever wonder how your life would be different if you hadn't met Mr Murty in college?'

Sriram nodded. 'I think about that all the time.'

'You could still be living in India instead of in America. I'd call that lucky.'

5

Sriram considered the idea and after draining his beer said, 'Yes, I guess you would say that.'

'Okay, enough shop talk.' Vidya jumped up from her seat. Dressed in black jeans and a gray sweatshirt she looked more like a co-ed than a thirty-year-old substitute teacher, her degrees in classical Indian literature from an unpronounceable university more of a résumé liability than an asset. 'I have two choices for dessert. The first is keer, a soupy rice pudding based on a recipe I learned from an old blind woman from Jaisalmer. The second is an apple pie I picked up at the supermarket this afternoon.'

Sriram leaned back in his chair till he was balancing on two creaking legs. 'My dear, you are wasting your breath. Bring Mr All-American his over-processed, chemically enhanced apple pie and bring your loving husband enough keer to make me seriously think about getting a membership at the health club.' He patted his stomach, the soft base of a future beer belly already in place.

'If I knew that's all it took to get you to join a gym I would have made keer ages ago,' Vidya said, kissing her husband on the forehead before returning to the kitchen.

'Please note,' Sriram winked at Jason, 'the clever use of the verb 'think' in that sentence.'

Two hours and three cups of herbal tea later, Jason stretched his arms above his head and stood to leave. With the entire couch now to itself — not just the three quarters it had claimed when it leapt down from the windowsill — Bindi, Vidya's gray and white cat, mimicked Jason's stretch, adding a haughty tail flick.

'You should get a cat.' Sriram bent down to scratch behind Bindi's ears. 'Women trust men who have cats, a real sign that they are secure in their manhood,' he said before heading to the kitchen.

'I don't think a cat and I would get along.' Jason watched the cat watch him, its green eyes locked on his.

'He couldn't tolerate a cat like Bindi.' Vidya gave a dismissive wave. 'Far too independent and absolutely can not be trained. You couldn't take the ambiguity that comes with a cat.'

'Actually the cat wouldn't tolerate him,' Sriram said from the kitchen. 'Not with his mind-numbing predictability. Cats need mental stimulation. Living with Jason would be like watching paint dry. The poor thing would go batty.' The white plastic bag made a loud sucking sound as Sriram pulled it free from the tall garbage can.

'I hate to disappoint you both by being so predictable,' Jason said, checking his watch against the digital display on the DVD player, 'but I got to head downstairs. Tomorrow's the last day to get loans packaged for closing this month and every real estate agent for a hundred miles around will be calling.'

'You should quit that job,' Sriram said over the noise he made in the kitchen. 'If they haven't noticed you by now they never will. And what's the best they could do for you, some dead-end middle management position in the same office? You have a degree . . . '

'Just an associate's,' Jason said.

' . . . and you are a hard worker,' Sriram said, ignoring the self-depreciating comment. 'Get a job with some multi-path mobility options that maximizes your earning and productivity potential.'

'Does he always talk like that?' Jason said to Vidya.

'Sad but true. You should hear it when he tries to get romantic.'

'Maybe I should apply for a job at Raj-Tech,' Jason said. 'Use you as a reference.'

Sriram's booming laugh echoed off the kitchen's tin cabinets. 'You don't want to do that.'

'Perhaps Jason is happy where he's at,

Sriram. He is, after all, the only male in the office of what, fifteen women?'

'Ten,' Jason corrected. 'And if I was looking for a pear-shaped, middle-aged woman with two or more kids, I'd be in heaven. Any good-looking young women at Raj-Tech?'

'No, just devilishly handsome men like Sriram.' Vidya looked towards the kitchen. 'And as for you, don't think you're going empty handed.' She reached around into the kitchen and retrieved a shopping bag filled with a half dozen Tupperware bowls of various sizes and shapes.

'Vidya, I still have the containers from last week.'

'Do you have any idea how many extra containers a determined Indian housewife can fit in one kitchen?' she said, spinning the bag shut and tying it with a flick of the wrist as she walked across the room. She hung the bag's handles over Jason's wrist and planted a quick kiss on the cheek. 'Thank you for enduring yet another one of my culinary adventures.'

Jason shifted the bag to his fingers, wrapped his free arm around her narrow shoulders and gave her a hug. 'Vidya, if it wasn't for you I might have starved to death months ago.'

'What's this, what's this?' Sriram said. 'My

wife and my dear friend cavorting in my very own living room? Have you no shame? Get a hotel room like all respectable adulterers.' He held two trash bags closed in his fists, a smaller bag tucked under his arm. 'At least be so kind as to get the door for me.' He pointed with his dimpled chin.

Jason gave Vidya's shoulders one last squeeze, then held the door open as Sriram edged past blowing kisses to his wife. 'Don't lock me out, dearest.'

'Too late,' she said with a laugh and shut the door.

The apartment building, identical to every building in the complex, consisted of four units — two one-bedroom apartments on the left-hand side and two two-bedroom apartments on the right. Across the hall from the Sundarams' large second-floor apartment, Mrs Dettori was already asleep. An ancient woman who lived alone, Mrs Dettori spent much of her day watching television, the volume so loud it rattled the lone picture frame on Jason's living room wall. Down the split-level flight of hallway stairs, the garden view apartments looked out into the roots and twisted trunks of the thick yews that ringed each building in the complex. In the winter, when the snow drifted up every vertical surface, it could be months before low-angled natural light shone through the windows. The basement apartment across the hall — two bedrooms and almost twice as expensive — was vacant.

Jason went down the stairs first, setting the bag of leftovers by his apartment before pushing open the spring-loaded metal fire door that led to the building's coin-operated washing machines and trash containers. Sriram followed behind, letting the heavy door bounce once against the white garbage bag before it closed behind him. Jason held open the lid of the chest-high container while Sriram swung first one then the other trash bag up and inside, the small bag under his arm dropping to the floor. Jason scooped the bag up off the floor, banking it off the row of humming electric meters and into the still open trashcan.

'Hey, watch it.' Sriram snatched the bag out as soon as it landed. 'This is expensive.'

'What? It's *special* garbage?'

Sriram held the bag up to the light, checking to ensure that no grime from the trashcan stuck to the plastic. 'This is not garbage, it's a gift for my mother.'

'So what are you doing taking it out with the trash?'

Satisfied the bag was still clean, he said, 'I'm not throwing it out, I'm sneaking it out.'

'Of your own house?'

'I don't want to get Vidya upset. If she sees it she'll be crying all night.'

Jason shook his head. 'She's jealous of your mother? That's weird.'

'She's not jealous, you idiot. If Vidya sees this, she'll know that I'm going to India. She gets very upset when we are separated like that.'

Jason put on his most sarcastic smile. 'Gee, won't she know eventually? She's a bright woman. She'll catch on after, oh, a couple days.'

'Yes, I'm going to tell her. Tomorrow. But if she sees it tonight . . . ' He shook his head to indicate the trouble it would cause.

'So what are you going to do, leave it here in the basement?'

Sriram rolled his eyes. 'Yes, I'm going to stuff a specially woven, hand-embroidered gift behind the dryer. Here,' he said, holding the bag out to Jason. 'Hold on to this for me until tomorrow night.'

'Can't you just hide it in your apartment?'

'Can't you just not be an ass? Here.' Sriram gave the bag a shake.

Jason sighed as he took the bag. 'What is it anyway?' he said, peering inside.

'It's a sari,' Sriram said. 'It's what women wear in India.'

Inside the bag Jason could see a tightly wound bundle of rich, red fabric with thin lines of an intricate gold and silver embroidery just visible on the edge. He didn't want to be in the middle of a domestic deception, helping a husband hide things from his wife, afraid of losing the friendship of either. 'Do you really have to go all the way to India? Wouldn't it be simpler just to mail it? What would it cost, like twenty bucks, maybe fifty if you Fed Ex-ed it?'

Sriram looked up at the ceiling, his hands coming up to cover his face then dropping back down to his sides. 'Not everything in life is so simple, Jason. I don't expect you to understand, but this is an important Hindi tradition and it absolutely must be hand delivered. Vidya would agree — I must take this to India.'

'Why doesn't she go with you? I'm sure the school district could get by with one less substitute for a while.'

'It's something I must do alone. Part of the tradition. Sons go to great lengths to hide the sari from sight, never letting on to anyone where he's hidden it, never telling anyone about it.'

'But you're telling me all about it. Don't I count?'

Sriram didn't say anything but smiled in a

way that Jason could read many ways. Jason looked at the package, 'Well, if it's that important to you . . . '

'It is truly that important to me.'

'Just make sure you get it tomorrow and don't tell Vidya I had it.' Jason turned to open the service room door.

'You have my word, my friend,' Sriram said. 'I will never tell a soul. Just be sure that you do the same.'

# 2

When Jason Talley saw the police cars in the parking lot in front of his apartment building the first thing he thought about was his bathroom window.

That morning after showering he had opened the lone window over the tub, the wet, steamy air forced out as the cold spring air poured into the room. Now, with six white and green Corning police cars and two dark blue state trooper vehicles bunched near the apartment walkway, he couldn't remember closing the window when he left for work.

The day had been as busy as he had predicted. He started off with fifteen file folders on his desk, each needing columns of numbers verified and a half-inch thick stack of forms and releases customized before it could be shipped off to the proper attorneys who, with pens flying and papers shuffling, would turn innocent couples into thirty-year mortgage holders. If the correct paperwork was in place and if the real estate agents and loan processors had done their jobs right, he could knock out three loans an hour, a pace that had twice earned him a certificate of merit from the home office. But each file came with problems — missing bank statements, misspelled names, addresses that didn't match, illegible hand-scrawled notes with unknown words underlined a half-dozen times and a string of exclamation points that ran off the page. His reputation for speed and accuracy meant that Jason was assigned the 'tough' loans, ones involving short-tempered agents and condescending lawyers, the kind who made some of the younger women cry with their cutting remarks. They were no less condescending when dealing with Jason but, surprised to find a male on the other end of the phone, their comments lacked their usual sting.

The last loan — passed to him at four by a harried co-worker two cubicles down, a yellow Post-it note with HELP! written under a smiley face stuck to the plastic cover — dropped into the completed pile just as the Fed-Ex man came in for the day's final pickup. By the time he straightened up his desk, washed out his coffee mug, and shared his horror stories with the other loan closers in the office it was almost five-thirty. What passed for rush-hour traffic in Corning was long over and he made it home in five minutes, only to find the lot filled with police cars.

The apartment buildings were bunched together like covered wagons huddled in a circle around the parking lot. As if it had wandered off during construction, Jason's building stood apart from the others, backed up against a steep, wooded hill that was crisscrossed with hiking trails and access roads. With the building as cover, you could unload an entire apartment out a rear window. Jason tried to remember if he had turned the latch and had wedged the security bar into place, but his mind kept calling up images of his stereo, computer, and flat-screen TV disappearing up the hill-side. He parked as close as he could and as he headed up the walkway to his building, the glass door swung open and the town's sheriff stepped out on the landing.

Jason was still in high school when patrolman Frank Neville ran for sheriff. Back then he was known to most students as Officer Frank, dropping in every year around prom season to talk about the dangers of drunk driving. Although they knew the message by heart, the students enjoyed his visits since it got them out of class and they got to see the wonderfully graphic videos designed to scare them into sobriety. In the ten years since he had won the election, Sheriff Neville had put on a few pounds and had lost much of his already thin hair, but he still had the easy smile that made you want to confide everything. As he started up the steps Jason noticed that that easy smile was missing from Sheriff Neville's face.

'You must be apartment D,' Sheriff Neville said, extending his hand as he spoke.

Jason shook the man's hand, surprised by how large and soft it felt. 'That's me. Jason Talley. I guess they got my TV, huh?'

The sheriff tilted his head to the side as he looked at Jason, his handshake slowing with each pump. 'Who?'

'The people who broke in.' Jason used the corner of the briefcase in his left hand to indicate his apartment. 'I think I left my bathroom window open and that's probably how they got in.'

The Sheriff turned to look where Jason pointed. 'I don't think so. But if you don't mind we'd better take a look in your apartment.'

'Sure, no problem.' Jason dug his keys back out of his pocket. 'What's going on?'

The sheriff looked up to the roofline of the brick building, adjusting the glossy black bill on the front of his cap before he spoke. 'It's the apartment upstairs.'

'Something happened to Mrs Dettori?' Jason said and suddenly felt guilty for not stopping up to check on the old woman as he had promised her he would when he first moved in.

'No, she's fine. It's the husband and wife.' The sheriff looked down at his notebook, sounding out each syllable of the strange words. 'Sundaram. Sriram and Vidya Sundaram.'

'Sriram and Vidya,' Jason said, smoothing out the sheriff's rough pronunciation. 'What's wrong?'

The sheriff turned to meet Jason's stare. 'I'm afraid they're dead.'

Jason felt his mouth open, felt his lips trembling, felt his tongue move but no sound came out. He dropped his briefcase, the cheap locks snapping open, spilling manila folders down the steps. He felt the sheriff grab his upper arm and heard him say something about being careful and taking deep breaths, the man's voice muffled by the roar in his ears. A metallic-tasting bile rose up his throat and Jason fought to keep down his late lunch.

'Here, I'll get this stuff. Why don't we go sit inside. You don't mind us going in your apartment, do you?' Sheriff Neville stuffed the papers back in the briefcase.

'No,' Jason whispered. 'No, it's okay.' The sheriff handed him the briefcase and they started up the walkway. As he stepped through the front door he could see the yellow police tape across the open doorway. The sound of low, deep voices that didn't belong in his friends' apartment filled the hallway, a half-dozen police radios squawking in surround-sound. From the angle of the stairs he could only see the ceiling and part of a painting that hung on the living room wall. He tried to remember what the painting looked like, tried to crystallize every memory of their home, realizing he'd never be in the apartment again.

'Why don't we come down here,' Sheriff Neville said, guiding Jason down the stairs. 'Hey Derrick,' he shouted up the stairway, one of the low, deep voices answering back through the open door.

'Derrick, we're going to be down in Mr Talley's apartment. Why don't you stop down in a bit?' The sheriff stepped out of the way as Jason unlocked his apartment door. Inside Jason dropped the briefcase by the coffee table, only one of its locks popping open this time, and slumped down in the recliner that stood across from his new TV.

'Mind if I have a seat?' The sheriff, not waiting for a reply, moved a pillow off to the side of the couch. He pulled a pen from his front pocket and clicked the point out. 'How long did you know the . . . ' He flipped back a

20

page in his notebook. 'The Sundarams?'

Jason had to count back through the months, adding up the exotic meals, foods he had never tried before and would never have again, before answering. 'About nine months.' He was surprised. It felt like they'd been neighbors for years.

'Did you know them well?'

'Yeah,' Jason said. He paused and started again, 'I guess. I mean I saw them about once a week. We had dinner together last night,' realizing that, other than those weekly dinners, he seldom saw them in the building.

'What were they like?' The sheriff looked up as a pair of police officers entered the apartment. One was a Corning cop Jason had seen around town a hundred times, the other wore the slate-gray and blue uniform of a state trooper. They nodded first to the chief, then to Jason before glancing around the apartment. 'You don't mind if they look around, do you?' Sheriff Neville had his easy smile back in place.

Jason had seen a thousand episodes of *Law and Order* and knew all about warrants and probable cause and how the smallest thing might be seen as incriminating evidence. He nodded anyway. The sheriff told the men to check the windows in the other rooms but as soon as they rounded the corner he could hear them opening closets and dresser drawers.

'What I mean,' the sheriff said, clarifying the unanswered question, 'is how did they get along? They fight much?'

Jason laughed but, slouched in the chair, it sounded like a deep cough. Did they fight? They fought all the time, he thought. Fought like Cary Grant and Katherine Hepburn, like Nick and Nora Charles, like Burns and Allen. They fought like he dreamed of fighting, with a beautiful woman, all witty comments and clever retorts, each threat delivered in a matter-of-fact tone that couldn't disguise the all-consuming affection that shouted a love so profound it seemed magical. He smiled as he recalled hearing Sriram, locked out of his apartment, singing Hindi movie love songs in the hallway, convincing Vidya it wasn't some Himalayan bandit at the door, her laughter even louder than his wavering falsetto. 'No,' he said smiling. 'They never fought.'

The sheriff looked up from his notes. 'You sure about that? There wasn't a lot of tension between them?'

Jason shook his head. 'They were the happiest people I knew.'

Sheriff Neville took in a deep breath, filling his cheeks before he let it out in a long stream. He flipped a few pages and paused while he re-read his notes. Jason stared out the open door of his apartment at the metal door of the laundry room.

'You say they were happy, huh?' the sheriff said, not looking up from his notes. Jason let the silence answer the question.

'You see the problem I've got with that.' The sheriff tapped his pen against the side of the notebook. 'All the signs point to a domestic dispute.'

'Not possible,' Jason said, more to himself than the sheriff.

'We still got a lot of work to do but I gotta tell you it looks like a classic murder-suicide.'

Jason turned his head to the side until he could look straight into the sheriff's hazel eyes, holding them steady for ten seconds before slumping deeper into the chair. 'You're wrong.'

Sheriff Neville sighed as he slid the notebook into his shirt pocket. 'Maybe. I've been wrong plenty of times before. And like I said, we still have work to do.' He stood just as Derrick and the trooper stepped out of the hallway, each giving their head a tiny side-to-side shake, a signal that the sheriff returned with a quick nod. Jason considered standing but doubted his legs could hold him up for long.

'Jason, do you know of anyone who would

want to hurt the, the . . . ' He started fishing his notebook back out of his pocket.

'The Sundarams,' Jason said, saving the sheriff the effort. 'No. No one.'

'All right. Last question — do you know of any of their family members we can contact?'

'Sorry, sheriff. They mentioned family in different parts of India but I don't know of anybody here. You might want to check with Sriram's boss over at Raj-Tech. They knew each other in India, he might know somebody.'

'We've already been in touch with Mr Murty,' the sheriff said. 'I'm on my way over to see him just as soon as we finish up here. He took the news a bit hard but he's promised to do everything he can to help. Apparently there are all these Hindu religious rites.' He waved his hand to indicate scores of mysterious ceremonies, incomprehensible to the uninitiated. 'Anyway, Jason,' the sheriff said, 'if you think of anything, give us a call down at the station.'

'I will, sheriff,' he said, thinking there was nothing else to add. 'And if you find out anything, can you let me know?'

'Sure thing,' Sheriff Neville said. Despite the smile and the assurances, Jason knew that the sheriff would never call.

For the next two hours Jason sat

motionless in the leather recliner. He listened as the police wrapped up their investigation, listened as the apartment complex manager made arrangements to have the apartment painted, listened as Mrs Dettori settled in for a night of high-volume Must See TV.

From snippets of police conversations in the hall, Jason learned that it was Mrs Dettori who had first called 911. She had noticed the door of apartment A was open when she made her daily trek down the stairs to get the mail. In the twenty minutes it took her to get down and back, the door remained open. She was going to pull it shut on her way to her apartment and that's when she saw the blood on the walls. He listened as the police questioned her yet again, asking if she heard anything unusual. 'Not since 1992,' she shouted.

He listened for the correct final question on *Jeopardy!* — Who was Melville? — before getting up to close the door.

★   ★   ★

The second time he heard the noise, a sharp click that was muffled by the curtain, Jason knew someone was trying to open the bedroom window.

He sat up and eased himself across the bed,

his eyes never leaving the dark corner, trying to pick up any movement in the curtain's thick fabric. He sidestepped across the room and felt for his jeans, folded atop the wicker hamper by the closet as if dressed he would somehow be less vulnerable. The sound continued and Jason could envision the tip of a knife being pried under the frame of the screen, slipping off to click against the glass. He stepped into his jeans then slid his hand across the top of the dresser till his fingers found his cell phone. He flicked it open, feeling for the small keys with his thumb. He pushed down the nine, then ran his thumb up past the six to the three. The clicking stopped before his thumb found the one and in the heavy late-night silence Jason heard an impatient meow.

Jason turned on the bedside lamp and drew back the curtain with his hand. Outside Bindi's eyes glowed green in the glare of the light. She fixed a single claw into the screen and gave it a tug, the click louder now with the curtain out of the way. When she was sure she had his full attention she gave a second commanding meow.

'Any other cat . . . ' Jason said as he undid the lock and removed the security bar. Closed since late fall, the window needed an extra shove before it opened. Jason had the screen half off when Bindi squeezed her way through and leapt on to his bed. By the time he had the window closed, she had settled in at the center of the bed.

'Don't get too comfortable, cat,' he said. He took off his jeans and refolded them before turning off the light and slipping back into bed. 'You can stay the night but tomorrow . . . '

But tomorrow what? He imagined what Vidya would have said about his finding the cat at three a.m. He had to take her in, he could hear Sriram saying, it was out of place and you know how Jason feels about things out of place. They would joke about having to add pizza to the cat's diet and Sriram would make some comment about Jason finally getting someone to spend the night and somehow they'd all end up laughing.

But not tomorrow.

Jason lay on his back, his eyes open, nothing to see in the predawn darkness, his dead friends' cat purring at his side.

# 3

'The airline tickets and hotel vouchers are all in here.' The girl tapped a bright pink nail on the complimentary plastic document folder, by chance or design striking the center of the round Bonnell Travel Agency logo. 'The itinerary is in the Freedom Tour's main brochure,' shifting her tapping to the glossy magazine to her right, 'but I'll print you out a text version. You don't want to be lugging this all over India.'

'I don't know,' Jason said, 'I may need something to read at night.' He did his best to sound dashing and nonchalant.

Although it was only her first month on the job, Katie Phelps had an innate sense of salesmanship and, thanks to four notorious years in a party-crazed sorority, enough experience with men to know how to respond. She tilted her head down and to the side, her shoulder-length blonde-white hair framing her artificial tan, darted a quick look up under her long black lashes, and smiled a six-point-five percent agency commission smile.

It was just an idea when he walked in, an

option he mentioned as he planned his spring trip to Daytona. Before he could stop her, Katie had covered the desk with oversized brochures and foldout maps, ooh-ing and ahh-ing at the moonlit photos of the Taj Mahal, the golden beaches, the gaily decorated elephants and the action shot of the Bengal tiger leaping into a pristine lake. India had been just a word in a pick-up line. Now it was a non-refundable deposit reality.

'Anyway,' Katie said, giving her hair a playful toss, 'you shouldn't have any problems at all. Freedom Tours is a really great company. We book a lot with them.' She noticed Jason's smile sag and quickly added, 'But never to any place so cool. I have to tell you, I am impressed.'

Jason felt himself grinning like an idiot and ran his hand across the stubble on his chin to cover his mouth. 'I've always meant to get there,' he said, hinting at countless trips that brought him so close to the sub-continent, but other than annual treks to Florida, a high school field trip to D.C., and a ten-day Caribbean cruise with an ex-girlfriend, Jason's traveling had been limited to car-based daytrips and the occasional Yankees weekend in New York City.

'My friends talk about India so much that I figure I might as well see it for myself.' A week after the memorial service and three weeks after he had found Sheriff Neville waiting for him on his apartment steps, Jason still spoke of Sriram and Vidya as if they were getting together that night.

When he saw the information in their obituaries, Jason had thought about taking the day off and making the two-hour run up to the Hindu temple in Rochester. But funerals made him uncomfortable as it was and not knowing the religion or the language or the family, if there was any, would only make it worse. Besides, he reasoned, as a non-Hindu they might not want him there at all.

Later that week Ravi Murty had held a memorial service in one of the meeting rooms at Raj-Tech, attended by Sriram's co-workers and people from the public library where, Jason learned, Vidya volunteered three days a week. There were no religious symbols, no many-armed statues of gods that might shock the mourners, just a few candles and a framed picture of Sriram and Vidya that Jason recognized from their living room.

'I first met Sriram in college in Bangalore,' Ravi had said in his brief eulogy. 'I was always impressed with his quick mind, his eagerness to learn, and his dedication to his work.'

It was probably true, Jason had thought, but he would have mentioned Sriram's sense of humor and friendship. Ravi then described Vidya as well educated and cultured, missing, Jason believed, everything that had made her special.

To everyone's relief, Ravi did not mention the graphic details that had covered page one in *The Leader* — the long, rambling suicide note on Sriram's computer, the unregistered handgun, the blood.

Corning was small enough that Jason had recognized some of the faces at the reception but didn't know any by name. He was standing off to one side of the room, sipping a glass of fruit punch and thinking about leaving when Ravi Murty approached.

'Thank you so much for coming,' Ravi had said, extending his hand. Unlike Sriram, with his subtle accent and exact pronunciation, each word clipped clean, Ravi had a middle-America dialect that made him sound like a local news anchor. 'I'm Ravi Murty. Sriram worked for me at Raj-Tech.'

'Jason Talley. I live in their apartment building. Thank you for arranging all this.' He matched Ravi's firm, corporate, three-beat handshake. 'I'm sorry I didn't get up to Rochester for the funeral,' he had said, fumbling with the last word, unsure if that's what it was called when Hindus did whatever it was they did with their dead.

'It was nice. The people at the temple were most helpful,' Ravi had said, and Jason realized then that no one else had shown up. 'It's funny — you meet someone in college, you never think you'll be the one making their funeral arrangements.'

'I didn't know that Sriram went to school in America.'

'He didn't. I went to university in India — sent, really. My parents' last attempt to get me in touch with my roots.' The way he had said it — his tone sarcastic, his fingers waving — made it clear what he thought of the idea. 'I guess I stood in for all of his college friends as well.'

'I still have a hard time believing it,' Jason had said, trying to ignore a rising sense of shame. 'I know what the papers say but they were the happiest people I knew.'

The man gave a slight sigh. 'Well, I'm glad that's how you'll remember them.'

'I think that's how most people will remember them.'

'That and the cookies,' Ravi said. 'Every Monday morning Sriram would bring in a batch of cookies, put them in the break room. Oatmeal raisin, peanut butter chocolate chip, sugar cookies with those sprinkles on them . . . let me tell you it made the work week a lot easier to face.'

32

Jason had laughed, remembering the dark Monday mornings and the still-warm bags of cookies on the front seat of his car. 'So that's why you hired him.'

'Yeah,' Ravi said, 'that and the fact that the man was good. I worked with him in a mentor program at the University, taught him a few tricks, nothing he wouldn't have learned on his own. Quick learner, too. Show him something once and the next day he's teaching you.'

'Is that when you decided to hire him?'

Ravi shook his head, laughing again. 'No, I wasn't that smart. Besides, at the time Sriram had formed a small software development company with several of his classmates. It was not unusual. We were fresh out of college, we all wanted to be the next Bill Gates.'

Jason recalled a profile on Ravi in the Lifestyles section of *The Leader*. It had talked about how this thirty-something computer genius had begun Raj-Tech, borrowing five dollars to type up the company plan on a rented cyber-café computer. Ten years later that same company was poised to release a new program that could be worth millions.

'They worked hard but Sriram realized that his little group lacked the vision needed to take it to the next level. By this time I had already established Raj-Tech here in Corning. Sriram contacted me. I recalled that he had shown some potential and I agreed to hire him on and help him get his green card.'

'How'd his friends take it, him leaving them like that?'

Ravi shrugged his shoulders. 'That's exactly what they wanted for themselves. Some were upset — a couple *really* upset — but that's business, right?'

Jason swirled the last of the fruit punch in his glass and thought about disgruntled partners and business deals gone sour. 'Is there a chance it may not have happened the way the police described it?'

Ravi tilted his head to one side. 'You mean to Sriram and Vidya? Oh, I don't think so.'

'Anyway, I'm glad you gave him the job,' Jason had said, sensing the conversation had gone too far into areas neither of them wanted to talk about.

'Sriram was a good nuts and bolts man. He was good at cleaning up a rough program, working out some of the tedious details.'

'And I'll miss Vidya's cooking,' Jason said, his voice lightening as he remembered the foods he didn't think he'd come to love.

'You can't go wrong with Indian cuisine,' Ravi said, taking up Jason's tone. 'Actually, you can't go wrong with anything Indian.

Personally I prefer my India imported but it's becoming quite the popular tourist destination.'

'Hey, I've got lots of time to use up,' Jason had said. 'Maybe that's where I'll go next.'

Now, a week after the memorial service and a half hour after walking into the Bonnell Travel Agency to book a flight to Florida, Jason was finalizing a fourteen-day, thirteen-night all-inclusive package tour of a place that up to that moment had been a V-shaped mass on a map.

'You were smart to jump on that last-minute opening,' Katie said, checking her computer screen. 'You saved about fifteen percent. But that puts the pressure on you. We'll take care of the visa, that'll be easy. I just hope they understand at your job.'

'Oh, that won't be a problem,' Jason said, still looking at the list, wondering now if it would be a problem.

Katie sighed as she looked at the cover photo on the brochure, a sunset shot of the Taj Mahal. 'You are going to have *such* a good time.'

# 4

'On behalf of everyone at Freedom Tours let me officially welcome you to India and say *nameste*.' As he said the last word the handsome, pencil-thin man placed his palms together below his nose and angled his head forward with a practiced solemnity. Jason noticed that several in the group returned the gesture while others recorded the moment in both digital and standard film format.

'My name is Dayama Panjaj Satyanarayan.' He paused as the tourists mumbled astonished remarks, then grinned and added, 'But you can call me Danny.' Most of the thirty-five members of the Freedom Tours' spring excursion chuckled, saying that it was a darn good thing while others tapped their hearing aides or shouted from the third row that he needed to speak up. Jason smiled as well, but only because his new roommate had stopped patting his knee long enough to cup a hand behind his ear to listen as Danny spoke.

The Air India flight had taken off from JFK Friday night, touched down for a three-hour layover in London just after dawn, and had flown all day Saturday, arriving at the Indira Gandhi International Airport early Sunday morning. By the time they had recovered their luggage, cleared customs, and piled on the Trailways-style tour bus it was close to three in the morning. It was a forty-minute ride to the hotel, the windows tinted so thick that all he could make out were the hazy glows around streetlights and roadside campfires. When they arrived at the gated entrance of the Holiday Inn in Connaught Place there was a pinkish hint of dawn in the sky and Jason realized that it was already the third day of his trip and he was just arriving.

It was in the lobby of the Holiday Inn that he also learned that the great deal that Katie the travel agent had secured for him was based on double occupancy. 'I hope you don't snore,' was all his new roommate had said as they passed out the keys.

Jason knew that people didn't look their best at four in the morning, especially after spending the better part of twenty hours in coach class seats, but looking around the lobby he realized he could have done worse than drawing Bob Froman as his roommate. Bob didn't need a walker, didn't wheeze, and unlike most of the other single men, he spoke — when he spoke at all — in a normal, conversational tone, never asking people to

37

repeat their already deafening comments. Even when he woke up three hours later in their hotel room to find Bob, fully dressed, sitting on the edge of his bed watching him sleep, Jason knew his roommate wasn't the worst of the lot.

'I'm sure that you are all a bit tired this morning,' Danny was saying now, standing behind the music stand that served as a podium. 'You may find that the real effects of jetlag won't be apparent for several days,' he continued, saying *jetlag* as if it were italicized. He paused again as the tourists agreed and exchanged red-eyed travel anecdotes. His fifteenth tour with Freedom Tours, Danny Panjaj Satyanarayan knew his audience.

Looking around the meeting room — a room that looked just like the meeting rooms he had seen at the Holiday Inn in Corning — Jason worked some numbers in his head. Adding in his statistically anomalous twenty-seven as well as an estimated twenty-five for the auburn-haired girl in the front row, Jason put the average age of his fellow Freedom Tourists at an even sixty. He flipped through the glossy brochure the travel agent had given him, noticing for the first time all the pictures of laughing, gray-haired travelers.

'After we enjoy a light brunch here at the hotel,' Danny was saying, 'we'll head out for a pleasant day of sightseeing. We'll start with a visit to an authentic Rajasthaani silversmith workshop where you will see traditional designs worked into elaborate patterns before your very eyes.' He waited for the women of the group to nudge their husbands and joke about needing the credit cards.

'We will then visit my nation's capital building, where, due to post September Eleven security measures, we will unfortunately be unable to disembark. But that will mean we will have more time when we visit the Modern School of Mughal Art, where you will have the opportunity to see with your very eyes the ancient traditions of Mughal miniature portrait painting continued to this present day,' Danny said, adding that the school was equipped to take U.S. dollars, travelers checks, Visa and MasterCard.

'By then we'll be ready for a break, so we'll enjoy our late afternoon tea in the shady courtyard of a nineteenth-century villa, previously owned by a British government official and now home to the silk-weavers cooperative, and I must say home, too, to the finest bargains on traditionally dyed and adorned scarves in all of Delhi. We'll finish our first day off with a true Indian feast here at the hotel, followed by a multimedia presentation in this room on the history of

Delhi's Red Fort.'

The auburn-haired woman raised her hand. 'Why don't we just go to the real Red Fort and see their sound and light show?' She glanced down to the Lonely Planet guidebook in her lap. 'Nine-thirty p.m. One hour. Fifty rupees.'

Although his smile stayed in place, Danny's narrow shoulders dipped. 'I'm afraid that show doesn't run on Sundays.'

'It says nightly,' the woman said, her finger pointing out the word as she held up the book.

'We've found,' Danny said, speaking to his main audience and over the head of the troublemaker, 'that after such a long flight and such an adventure-filled day, most people prefer to relax here in the hotel.'

'Shopping is hardly an adventure-filled day and I don't think any of us flew halfway around the world to see a stupid video with the real thing a couple miles away.' There was a sharp edge to the woman's tone and Jason could feel the nervous tension begin to radiate off the members of the tour group who found shopping and movies quite adventurous enough.

'Well, it's a *bit* more than a couple miles and it *is* in a less *safe* area of town and traffic at night is tricky, and there is the jetlag to consider . . . ' Danny paused as if he were considering the idea. 'I suppose we *might* be able to do it, that is if that's what you *all* want.' The way he said it let the group know that it was definitely not what they wanted and the group was quick to agree.

The matter settled, Danny gathered up his papers. 'There are fresh bagels, pastry, and toast in the buffet line as well as coffee and Sanka, so please, help yourself.' He smiled at his audience and said, 'We have quite an adventure-filled day ahead.'

★  ★  ★

'Well, this sucks,' the auburn-haired girl said as she plopped down hard in the open seat next to Jason. They had just finished their tour of the silk cooperative, a fifty-minute scripted sales presentation that had proven to be effective with most of the tour, and were climbing aboard the bus for the ride back to the hotel. 'I didn't come to India to go shopping,' she said, reaching up to feel if there was anything coming out of the round air-conditioning vent.

Jason had only caught a few glimpses of her as they were shuttled from shop to shop but now, with her sitting next to him, he was surprised to see how attractive she was. Her clear, brown eyes were several shades lighter than her shoulder-length hair, pulled back into a ponytail that poked out through the back of a Toronto Blue Jays baseball cap. Her skin, flushed from the late afternoon sun, was smooth, and a thin line of sweat beaded up on the ridge above her lip. Despite an oversized tee shirt and a pair of khakis just baggy enough to be in style, Jason could see that she had the lean body of an athlete, the small bump on her nose the souvenir of a home-plate collision or a well-spiked volley-ball. She pulled a water bottle out of her backpack and, after taking a long pull, offered it to Jason saying, 'We gotta get outta here.'

Jason waved off the bottle, holding up one of his own. 'Get out of where? India?'

'This bus. This whole tour thing,' she said, gesturing with the bottle before taking another drink.

'It's just the first day,' Jason said. 'I'm sure it'll get better.' He didn't know if he believed it but he was hoping it was true.

'I doubt it. I asked Danny Boy if the whole trip was like this and he said that no, in some places the shopping is even better. This is what I get for buying a raffle ticket from a nursing home.'

'You won this trip?' Jason said, thinking about how much he had paid.

'Yeah, go figure. A two-dollar ticket and I win India. If it's all like today I got ripped off. I'm sorry,' she said, turning to face him. 'I'm not usually like this. I'm Rachel.'

'Jason,' he said, offering her his hand. 'What part of Canada are you from?'

'Brockville. Up on the St Lawrence, the Thousand Islands area.' She paused and looked at him sideways.

'It's your accent. The way you said *dollar* and *sorry*,' he said, accentuating the Os in both words. 'That and the Canadian flag pin on your backpack.'

'Clever. You from the States?'

'New York — but not the city. A small town called Corning.'

She nodded. 'It's a pretty area. I rode my bike down your way back in high school. So did you win this trip, too?'

'I'm not that lucky. I got it through a travel agent who has some explaining to do when I get back.'

Danny came down the aisle of the bus counting the heads of his charges before shouting something up to the driver in Hindi, the driver responding by pulling the door shut and easing the engine into gear. The afternoon sun was blinding but the thick polarized tint on the windows made it look like midnight.

'Well,' Jason said with an exaggerated sigh, 'at least we get to see the Taj Mahal tomorrow. That ought to be cool.'

Rachel shook her head. 'Not me.'

'It's part of the tour. We leave the hotel at six a.m . . . '

'I know. I just don't want to see it.' She unzipped her backpack and shoved the water bottle inside, crushing down wads of papers and loose camera gear.

'You come all the way to India on a free trip and you don't want to see the most famous thing in the whole country?'

'It's not that I don't want to see it,' she said. 'It's just that I can't. There's an old legend that says that the first time you see the Taj Mahal it should be with someone you love.' She shrugged, a comment on the stupidity of the idea or her romantic nature, Jason wasn't sure. 'I'll see it someday,' she said, as if it were an art-house movie that might turn up on video.

'I'm not so sure about me,' Jason said, adding a self-mocking laugh. 'I'd better see it while I can. What *do* you want to see then?'

Rachel drew in a breath and held it a moment before she answered. 'Trains.'

'Trains?'

'This is the point when most guys I meet

44

suddenly see a friend at the other side of the bar or remember that they had to rush off for surgery. I like trains,' she said, her voice taking on the quality of an apology. 'I like spotting trains, I like riding trains, I even have a five track setup in my apartment.'

'Trains, huh? That's sort of . . . '

'Strange? Creepy? You can say it, I'm used to it.'

Jason found her confident smile sexy. 'No, I find it fascinating,' he lied. 'It's not something I'm into myself . . . '

'I know, I know. I promise I won't try to convert you.'

Jason pulled the folded itinerary from his shirt pocket. 'You're in luck. We take at least two train trips.'

She looked down at the wrinkled paper. 'Oh, I think there may be a few more that aren't on the list yet.'

★ ★ ★

Catering to the changing needs of the international business traveler, the Holiday Inn had converted its little-used barbershop into a business center, complete with photocopiers, fax machines, scanners, and ten computer stations, everything state-of-the-art and available at a competitive rate to registered guests. After watching the first few minutes of Freedom Tours' multimedia presentation, Jason had paid the concierge five hundred rupees for ten minutes of high-speed Internet access. At a dollar a minute, Jason typed quickly.

He found ninety-five new emails in his Hotmail account. He skimmed down the list, deleting the obvious junk mail, leaving twenty messages, all but one from people he did not know.

When he had realized that there was no way to back out of the contract without losing more than a vacation should cost, Jason had focused on organizing the few non-structured moments on the package tour, including 'a morning on your own to discover the surprises of Bangalore.' Using addresses pulled from a mass email Sriram had sent — a collection of funny headlines from the local paper — Jason wrote an open letter explaining that he would be traveling through India and would like to meet any of the couple's friends and family along the way. He had included his flight information as well as a link to the Freedom Tours' website.

With screen names like Currycrazy, way2fast4u, Tigerlilly, and namapuraturum, and most of them Hotmail or Yahoo accounts, Jason had no way of knowing if the recipients were in

India or down the road in Corning, but the first email he opened let him know it had been a good idea.

'I am Ram Shankar and I attended college with Sriram. If your travels chance to bring you to Trivandrum, please ring me up.' A row of winking smile faces was followed by a phone number and street address. He wasn't sure where Trivandrum was or if his travels would take him there, but Jason printed out the message and continued down the list. Most of the letters were from people living outside of India — Boston, San Francisco, Dubai, London — wishing him luck or suggesting sites to see on his trip. Out of the twenty letters in his inbox, five came with offers to help, and Jason added each to the printing queue.

It was the last email that made his heart race.

'I wish you would have contacted me before you sent that letter,' Ravi Murty had written. 'There were things I didn't tell you about Sriram, things that have to do with that computer company he helped start. It's too complicated to get into, but there are people out there who still blame Sriram for destroying their dreams and I'm afraid they might take their frustrations out on you.' Jason smiled at first as he read the line, Ravi sounding like an old woman who watched one too many spy movies. The smile disappeared as he read the rest of the message.

'You have no idea of the role honor and revenge plays in Indian society. Families nurse grudges for centuries, striking out at seemingly innocent bystanders who had the most tenuous link to the offense. In India a laborer will break rocks for fourteen hours a day for less than the cost of lunch at McDonalds. Five dollars would get a man pushed in front of a train, for ten they'd slit his throat in broad daylight.'

Jason felt his hand sweat as he gripped the computer mouse, his mouth drying with each open-mouthed breath.

'To make it even worse, you tell them right where to find you. They could have spotted you at the airport and could be following you right now. You're tall and you're white. The light-brown color of your hair alone is enough to set you apart. You are hard to miss.'

He thought about the tour group, how Danny carried that red golf umbrella, how they drove around in the largest vehicle on the streets.

'It was a foolish thing you did and I hope it does not bring you to harm. Take my advice, trust no one you meet in India.' A postscript under the computer-generated signature provided contact information for the Raj-Tech offices in Bangalore and a final piece of advice. 'Be damn careful.'

# 5

Although the plants were larger and more lush and the uniformed staff more numerous and subservient, the lobby of the Holiday Inn in New Delhi looked like the lobby at any Holiday Inn Jason had ever seen. This one had more old people than most, but aesthetically it was cut from the same corporate-designed cloth.

He was sipping his first coffee and looking over the day's itinerary when Rachel appeared in front of him, her backpack slung on her shoulder. She wore the same baggy khakis but instead of a tee shirt she wore a man's dress shirt with the sleeves rolled up. With her hair tucked under her Blue Jays cap and her hands dug deep in her pockets, she managed to look sloppy and fashionable at the same time.

'Grab your bag,' she said, kicking at his foot. 'We're hitting the road.'

'Well, good morning to you, too.' Jason looked up to see her smiling and wondered if she realized how attractive she was. He held up the folded itinerary for her to see and said, 'We've got another five minutes before they start packing us on the bus.'

'We're not taking the bus. We've got to grab a cab to the station if we're going to catch the next train to Jaipur.'

'That's not on here,' Jason said, running his finger down the typed lines.

'Remember yesterday how we said we wanted to get out of this tour?'

'I remember that's what you said.'

'Anyways,' she said, ignoring his correction, 'I got us out of the tour. We took quite a hit on the buyback but Danny Boy added in a pair of India Rail passes so it almost worked out okay.'

Jason looked at her but didn't say anything so she continued explaining.

'We won't be able to stay at these four-star palaces and we'll have to eat on the cheap, but we'll do all right as long as we split the costs.'

'What are you talking about?'

Rachel brought her hands out of her pockets to help her tell the story. 'Danny,' she said, pointing him out across the lobby, 'bought our tour packages off us. We can go wherever we want.' She waved her arms out wide, symbolizing, Jason guessed, both the sale of the tour packages and their new independence.

'We can't leave the tour. It's not right.' He didn't think it was that funny but it made

Rachel laugh a light, cheery, beautiful smile laugh.

'It's not right? What's not right is that a couple of healthy twenty-somethings are traveling around with a herd of retirees when there's a really cool country to explore. Now come on,' she said, shrugging her shoulders to readjust her backpack, 'we've got to get moving to get that train.'

'Wait a second,' Jason said. 'I can't just . . . '

'Yes, you can,' Rachel said. 'And you sort of have to. Danny Boy's already sold our spots to an Australian couple visiting India for their fiftieth anniversary. Pretty romantic, actually. Besides,' she added, her voice dropping as she turned to look at him, 'he refused to let me out of the tour unless you went with me. They're still really sexist here.' She waited a half-minute for Jason to make up his mind before saying, 'Well? We going?'

Jason sighed and stood up. 'Do I have a choice?' He grabbed his backpack and followed her through the lobby and out the front door of the hotel.

★ ★ ★

Five hours later, his jaw hanging slack, his arms too heavy to lift, Jason fought to keep his eyes closed.

He'd been trying to fall asleep for hours but, just as he'd feel his muscles relax and his breathing deepen, every synapse in his brain would light up and with a frightened gasp he'd snap awake. In a moment of adrenaline-infused clarity he weighed the two possible causes.

The first was jetlag. Yes, his internal clock was all screwed up and, yes, he'd drunk way too much coffee at the hotel, but as he felt his brain spasm and race he knew that this was not the reason.

The second was India, and he knew that this was the cause.

The moment they stepped out of the air-conditioned hotel into the early morning sun, Freedom Tours' version of India ended and the real India began. Rachel waved off the doorman's offer to hail a taxi as she led the way out past the gate to the main road where a swarm of three-wheeled, black and yellow cabs crowded the entranceway. When they spotted their bags, twenty men leapt out of the open sides of their cabs and raced towards them, each shouting offers in their own version of English, wading through a mob of young boys that flew in from the streets, some waving tourist maps, some fanning picture postcards, one holding up a classroom globe.

Jason gripped his backpack with both arms, his eyes wide as a score of hands reached out to him. The cab drivers responded, snapping thin leather straps across the boys' legs, and Jason watched as they jumped in pain or in sport, laughing and kicking out at the old men before sprinting away. Then the men were on him, each shouting that his was the best cab in all of Delhi and that the others were thieves and liars. At six feet even, he towered over most of the men, all dressed in button-down shirts and pants that were at one time black but now faded to gray, and all of them fighting to be heard. At the fringe of the crowd he spotted Rachel as she climbed into a cab. She gave an impatient wave and tapped her finger on an imaginary wrist-watch.

Jason turned back to see his former companions making their way on to the Freedom Tours bus, and he wondered who would room with Bob Froman.

'Come on already.' Rachel's high voice cut through the din and Jason turned back, the crowd parting as he walked to the cab, scanning the hotel entrance for other tourists willing to wander off on their own.

'It's not a cab per se,' Rachel said after the driver kick-started the engine and U-turned his way through four lanes of traffic. 'It's called an auto-rickshaw. They say they're the best way to get around in the cities. Oh, and it's not the wrong way,' she added, noticing the panic in his eyes. 'They drive on the left here. It's an old British thing.'

Stuffed in behind the driver and sharing a narrow bench seat made for one, there was little chance they would be thrown out the open sides despite the jerky last-second turns. The overtaxed engine screamed its way through the gears while the rounded shape of the roof and the placement of the tail pipe ensured that little of the leaded gasoline fumes escaped.

He watched as the four-star hotels gave way to no-star flop-houses, a mile of road and a ten-million dollar drop in value. Concrete office buildings, their faded white paint peeling off in newspaper-sized sheets, lined the street, hand-lettered signs covered in the squiggly lines of Hindi tacked up on the walls.

Although they passed within an inch of the tin sides of the auto-rickshaw, Jason couldn't identify any of the cars that muscled their way down the street, squat rounded boxes that were not much larger than his golf cart-sized cab, their fenders and doors dented from countless commutes. Delivery trucks, tarted up with bright paint, lights and bits of shiny metal, coughed out hot coils of black smoke while on the left a bus crept by, every seat full with another forty passengers clinging to the sides like army ants pulling down a doomed beetle. An endless stream of scooters weaved through the traffic carrying sari-clad women sitting sidesaddle behind the stern-faced drivers or families of eight stacked on like a circus act out for a ride, the smallest toddler astride the handlebars. Seeming to flow backwards through the traffic were the bicycle rickshaws, their sweating drivers hauling passengers and cargo many times their own weight.

Despite the images recalled from a high school social studies filmstrip, there were no cows wandering the streets, but as the driver bounced his dented cab against the side of a truck and up on to the sidewalk to avoid a lost rear axle rolling down the street, Jason felt that this said something about the wisdom of the cow.

And everywhere — squeezing between the auto-rickshaws, cutting in front of brake-less trucks, darting out from behind parked cars — everywhere there were people. They spilled off the sidewalks, poured in and out of the buildings, and filled up every space not taken by something larger or immoveable. Most of the men were dressed in long-sleeved shirts

56

and slacks, the styles five years out of fashion. Some wore designer suits, some wore knock-off NBA jerseys, and some wore a matching two-piece outfit that looked to Jason like a cross between hospital scrubs and pajamas.

Most of the women he saw wore a *shalwar kamiz*, the female version of the scrub/pajama hybrid, theirs adding a scarf draped stylishly down the front with the tail ends tossed over each shoulder. There were teenagers in jeans and roaming pockets of girls in bright school uniforms, but fewer women in saris than he had expected and none who wore a sari as elaborate as the one bundled in the bottom of his backpack.

Where the buildings near the hotel had been shabby and neglected, the ones they passed on the way to the station were decrepit and best forgotten. The traffic thinned out, but there was more trash in the streets, and gaping potholes threatened to swallow their cab. The suits and designer clothes were gone, replaced by ill-fitting and dirty castoffs, flip-flops or bare skin replacing the leather sandals. The people here moved at a different pace, the shuffling, nowhere-to-go gait of the unemployed. There were fewer smiles, but the ones he spotted seemed somehow more real.

Mixed in with the pedestrians who crowded the streets, beggars approached the cars, tapping on the windows of the larger sedans, pre-teens holding up dirt-smeared babies in tattered rags as they stared into the air-conditioned cars. He felt Rachel draw back against him as a leather-faced old woman approached the cab, mouthing her toothless request for rupees. Two small boys appeared on his side of the open vehicle, one holding the stump of his arm, the other saying, 'Mister look' while he balanced himself on his cane, his withered leg dragging across the pavement.

He didn't know what to do, didn't know how to feel. He recalled a notice he had seen in a New York City subway: 'Giving money to beggars keeps them beggars.' He wanted to believe it was true, but as a sideways glance caught the milky eye of the old woman, he wasn't so sure. A break in the traffic ended his moral dilemma as the auto-rickshaw rocketed ahead.

'There's the train station there,' Rachel said, pointing at the image in her guidebook and then at the massive red brick building at the end of the block, a second fleet of yellow and black auto-rickshaws lined up ten deep out front. He paid the driver with a wad of multi-colored bills and together they worked through the maze of cabs to the main entrance.

Although it was busy, with luggage-laden passengers criss-crossing from every direction in the open lobby and porters in sweat-stained red smocks pushing handcarts stacked ten feet tall with taped-together suitcases, after the cab ride Jason found the train station calming. Rachel insisted on getting the tickets, not wanting to miss a moment of the train experience, and, despite the signs that stated that the taking of photography was strictly not to be advisable, she snapped a dozen shots, half of trains, the other half of empty tracks. They found their train — the Pink City Express — just as it started to lurch forward, laughing as they stumbled aboard.

Now, as Rachel stood in the open doorway, the train racing past miles of treeless farmland, Jason gave up on sleep and pondered his stupidity.

The trip had been a mistake, something he knew before he had even left Corning. He wasn't the kind of guy who got off on exotic passport stamps and tales of white-knuckle escapades in strange-sounding places. He was a relax-by-the-hotel-pool-and-build-an-impressive-bar-tab-while-working-on-your-tan kind of guy. With just ten vacation days a year, he didn't have room in his life for an adventure. He thought about the time difference, wondering what was happening at the clubs he always hit at Daytona Beach, but gave up when he decided that no matter what it was it was better than riding a train in India.

He didn't have to stay with Rachel. He could take his share of the buyout and hook up with another tour group, one that had a set itinerary and no auto-rickshaw rides, and leave her to her trains, salvaging something out of this mess. But as he watched her holding tight to the handrails, her ponytail bouncing as she leaned out into the desert-dry wind, the back of her pants dipping down to expose the swirls of a tribal-style tattoo on tanned skin, he knew the trip would be better with her around.

The car was only half-filled, the airline-style chairs tilted back as the other riders — families, business types, and a few tourists — were lulled asleep by the hypnotic clacking of the rails. Across the aisle an older woman stood to remove a water bottle from the open, overhead luggage rack. She wore a green, tight-fitting tee shirt under a lighter green sari, part of which she draped over her shoulder, adjusting the end to serve as a headscarf. The material was a light cotton, the simple pattern machined along with the cloth. Jason pictured the sari he was carrying with its heavy silk and detailed embroidery and thought about its significance.

When Jason had unrolled the bundle back in Corning he was amazed at what he found. It was a little more than a yard wide, but it stretched from the front door of his apartment, past the kitchen, down the hallway and halfway into his bedroom. The intricate, hand-stitched gold and silver design filled only the last three feet of the fabric, but a thin-lined yellow and black pattern ran the entire length of the sari, ending at a cloth-covered button at the corner. There was something familiar to the designs, something in the pattern he had seen before. He studied it for an hour before giving up and refolding the sari, the bundle somehow larger than the one he had unwrapped.

Sriram had said it was a tradition for sons to give their mothers saris but Jason wondered if the tradition changed when the son died and a stranger delivered the gift. He still did not have an address for Sriram's family in Bangalore or any idea what he would say when they asked him how their son and his wife had died. He didn't have a four-star hotel bed waiting for him in Jaipur, didn't have as much money as he feared he would end up needing, and he didn't have a clue why he found himself drawn to this bossy Canadian.

What he did have were emails from people who seemed quite eager to help, any one of whom, Ravi had warned, might be waiting to kill him.

# 6

'This is why I came to India,' Rachel said as she leaned over Jason to get a better view of the Jaipur train station. Despite day-long temperatures in the eighties and the dirt blown in through the open windows, her hair still smelled of citrus shampoo. 'Forget the tourist crap, give me trains.'

'From what I've seen,' Jason said, looking between the bars on the window as the grimy walls of the station's outer buildings came into view, 'you can have 'em.'

She pulled her thick guidebook from her pack. 'Cute. But you'll learn to love it yet.'

The locals began jumping off the train as it was still pulling into the station, a good way to twist an ankle, Jason thought. He kept his seat, watching the crowd that stood waiting on the long concrete platform, everyone scanning the windows of the incoming train for a face they knew. A white-haired old man pulled his extended family down the line, laughing, crying, shouting greetings to someone Jason couldn't see while nearby a teenaged boy stooped down to touch the cuff of his father's trousers, the man placing his hand on the boy's head to complete the silent greeting. A young bride, holding a naked infant, waited as her husband pushed through the crowd, their public greeting limited to an exchange of smiles. There were dozens of men watching the train, any one of whom, Jason realized, might be waiting for him.

Jason sat until the train came to a complete stop, stood up, stretched and made his way to the door, Rachel close behind him.

'It says there're lots of places to stay, some with their own toilets. Remember,' she said, bumping into him as the train gave one last jolt, 'we've got to keep it on the cheap. Any way we can save a few rupees will help us out in the long run.'

Jason ran several responses through his head, deciding it was best to say nothing. He stepped off the train and turned to wait as Rachel stopped to take one last interior shot. As he watched her camera flash light up the empty compartment, he sensed someone step up behind him.

'This is for you, Mr Jason Talley,' the man said and Jason spun around, expecting the point of a stiletto or the black hole of a gun barrel.

In his right hand the man held a small bouquet of fresh flowers.

'Not for you so much as for your wife,' the

man said, nodding as Rachel joined them.

'They're beautiful,' Rachel said, accepting the flowers.

The man smiled a nervous smile. 'I am afraid that they will wilt before long in this heat.' Despite his concern for the flowers, the man was wearing a navy blazer, white shirt and a striped tie, the sandals that poked out from under the cuffed khakis his only concession to the weather. His hair was jet black, parted on the side, the sharp lines of recent haircut visible around his large ears.

'Then I'll enjoy them while they last,' Rachel said, closing her eyes as she inhaled their fragrance.

Jason lowered his backpack, holding it so that it hid his shaking knees. He forced a dry swallow before saying, 'How did you know my name?'

The man smiled again, thin lines appearing at the corner of his eyes, hinting at his age. 'You sent an email saying you would be coming to India. I am cyberchief twenty-two at Hotmail dot com, also known as A.S. Singh, but you can call me Attar.' He held out his arm as he spoke, and Jason had to drop his backpack to shake his hand.

'Well, you know who I am,' Jason said. 'But I wasn't supposed to be on this train. How'd you know I'd be here?'

Attar held up a finger, excited to explain. 'I received a text message from my friend in Delhi, Bahadur Godara. You may know him better as B underscore godara at Inrail dot com. He, too, was one of the people you emailed before arriving in India. He met your tour bus at the sandalwood carving center this morning — it was listed as today's first stop on the Freedom Tours website — but a Mr D. P. Satyanarayan explained that you had left the tour. He told my friend that you were traveling by train. After that it was a simple matter of hacking into the India Rail system. There you were, Mr Jason Talley and his wife, Rachel Moore, Pink City Express, chair car number seven. And, *ahcha*, here you are now.' His head bobbed as he spoke, a gesture somewhere between a nodded yes and a shaken no.

'And now that you are here,' Attar continued, 'you are my very special guests. Come, I will take you to my apartment where you and your wife are free to stay as long as you wish.'

Jason laughed. 'Oh, we're not . . . '

'We're not going to pass up your kind hospitality, Mr Singh,' Rachel said, stepping in front of Jason. 'My husband and I would be honored.'

'Please, call me Attar,' he said. 'I hope you

66

are hungry. My wife is a most excellent cook.'

'That's so kind of you,' Rachel said as they crossed the concrete platform to the soot-stained brick station. 'Tell me, Attar,' Rachel said, stepping ahead to look around her new husband, 'would you know where a girl could get a copy of the India Railway timetables?'

★ ★ ★

Attar pushed in the clutch and downshifted, the engine revving as he passed a bicycle stacked high with empty burlap bags that inched up the winding, hillside road. He tapped the horn as he went by, tapped it again when he reached the open road and again for no apparent reason.

They were twenty miles out of Jaipur and, other than the bicycle, they hadn't seen another vehicle in miles. Still, Attar kept one hand on the horn, tapping out cautionary beeps as he drove.

'Amber Palace is only eleven kilometers from the city center,' Attar had said when they had climbed into his bulbous white Ambassador after lunch, 'but on such a beautiful day I would be a poor host if I did not take the scenic route.'

Jason let his arm hang out the open window, reaching now and then for the

67

steering wheel that should be in front of him but instead was far to his right, his foot slamming down on the missing brake pedal.

'Right-handed driving,' Attar said, chuckling each time Jason flinched. 'One of the lasting legacies of British rule.'

Jason leaned back in the seat catching both the cooling breeze and the warming rays of the sun and took in the scenery. The rolling hills reminded him of Corning but the desert rock formations and the patchy greenery looked like pictures he'd seen of New Mexico and Texas. When the road dipped down into a ravine or when they passed a small pond, the vegetation was lush and thick, and Jason caught glimpses of handholding couples strolling in the cool and secretive shadows. There were no maniacal auto-rickshaw drivers, no ancient donkey carts, and the pungent aroma that slapped him in the face as they left the station — a curdling blend of diesel fumes, cooking spices, piss and dirt — had dissipated, leaving the air as fresh as it was going to get. He saw his face in the shiny metal dashboard, surprised to see the smile.

The area around the train station in Jaipur had looked like the area around the train station in Delhi, with the same pack of noisy auto-rickshaws and, Jason was sure, the same pack of noisy auto-rickshaw drivers. The buildings were just as dirty, the signs just as indecipherable, and the pedestrians just as suicidal. Attar beeped his way around the congestion, steering his car on to the wider streets that led through the city.

It had taken them twenty minutes to reach the six-story Vina Yak apartment building, located in what Attar was proud to point out as the better part of the city. The mounds of trash were less frequent here and streets were devoid of the squatters' shanties and half-naked beggar children that infiltrated other neighborhoods, but the same covered sewer ran down both sides of the street, the slabs of cut stone offering little protection from the wafting smells. Single-family bungalows of concrete and brick ducked from view behind chest-high walls while boxy two-story apartment blocks crowded near the intersections. Clustered at the end of the street with other recent additions, the Vina Yak apartment building towered over its neighbors.

Characterless architecture and shoddy construction methods allowed the building to look both almost completed and ready to be condemned at the same time. The natural tones of the gray concrete bled through the cheap white paint, and reinforcing rods poked straight out at irregular intervals, rust-colored streaks washing down the walls. In the windows of the rented apartments, drying laundry hung limp out of half-open windows and rows of potted plants served as a warning track on the rail-less balconies. Through open windows he could see Ikea-style entertainment centers and from one he could hear the roar of an F-16 fighter as it gunned down PlayStation bogies in surround sound.

In the lobby, carts loaded with ceramic tiles and bags of cement gave the impression that the construction crew had just stepped out for lunch. The peeling paint, the busted window frames and the elevator door that refused to close as they rode up six flights suggested a much longer break.

When they entered the apartment there was little doubt about Attar's background in computers. A jury-rigged workbench ran the length of one of the living room's long walls, and a dozen computer towers in various states of repair sat cracked open among miles of cables and reams of schematics and photocopied instruction manuals. On the glass-topped coffee table Jason spotted a pair of laptop computers, while on the dining room table twin monitors ran tranquil images of a cyber fish tank, complete with a screen-sucking plecostomus. Two small boys peeked through a crack in the bedroom door, giggling every time they were spotted. A slight

70

woman in a blue *shalwar kamiz* came out from the kitchen long enough to be introduced as Attar's wife, Pravi, before disappearing back through the swinging door, only to return moments later with tin plates laden with spicy foods. As soon as they finished eating, Attar had them back in the car and heading out on his scenic ride to Jaipur's main tourist attraction.

'I guess the jetlag has caught up with your wife,' Attar said, pointing at his rearview mirror as the car swerved along the hillside road. Curled up on the back seat, Rachel wore her hat down over her eyes, her head resting on the soft spot that six yards of silk made in his backpack.

Jason was tempted to tell him that they weren't married, that they weren't a couple, and that he didn't even know her last name was Moore until Attar had told him at the train station. But through lunch Rachel had explained to their hosts how she and Jason had met at her cousin's wedding, how they dated for a year while she finished her degree, explained all about the big wedding and how they bought the farmhouse where Jason had grown up, and why they decided to travel to India before settling down to start a family in Corning. And, when Attar mentioned family members in nearby Binghamton, Rachel took

71

down their names, promising to look them up.

Jason had been amazed at the effortless way she rambled on, sounding as if she were recalling vivid memories instead of making it up as she went, creating in the process a fictitious life that was far more interesting than his reality. He laughed along with Attar and Pravi as she described how they had both been tossed into the icy Black River while whitewater rafting on their honeymoon, and how she had talked him into climbing onstage to sing along with the Tragically Hip at a concert in Hamilton, adding in the appropriate 'my crazy wife' shrugs and smiles.

Jason looked back at Rachel. Her mouth was just visible under the bill of her cap, her hands balled up under her chin. Even asleep and half hidden, Jason found himself drawn to her and he wondered what their wedding night had been like.

'She can sleep anywhere,' Jason said, turning back to watch for traffic coming down the wrong side of the road. 'So how did you know Sriram?'

'Five years ago. We were in university together down in Bangalore earning our masters degrees, learning to make magic, as Sriram used to say. After uni we were together in a business venture, Sriram and I and a few others from our class. Bangalore Worldwide Systems, L.C.C.'

'Yeah, I remember hearing something about it,' Jason said, thinking about his memorial service conversation with Ravi. 'But didn't he leave just as you were about to make it big?'

Attar laughed, his head bobbing. 'Oh, I do not think we would have ever made it big. There was a great deal of immaturity and hotheadedness in that group. But yes, Sriram disappeared one day and we learned that he had taken a job in America.'

'At Raj-Tech. So you knew Ravi Murty, too.'

'We were in several of the same labs. He was a few years ahead of me, a bit aloof but he could be fun. He was more of Sriram's friend, his mentor, really. Still, it was quite a surprise when Sriram decided to go to work for him. But we were happy for Sriram. At first anyway.'

Jason looked over at Attar and waited for the explanation Ravi had warned him he would hear.

'He had not been gone a week when a computer virus wiped out all the files at BWS. Our backup files as well, most unusual. When the virus showed up on our home computers we knew that something was going on. Sriram of course denied everything and for several months we were willing to accept that it was just an unfortunate accident, the cost of doing business in the Information Age. But then we heard that some of BWS's innovations were turning up in Raj-Tech's programs . . . ' He let the sentence trail off, its meaning clear.

A clump of flat-roofed houses appeared on the right. Jason could see a dozen women, all in bright saris, filling water jugs at a communal tap, then hoisting the full containers on to their heads for the walk back home. A cow strolled down the center of the road, withered and bony with a narrow hump on its shoulder that flopped to one side like a jaunty beret. Attar gave the sacred animal a polite beep and sped past while Jason sat thinking about how little he knew his dead friend.

'I was quite angry with Sriram.' Attar tapped his horn, harder this time. The traffic — animal and vehicle — picked up, and the beeping became more consistent. 'Whether our ideas were any good or not makes no difference whatsoever. And it is not just the money I had invested in BWS that he robbed me of. No, it was the intellectual spirit, my creativity, which he stole. I felt violated, raped in a way that only would make sense to another program designer,' Attar said, his words rushing together as he spoke. 'That work was my world — my religion — and he reached in and snatched it away.'

Jason shifted in his seat, keeping his eyes fixed on the truck in front of them, waiting for Attar to break the silence. After down-shifting and darting into the wrong lane till he was well past the speeding truck, Attar's breathing slowed. 'But you can not live in the past,' he said, his voice now serene. 'According to Krishnamurti, without freedom from the past there is no freedom at all.'

Jason nodded, wondering who or what a Krishnamurti was. 'The old forgive and forget, huh?'

Attar thought for a moment then shook his head. 'Forgiveness and forgetfulness are irrelevant. It is all about accepting what has been and moving on to what is now.'

'Well, I'm still impressed. If that had been me that had been cheated I'd still be mad.'

'Oh, some of the others remain most sincerely disturbed, I assure you. But their anger, as Krishnamurti has shown, is based on their fears, fears about their past mistakes, and their uncertain future. By accepting what is and not obsessing on what might have been or what might yet come, you defeat fear. Without fear there is no anger, without anger

75

there is no violence.'

'Violence? You think these friends of yours are capable of violence?' Lines from Ravi's email buzzed in his memory.

'*Absolutely,*' Attar said, tapping the horn to emphasize the point. 'We are capable of extreme violence. We just need the right push.'

'But Sriram's dead.'

'But the fear he caused lives on. And with fear there is the inevitability of violence. And for my old acquaintances, you now represent that fear, and in their eyes that fear must be destroyed. So with that, if you will please awaken your wife . . . '

Jason felt his hand grip the doorframe and his leg muscles tense. 'Why?'

'Because when we get to the top of this hill,' Attar said, 'there is a most spectacular view of the Amber Palace.'

# 7

The cobra reared two feet above the rim of the basket, its hood wide as it swayed in time to the tuneless music. Without thinking, Jason took a step back.

'Don't worry. It can't bite you,' Rachel said, stooping down to the snake's level to get a picture. 'My guidebook says that the charmer sews the snake's mouth shut before a performance.' She framed the shot on the small screen before digitally saving the image. 'One stitch and it can't open its mouth.'

Attar spoke with the snake charmer, who rocked from side to side, tempting the fat black snake to strike. He slipped the wood flute from his mouth to speak but kept it moving in front of him, returning to his high-pitched wailing song as Rachel moved in for a tighter shot.

'The snake charmer wants me to ask you if you would like to sew a deadly cobra's mouth shut.'

Rachel laughed as she schooched closer to the snake. 'What are you, nuts? There's no way I'd do that.'

'Interesting,' Attar said after relaying the

comment. 'That's exactly what he says.'

It took a moment, but when it sunk in Rachel stumbled to her feet and ducked behind Jason, her hands reaching around his chest as she peeked over his shoulders. The snake charmer eased the lid down on the snake's head and it disappeared into the low, round basket. He smiled up to Jason, who handed the man a handful of rupee notes.

'You could have bought the snake for that much,' Attar said, shaking his head.

'It was worth it,' Jason said, feeling Rachel's warm body tight against his.

They had spent most of the afternoon at the hilltop Amber Palace, wandering though its ornate and empty rooms, Rachel providing background information summarized in her guidebook, Attar chuckling as he corrected her pronunciation. Jason struggled to make sense of it all — the massive palace gates, every inch covered with symmetrical eight-fold designs, the crooked passages that ended in hidden rooms, secret balconies with epic views of the valley below and everything older than the oldest building he'd ever seen. For all its age and beauty it lacked a logical layout, its ornamental symmetry lost in a fun house maze of dead-end hallways, slanting floors and off-centered windows. It was impressive, he heard himself saying, but with a little more planning and organization it could have been awesome.

The sun was low on the horizon when they reentered the city, Attar joining in the chorus of tinny beeps and screeching brakes, but he insisted that they make one last stop. From the street the Palace of Winds promised to be the most breathtaking site of the day, five stories of rounded cupolas, lattice-covered balconies, stacked domes and repeating niches, all carved from a pink-red sandstone and accented in delicate white highlights. Now, as they stood inside, the snake charmer stacking snake-filled baskets on his head, Jason wondered if they had taken a wrong turn.

Unlike the Amber Palace, with its majestic chambers and its rich decorations, the Palace of Winds was more like a giant Hollywood set, a stunning façade held up by utilitarian supports, crammed into the middle of a busy market street. There were stone staircases to climb and plenty of windows to look out, all of them providing lattice-obstructed views of the dirty and crowded street below, but other than the large gray monkeys, the palace was empty.

'Known as the Pink City, Jaipur was founded in AD seventeen twenty-seven by the astronomer king Sawai Jai Singh,' Rachel said, reading the faded sign posted next to one of the dark, sloping ramps that led to the upper floors. 'A royal decree mandated that all the buildings within the city walls be painted pink to simulate the red sandstone buildings of Mughal cities.'

'There's no 'u' in color,' Jason said, reading ahead.

'There is if you went to school in India. Another holdover from the days of the Raj,' Attar said with an exaggerated British accent.

Rachel took a sip from her water bottle before continuing. 'The Hawa Mahal, known popularly as the Palace of Winds . . . blah blah blah . . . nine hundred and fifty-three windows . . . yada yada yada . . . lace-fine carved screens . . . royal ladies watch the street hidden from view . . . today stands as a reminder . . . yeah, whatever.'

'You have to forgive her,' Jason said to Attar as they climbed a twisting staircase to the second floor. 'If it's not a train she's not interested.'

Shafts of sunlight wedged through the narrow windows, spotlighting sections of carved white marble pillars and lobed arches that suggested that the palace wasn't always so barren. The air on the street had been sluggish, weighed down by exhaust fumes and spices, but a light and steady breeze kept the hall cool. Darting in and out the windows, young monkeys tested their agility while their parents were content to sit on balcony railings and scratch at fleas.

'You can feed them peanuts,' Attar said, reaching into his pocket to produce a small white paper bag. 'Just hold your hand flat and do not make any sudden movements.' He held his hand out to a monkey that sat on the windowsill. The monkey eyed the lone peanut, deciding if it was worth the effort. Attar added a second nut to his hand and the monkey snatched them both, swinging out the open window and along the carved front of the palace. A group of small boys gathered around Attar and he supplied them with peanuts, half of which they gave to the monkeys and half they ate themselves.

'Come here, little guy,' Rachel said and held out her hand to coax a jittery monkey off a stone railing. Its large eyes were chocolate brown and its fur looked soft to the touch. The monkey reached out a paw, drawing it back twice before he picked up the peanut.

'You are *so* cute I could just kiss you,' Rachel said and for a moment Jason wished he were a monkey. He set his backpack on the ground, unzipping a side pocket to get his camera.

'Look this way,' he said and lined up

Rachel, the peanut and the monkey in the viewfinder. He pushed the shutter and a white flash lit up the dark alcove.

With the flash, the monkey's eyes widened and with a fang-bared howl it leapt from its perch and charged, its sharp claws clattering on the stone floor. Rachel screamed and covered her face but the monkey tore past her and threw himself at Jason, who stumbled backwards, his arms flailing as he fell. The monkey stood and showed his yellow teeth, grabbed the backpack, and raced up the red sandstone wall, leaping off the balcony and out into the street-side bazaar.

Jason scrambled to his feet, leaning over the railing far enough to see the monkey as it bounded across the tattered awning of a typewriter repair shop and on to the roof of an idling delivery truck, the backpack banging against its metal sides. The monkey paused long enough to look up at Jason, then jumped on to the hood of a passing Mercedes. The driver slammed on the brakes and hit the horn. The monkey glared at the driver, snapping off a windshield wiper before it climbed over the roof and on to a street sign. From there it scurried across a camel-driven cart hauling trash, bounced in and out of the seat of a bicycle rickshaw, along the tops of a row of tightly packed

Ambassador sedans and up a hand-lettered sign that was topped by a painting of a rotten tooth. Reaching the roof of the one-story building across the street, the monkey sat down to appraise its loot.

'Oh, shit,' Jason said, fixing the location of the thief before racing down the open stairs, Rachel right behind him.

'You are wasting your time,' Attar shouted to them from the balcony as they burst out on to the sidewalk, rushing headlong into the traffic. 'You will never see your luggage again.' Jason saw a few people pointing up at the monkey and a few more pointing at him, but for most Jaipurians the site of a felonious monkey or a panicked tourist did not merit attention.

'It's right there,' Rachel said, pointing over the roof of a bakery. Jason glanced up, nodded and ran into the shop.

'Excuse me,' he said, his words rushing together. 'There's a monkey. On your roof. Up there. He's got my bag. I need . . . '

The owner of the shop kept his eyes on his newspaper, jerking his thumb towards a dark stairwell that ran up the back wall. They stumbled up the tight stairway, spilling out on to the rooftop that served as a block-long patio for the pink-walled apartments set back on the building. Old men sat in folding chairs, spitting streams of red betel juice into plastic buckets while toddlers stood at the edge of the roof, tossing pebbles on to the cars below. A group of teenage boys, dressed in matching white shirts and blue trousers, sprawled on the blazing pink concrete, checking their cell phones and singing Indian pop tunes. When they noticed Jason and Rachel they stood up, shouting out the few English words they thought they knew.

'Over there,' Rachel said, spotting the monkey as it bit the top off a tube of Crest. It was sitting with its back to them, one leg dangling over the side of the building.

Jason held her back. 'If we scare it it'll just run away. You go that way,' he said, pointing far to the monkey's left. 'I'll come in from here. Try to box it in.'

'Then what? I'm not going to get rabies just to save your underwear.'

'Maybe he'll drop it. If you can, try to grab the bag.'

'Well, I'm sure as hell not going to grab the monkey,' she said and maneuvered her way across the roof.

Jason kept his eyes on the animal, trying to sneak up without tripping over the satellite dish wires and plastic piping that ran the length of the building. The monkey was busy tearing open a zippered-shut side pocket. He didn't want to think of what the razor-taloned thief would do with a red silk sari.

'Good morning mister sir,' one of the teens said, stepping up to walk with Jason.

'I'm kind of busy here,' Jason said. The monkey's tail gave a flick but the rest of the monkey sat still on the ledge.

'Part of this nutritional breakfast,' the teen replied. 'Merry Christmas. Star Wars. Michael Jordan.'

Jason watched the furry gray back as he continued his flanking movement, the monkey flinging a packet of disposable razors out into the street.

'Four, five, six, seven,' the teen said, adding 'Happy birthday' before breaking into a toothy grin.

'Shhhh,' Jason whispered. 'I need to get my backpack away from the monkey.' He pointed just as his travel alarm clock went ringing over the ledge.

'Oh, *kapi*,' the teen said, turning back to explain the situation to his friends, their English not as polished as his.

'Just stay back,' Jason said without looking at the boy. Across the roof he saw that Rachel was almost in position, the monkey busy licking Hawaiian Tropic sun block off its fingers.

He heard the footsteps behind him and

turned to see the schoolboys running towards him, sticks and rocks in their hands. 'No,' he shouted, putting his arms out to stop them, but they ran past him and headed to the monkey.

Intrigued by a toothbrush, the monkey didn't see the blitzing pack until it was almost on him. The monkey gave a high-pitched shriek and ran two steps at the boys, hoping to scare them off, then crouched as an empty water bottle whistled over its head. A broken broom handle cracked down as the monkey reached out for the backpack and a second stick, tossed like a spear, skidded across the roof, wide of its target. Gripping one of the padded shoulder straps, the monkey tried to pull the bag closer, the bag not moving, the bulk of the bag wedged under a bent piece of pipe that stuck out from the concrete. With the boys closing, the monkey gave the strap a second violent tug, the plastic clips shattering as the monkey scuttled sideways, the freed strap still in its paw. The monkey looked back at his lost prize, then at the boys, gave a spitty, yellow-fanged hiss and, waving the loose strap, leapt up and out to tightrope the jumble of wires strung along the street. Victorious, the boys gave a cheer and signaled to Jason and Rachel it was safe to approach.

'Call toll free one eight hundred,' the teen

said, stepping out of the way as Jason bent down to examine his pack. The side pockets had been torn open and there were long gashes in the top flap that exposed the extra tee shirts he packed, but, other than the smell, the pack had weathered the ordeal.

'Whoa,' Rachel said, waving her hand in front of her nose as she squatted down. 'What *is* that?'

'It *was* cologne,' Jason said, lifting shards of the glass bottle from the soaked-through side pocket. 'I guess it could have been worse.'

'Yeah, you could have worn the stuff. How's the rest of the bag?'

Jason pinched the plastic snap and stretched the bag open, pushing his folded clothes to the side to check on the sari. 'It's a bit damp but everything looks okay. I guess I ought to thank you guys,' he said, looking up at the schoolboys.

'Some restrictions may apply!' The teen held out his hand, his friends smiling as Jason took out his wallet.

# 8

The boy held the collapsing paper cup through the horizontal bars of the window in the second-class car of the six twenty-five express to Ahmadabad, walking along as the train began to lurch out of the station.

'Chai. Hot chai,' the boy shouted, determined to make one last five-rupee sale before departure. Jason took the folding cup from the boy's hand, not because he wanted a second cup of the milky, oversweet tea but because he knew if he didn't it would somehow end up on his lap. He handed the boy a crumpled fifty-rupee note and waited for change. The boy smiled and waved as the train picked up speed and the platform fell away.

There was a chill in the morning air he had not expected and the scalding chai warmed his hands through the thin cup and burned his tongue when he dared a tentative sip. He yawned and stretched, tensing his muscles in his back and his legs. Other than the late-night fight over the sari he had slept well.

Attar's wife had had a full meal prepared

for them when they arrived from their encounter with the backpack-stealing monkey. Just as she had done during lunch, Pravi Singh stayed cloistered in the kitchen, the children running out now and then to see the tall white man and his beautiful tanned wife. After the meal Attar had driven Jason to a store no larger than his cubicle at the mortgage office where he was able to replenish his supplies. A stroll down a side street led to an open-air market where a man with a foot-powered sewing machine repaired his torn pack for a handful of lightweight coins. The Hello Kitty replacement strap he threw in for free.

'Doesn't he have anything in black?' Jason had asked, examining the neon-pink padded strap.

'He says this is the only one that will fit your bag, that model being quite rare,' Attar explained, eyeing the new strap, doing his best not to laugh. 'He cautions that the clips have been damaged and you should not put too much strain on them or you will lose this strap as well.'

'Impossible,' Jason said, hefting the pack to his back. 'I couldn't be that lucky.'

Back at the apartment Rachel and Pravi were curled up on the sofa, watching a slide-show of baby pictures on a laptop computer, the boys squirming in to get a better view.

'Jason wants to name our first son Peter after his father, but I like Jason, junior,' he had heard Rachel say through the door before he turned on the shower, the drizzle of water splashing on the stone bathroom floor and running down the porcelain squat-style toilet behind him. By the time he was done drying his hair the thin towel was soaked and he felt his skin stick as he pulled on a clean Yankees tee shirt and gym shorts. He was climbing into bed when Rachel had entered the room.

'I hope you didn't use up all the warm water,' she had said as she dug through her bag.

'Nope. That was used up before I started.' The bed was comfortable and with his eyes shut he knew he'd be asleep in minutes.

'You know I usually sleep in the nude,' Rachel said, Jason's eyes popping back open.

'Well, don't change your routine on my account.' He leaned up on an elbow, just in case.

'But I knew we'd be sleeping on a lot of trains so I bought this.' She held up a Nike warm-up suit, the long-sleeved top matching the full-length bottoms. 'Cute, huh?'

'Adorable,' he said and settled back down, his head sinking deep in the feather pillow.

'What do you think you're doing?' Rachel said as she gathered up the things she would need in the shower.

'It's a little thing I like to do every night called sleep.' He had thought of adding something about being willing to change his plans if she had other ideas but it sounded wrong in his head.

'Not in that bed you're not.'

'Now that you've made us man and wife I think it'd look kinda strange if I slept out on the couch. And there's not enough room to sleep on the floor.' Jason waved a hand to take in the clutter of dark computer monitors and cannibalized mainframes that covered the room.

Rachel looked around, pushing a pile of broken keyboards under the bed with her foot before giving up. 'All right. You can sleep *on* the bed but you can't sleep *in* it.'

With a dramatic flourish, Jason threw back the covers and climbed out. He tucked the sheet and light blanket back in place on his side of the bed and lay back down under the thin top blanket. 'Better?'

'Much,' she said and ducked into the bathroom, closing the door behind her. By the time she had stepped under the shower's trickle, he was asleep.

It was dark when he woke, his body shaking in the arctic-cold air conditioning. Jason tried to slide under the covers only to find that, as a defensive measure or a reaction to the dropping temperature, Rachel had managed to wrap the free ends of the blanket tight around herself. He felt for his backpack, pulled the sari from the bottom and tossed it in the air, unfurling a few yards of fabric as it flew. In the dark he did his best to cover himself with the last gift his dead friend bought for his mother, his chattering teeth louder than his conscience.

An hour later he shook himself awake, the sari now part of Rachel's growing cocoon of blankets. He freed a section large enough to crawl under and fell back asleep only to wake up twenty minutes later, his small portion of the six-yard sari reclaimed. He sat up, grabbed the end of the sari, his fist tightening around the soft fabric and the button, and yanked it free, rolling Rachel on to the floor. Without a light on he could only guess at the dirty look she gave him as she crawled back in bed.

She didn't mention the sari incident as they packed to leave in the pre-dawn light, but as he brushed his teeth he caught her admiring the elaborate gold-thread embroidery. Now on the train, he noticed her eyeing the simple lever that kept the train's door shut.

'Once it warms up a bit I'm going to open

the door,' Rachel said. She glanced back at the half-empty car to see how many people it would upset. 'In Canada they'd never let you stand in an open doorway. Too many rules, everybody afraid of a lawsuit. Here, you want to stand in the doorway of a moving train, knock yourself out.'

'And how many people are killed falling off trains?' Jason was thumbing through Rachel's guidebook, looking for restaurants in Ahmadabad. 'Rules protect us from our own stupidity.'

'Okay, Dad. I get it,' Rachel said in an exaggerated teen voice.

'If you haven't noticed, safety isn't very high on the list here. It'd be smarter if you just stick to your toy trains.'

'They're not toys,' she said, this time in a voice that let Jason know she was done kidding. 'They are scale trains. One inch to eighty-seven point one inches.'

'HO scale,' Jason said. 'I used to build plastic car models. When I was a kid.'

Rachel sighed. 'Here it comes. You're going to make all sorts of smart-assed remarks about my hobby and I'm going to get pissed off and then you're going to feel sorry and I'm going to have to forgive you so why don't we just cut to the chase. I forgive you for being an insensitive jerk who thinks he has the right to belittle people just because they like things he doesn't.'

Jason smiled. 'Well, we got that out of the way. But come on. Trains?'

Rachel looked at him for a moment, trying to spot any hint of sarcasm in his expression. 'It started with my grandfather. My dad's dad. He worked for Canadian Rail as an engineer, worked the last steam lines in Ontario back in the fifties. Then he got hit in the face — some engine part flying off. Went blind in one eye.' Her finger came up involuntarily, touching her right cheek. 'That was the last day he drove a train. A full-scale one anyway. He was hoping for a grandson who he could share his passion for trains with but he ended up with me. I was ten when he died. Keep the trains going. That was the last thing he said to me. So I did.' She looked down at her hands.

Jason swallowed hard and took a breath before speaking. 'Wow.'

'You like it?' Rachel said, her whole face brightening as she popped up in her seat. 'I thought the bit about him dying was too much, but it seemed to fit. Usually I have him lose a leg in Manitoba but the eye was a nice touch.'

Jason felt his face redden. 'You made it all up?'

'Always tell people what they want to hear.

94

It makes them happy and it doesn't cost you a thing.'

'So there was no grandfather, no dying request?' His voice matched his waving hands, rising and dropping as he spoke.

'Of course there was a grandfather, silly. He sold insurance. Lives in Florida now. He likes my trains, at least I think he does, but he thinks *I'm* kind of weird.' She looked at him and smiled. 'Close your mouth before a fly lands in there.'

'You . . . but . . . why . . . '

'Why would I lie? Because the truth is never as interesting. Oh come on,' she said, giving his arm a playful punch, 'like you never made up a story when you were flirting with someone you liked.'

He drew in a breath to answer and held it, wondering what she had meant.

'Other than the Freudian 'trains into tunnels' thing,' she said as she stood up, 'I just think they're neat. Now I'm going to see if they'll let me do something stupid and climb up to the engine. I'd ask you to come along but I'm sure there's a rule against it.'

\* \* \*

Jason tied the grimy curtains together and wedged the knot under the top horizontal bar of the window. The side doors were propped open and the hot, dry air of the Rajasthani plains blew in, providing the sun-baked car with an illusion of relief. Although more passengers had boarded the train at the small stations along the route, the car was quiet, the midday heat and the gentle rocking of the train lulling the riders into a lethargic doze.

With variations on the theme, the view from the window remained the same. A line of hills was visible on the horizon, indicating where the flat farmland came to an end, and towns too small to earn a stop blurred by in seconds. Despite the heat and the dust, neat, green rows of some hearty crop ran away from the tracks, the mile-long fields separated by dirt roads or pump-fed irrigation ditches. Shacks appeared at unpredictable intervals, thrown up by the side of the tracks or plopped down in the middle of the field, not large enough to store a motorcycle, yet Jason knew they probably served as homes for the army of workers that dotted the landscape.

The few men he saw stood stork-like, with a bare foot propped against a bony knee, arms pulled tight across their chests as they leaned on homemade walking sticks. They watched as teams of women attacked the arid soil with pointed sticks or loaded the unknown harvest into the back of an ox-drawn cart, the tall wooden wheels replaced with bald truck tires. Some men chatted on cell phones and a few slept in the shade the rare tree provided, but most were content to just watch.

While the men wore an assortment of tattered slacks, tee shirts, jeans, and white cotton dhotis, the women all wore saris, the neon-bright colors and festive patterns shining through the dirt and sweat. Under their saris the women wore tight half-shirts that covered their shoulders and upper arms but left their stomachs bare.

Ancient women — one bracelet-covered arm balancing a heaping basket of dirt, the other drawing the end of the sari to veil a leathery face — snaked through the fields, the men pointing with their chins where each load should be dumped. Jason wondered if the saris they wore were the gift of a dutiful, stork-standing son.

Although no one seemed to have a problem staring at him, he felt uncomfortable studying the saris of the women who walked down the aisle of the train. At the station in Jaipur he had smiled when one girl, looking up suddenly, caught him admiring her form-fitting yellow sari. The girl's eyes widened in horror and, covering her face, she ducked into the crowd.

From what he could tell from his sidelong glances, the sari was wrapped around the waist, somehow creating a row of pleats in the process. The older the woman the higher up the waist the sari was wrapped, with girls in their twenties daring the sari in place on their hips. It took him an hour to notice that there were different ways of wearing the final length of fabric. The fashion conscious preferred a style that swung up from the left hip, across the chest and over the right shoulder, with the most elaborately decorated section of the sari hanging below the waist. The old women on the train — and everyone he saw in the field — passed the final yards of fabric around their backs and over their left shoulders, pulling a portion up on to their heads to serve as a veil, a toss of the fabric separating the trendy from the traditional.

Vidya had never worn a sari, happiest in tight jeans and midriff-baring tops, a look that matched her attitude.

He thought about the sari balled up in the bottom of his backpack and the friend who asked him to hold on to it, the friend he thought he knew.

Attar had made it clear that he believed Sriram had cheated him and his former classmates out of a fortune, his sudden move to the States evidence of his crime. And even

98

if the program was as 'academic' as Ravi had claimed, Sriram had still betrayed his friends for a chance to make it rich. Attar's faith — or whatever this Krishnamurti thing was — helped him, to a degree, move past the betrayal, to focus on today and forget about yesterday's lost millions, something Jason was sure few others would do. And he wasn't sure he could blame them.

Jason thought back to the dinners at the Sundarams' and how little Sriram had discussed his job. He loved to ramble on about the role of computers in society and the philosophy behind artificial intelligence and self-writing programs, but when it came down to what he did each day, Sriram had said little. If he was to believe Sheriff Neville and the reports in *The Leader*, there were a lot of things Sriram didn't share. Jason knew that his feelings towards his friend were shifting, that he was beginning to accept that Sriram had sold out his partners for thirty pieces of silver and a pair of green cards, but he still couldn't imagine Sriram murdering Vidya and then shooting himself. With the more he learned about Sriram he wondered if that, too, would start to shift. Maybe they weren't as happy as he thought, maybe there were passions he never imagined burning behind the smiling mask. He didn't know what went on when they shut their door.

And he still didn't know where to find Sriram's mother or what he would say when he handed her the gold-embroidered, blood-red sari.

A sari with a pattern he knew he had seen somewhere before.

A pattern that Rachel seemed to recognize as well, as she had folded the makeshift blanket early that morning.

# 9

With his spiral-bound notebook atop his carryall, M.V. Dharmadeep, Ph.D., rushed his hand along the page, documenting the conversation before it slipped from his memory. His penmanship was neat and tight and, although the train rocked heavily on this stretch of track, the notes on this page were as precise as those he had written yesterday in his university office, a skill acquired from decades of travel on India Railways.

When he had finished he reread his notes, placing a small star by the most salient passages. It was, as his students were wont to say, good stuff. Of course there was no place for anecdotal evidence in his monograph, but the interview was filled with the kind of trivial quotes that the general public lapped up, too undisciplined to understand that the truth was to be found not in the individual, but rather in the statistical collective. The kind of quotes that would help fill out that fluff piece he was ghostwriting for *The Express*.

He had spotted the couple before they had boarded the train, the man tall and proportionally built, his wife shorter, that silly cap making her look like the sport-mad co-eds he had seen around the university. She was attractive, yes, but her beauty was hidden by her slovenly appearance. He had planned to speak to them as soon as the train was underway, but, in typical liberated, western-feminist fashion, the woman was wandering about the train on her own, eventually opening one of the car's side doors to stand in the doorway for all the world to see. It wasn't till some time after noon that she settled back in her seat, and he had used that opportunity to introduce himself and conduct his research. He flipped back to the first page of his notes and read them through a third time.

**Question**: Is your marriage an arranged marriage or a love marriage?
**Answer**: (wife) It was definitely a love marriage. More like a love at first sight marriage.

Dr. Dharmadeep shook his head as he reread the line. They had seemed like such a nice couple.

He had been quite up front with them, explaining that he was the chair of the sociology department at the university in New Delhi, his specialization the statistical analysis of marital systems, specifically the inherent instability of love marriages, and yet, without hesitation, the wife proudly declared theirs to have been the worst kind of love marriage possible. His files were chock full of data that foretold the sad and predictable end of their relationship. A sixty-seven point nine two percent failure rate for love marriages in general, even higher when their youth and their self-described 'love at first sight' foundation were factored in.

**Question**: Did you ask your mother for her assistance in finding a husband?
**Answer**: (wife) You're kidding, right?

Each semester, Dr. Dharmadeep found himself having to defend the institution of arranged marriage, the students too easily seduced by the West's deceptive liberalism. They would bring up the same threadbare arguments — free-will, independence, human rights — the brighter among them quoting Shakespeare and that Friedan woman, the others spouting pop-culture clichés, some finding a way to twist Gandhi around to their side. But it made no difference. He had the statistical proof to dismantle each argument, the weight of tradition and common sense on his side. And, despite what they said in class, when the time came for marriage, ninety-five percent of his students would rely on their families to make the arrangements.

Question: Did you ask your father's permission to marry?
Answer: (husband) You mean ask her father?
Note — question was rephrased and repeated.
Answer: (laughing) My father would be shocked to hear I was married.

Marriage is not a union of two individuals, he would lecture his students, but rather a union of two entire families. Who loves you more than your family, who knows you better than the people who raised you? Finding a perfect match for one's child is the single most important task a parent must face. The process is not entered into lightly, the selection not the result of some chance encounter, some drunken meeting at a discotheque. An arranged marriage is a true marriage of love — the pure love of a parent for an offspring. This is why, he liked to point out, India enjoys a divorce rate of less than two percent, noting that that number included all the Indians living in the West, implying skewed results.

**Question**: How long have you been married?

**Answer**: (husband *did not know* and deferred to wife) Eighteen months.

**Question**: How does it feel to know that, statistically, your marriage has less than one year before it fails?

**Answer**: (husband — surprised) It seems like we just got married yesterday.

What was this obsession with love in a marriage? He had spent a lifetime studying marriage and was no closer to understanding why, from culture to culture, people assumed that love was the sign of a 'successful' marriage. No one spoke of responsibility or obligation, a few mentioned respect but seemed to equate the word with equality. His parents had raised nine children — *nine* — and he never heard the word used. And hadn't he himself been married for thirty years now, raising two sons, both engineers, and a daughter, happily married to a barrister, all without once telling his wife he loved her?

Although it was too late for them, he had taken a half hour to explain the superiority of the arranged marriage system, the husband interrupting with objections, the wife telling him to be quiet, her feminine nature sensing the truth.

The chai vendor made his way through the car and Dr. Dharmadeep waved him over with a five-rupee note. He sipped the steaming tea as the boy fished in his pockets for change, recalling the intent look in the young woman's eyes as she absorbed everything he said, nodding as she realized the logic of his arguments. In a way he felt sorry for her, forced by her culture into a marriage that she now saw for what it was — convenience and hormones, an exercise in myth-driven egocentrism.

Maybe there was hope after all, he thought as he read over the last page of his notes. Not for her, of course but for her children or her grandchildren. He put a large star next to the woman's final comment. He would use it in the article, a Western woman admitting that arranged marriages were indeed best.

It was exactly what he had wanted to hear.

★ ★ ★

'Hold on to this and don't run off,' Rachel said, holding her back-pack out by one of its straps. 'I want to get a shot of this train coming into the station.'

'Won't it look just like the last train?' Jason asked, surprised at the heavy weight of her bag, wondering what she could be hauling around India.

'It's an express,' she said, pointing at the fast approaching headlight down the tracks. 'It doesn't stop. I want to get an action shot.' She turned and he watched her as she walked down the platform, her low-slung khakis and her short shirt framing every move of her tight hips, the tattoo peeking over her waistband. He wondered if she knew what a great shot she was missing.

Their train from Delhi had stopped just long enough for them to climb off, pulling out of the station five minutes later and right on schedule, taking with it the bustle its arrival had caused. The few passengers who had gotten off had dragged their luggage through the turnstile and out into the late afternoon sun of Ahmadabad, leaving only transfer passengers and railway employees on the platform. The chai vendors had stopped shouting, the red-jacketed porters had slid back down against the station wall, and the shoeshine boys, spotting Jason's Nikes, had wandered off in search of more fashionable prospects. Down the platform Rachel was adjusting her camera, attracting the attention of a mangy puppy that sniffed at her feet. Other than the distant sounds of a hectic city, it was quiet and he was glad for the few seconds alone. He didn't notice the man behind him until he spoke.

'Mr Jason Talley?' the high-pitched voice said, cracking.

Jason sighed and closed his eyes, fighting the urge to ignore yet another Indian welcome his email message had caused. He forced on a smile and turned to meet his new friend. 'Yes, I'm Jason Talley.'

The knife was a blur in the man's hand as it swung up at his neck and Jason's back arched as his reflexes took control. The tip of the knife clipped his chin, splattering his attacker's shirt with bright red spots, the man shouting in Hindi as his arm swept past, paused, and came back again. Jason stumbled, his feet tangled in backpack straps, watching as his left arm shot up to block the blade. He saw the knife slow as it cut through his forearm, the blade pulling free and scratching the face of his watch, saw the stream of blood that trailed after the knife as the attacker's arm flew by, and watched as the man, wild-eyed, shifted the blade in his hand and charged.

Jason tumbled backwards, the packs skidding along the dusty concrete, his arms flailing to keep his balance, thick drops of blood forming curved patterns that seemed to hang in the air. The man leapt towards him, stabbing out with the knife as he came, forcing Jason to step back, his heel catching the edge of the platform.

The tin-roofed terminal shook as the express train roared into the station, horn blasting. In a frozen moment Jason could see the yellow and red engine closing, the conductor leaning out of the window, frantic, waving them away from the tracks, could see Rachel looking his way through the viewfinder of her camera while a wall of porters sprinted towards him, armed with brooms and handcarts, and could see the man, his shirt covered with Jason's blood, lunging, his shouts lost in the engine's diesel roar.

Jason launched himself forward towards the knife and away from the oncoming train. Startled, the man rose up on the balls of his feet, his momentum carrying him forward. Jason ducked to the side and the man spun to renew his attack, pivoting on his right foot, his left leg thrusting back, off the edge of the platform. Jason saw surprise in the man's eyes as he tumbled backwards in slow motion, his head catching on the train's iron bumper, yanking his body forward on to the tracks and under the steel wheels. The engine was fifty yards past the station before the airbrakes hissed, and screaming, the train began to slow.

Jason felt a dozen hands pull him back from the tracks, the train running just inches away, and he noticed that people were talking to him, rapid-fire in a language he didn't understand. Dark hands wrapped a dirty tee shirt around his left arm, one of the porters holding a damp sweat rag against his chin to stem the flow. They crowded around, grabbing at his clothes, helping to keep him on his feet as his knees buckled.

'What the hell are you doing?' Rachel said, elbowing her way through the knot of porters and train officials, stopping short when she saw all the blood. She looked at Jason, and he saw her lip tremble as her eyes welled up.

'It was an insane assassin,' a portly railway official said, his chubby hands brushing aside the porters. 'He tried to slice this man open and deposit him in front of the Avantika Express. We saw it but were unable to get to the poor blighter in time.' He looked over his shoulder to the pool of blood that dripped off the platform and down to the tracks, the open train window above the spot crowded with gawking passengers.

Rachel stepped closer, her hand reaching out for the bloody rag held against his face. 'What did you *do*?' she said in a half whisper.

'Me? I didn't do anything. I was just standing there and then this guy starts swinging a knife at me.'

'The man was most insane,' the official said to Rachel, lifting his eyes heavenward as he spoke, and the porters that had stayed close by nodded in agreement. 'Your friend is lucky to be among the living.' The man said something to the porters and, before he could protest, they had lifted Jason off his feet and were carrying him to the stationmaster's office. Behind them the Avantika Express started back down the track, a squad of railway workers with buckets and hoses waiting for the train to pass.

It was a large and well-lit office, the air conditioning set so low that Jason shivered from the cold. They hurried him to the back of the room, sticking his bloody arm under the tap on the small sink in the corner, red-tinted water splashing over the side and down on to the concrete floor.

At first Jason watched as the porters took turns holding his arm steady. There were moments when the water flushed the blood away and he could see deep inside the gash, the blood rushing back to fill the gap. He watched until his arm began to shake, recognizing at last whose arm he was looking at. He closed his eyes and focused on his breathing and swallowing down the sour taste in his mouth.

The porters pulled him away from the water, wrapping a clean, wet towel around his arm, four hands pressing it tight against his forearm as they led him to a wooden chair in the center of the room. Eyes shut, he heard the railway official reassuring Rachel that things like this just did not happen here at Ahmadabad, maybe in Jodpur or Alwar, yes definitely at Alwar, but not here at his station, and that help was coming in the form of a fully-licensed and board certified doctor from the clinic not two minutes away, and that she had nothing to fear, that she should just relax, asking if she would care for a cup of tea or some chocolate biscuits that were right here on his desk a moment ago.

Jason kept his eyes closed until the doctor arrived.

Groups of men in uniforms began passing through the office, the police officers the best dressed, wearing tailor-made and starched uniforms, their brass buttons and black leather boots gleaming, the clerks and officials of Indian Railways far behind in their company-issued suit coats and ties. The two medics who attended to his cut wore standard white smocks but the doctor, a tall man with a handlebar mustache and tobacco-stained teeth, made do with a nametag clipped to his plaid sport shirt.

'Shouldn't we get this done in a hospital?' Rachel asked, leaning over a dust-covered computer monitor to watch the doctor stitch the six-inch gash on Jason's arm. The cut on his chin had already stopped bleeding.

The doctor shook his head, the tails of his mustache bouncing. 'At the hospital they would charge you a hundred times as much as they charge the locals,' the doctor said as he worked. 'Here I will only charge you ten times as much.' He drew the black suture through a flap of skin, raising the hooked needle up past his shoulder, tugging the string taut before looping back and repeating the move on the other side of the thin, red line. 'Bite down,' the doctor said when he had finished, pouring half a bottle of hydrogen peroxide on the low ridge of skin and thread, sopping up the foaming runoff with the bloody towel.

There were not as many questions as Jason had expected, the porters and the sweating stationmaster explaining everything to the police. Outside he could see more uniformed men lifting a misshapen body bag on to the platform, a small crowd of onlookers kept back by sergeants wielding riding crops. He looked back in time to see the doctor tapping a long yellowed fingernail

113

against the side of a syringe.

'I will give you a tetanus shot, just in case, as well as some antibiotics to apply later. Keep your arm clean and avoid contact with animals.'

'See? It's a good thing you played tag with the monkey yesterday,' Rachel said, drawing his attention away from the needle.

'A monkey stole my backpack in Jaipur,' Jason explained. 'But we got it back.'

The doctor did not smile. 'Tourists get too close to the monkeys. A monkey bite is a serious thing, much worse than this.' He gestured with the dripping needle at Jason's arm, implying the pettiness of his wound. 'And if you had had a run-in with the monkey's owner it could have been very dangerous.'

'This was a wild monkey. It lived in the Palace of Winds.'

The stationmaster rested a heavy hand on Jason's back. 'Not all the monkeys you see are wild. Some are kept as pets and some are the property of unscrupulous individuals who train the monkeys to steal things and bring them back to their homes. Not so much here but in Jaipur . . . ' He raised his shoulders, hinting at the lawlessness of the fabled Pink City.

'My friend is right. Some entrepreneurs

even rent out their monkeys. You point out what you want and they get it for you. Now this will not hurt much,' the doctor lied, forcing the large-gauge needle into Jason's upper arm.

# 10

'Oh my God, that was amazing,' Rachel said as she swung her feet off the edge of the bed. 'That was an *incredible* night.' She smiled at Jason, reaching over to run a hand through his disheveled hair. 'You really know how to treat a woman.'

'You slept in your clothes on a fold-down bench on a train in India. How does that qualify as amazing?'

'Look at this,' she said holding her arms out to her sides. 'This is a first-class, AC sleeper for four. And it's just us.'

'Us and everybody who walks by,' Jason said, jerking a thumb at the sliding glass and metal door that separated the cabin from the narrow passageway that ran down the right side of the car. Two large windows on either side of the door gave anyone who cared to look an unobstructed view of the entire cabin.

'We didn't have to fold up the seat backs to make the bunk beds and we didn't have to do that stupid trick with the blanket so we could sleep together.'

'True,' Jason said. 'But that's because we slept on different beds.' He waved his hand in

116

the open area between the thick-cushioned bench seats that served as the bottom bunks in the box-sized cabin. There was a barred window opposite the glass door with the same dingy-brown curtain from the last train, and a small, hinged shelf was propped open under the window supporting Rachel's guidebook and an empty bottle of water. Outside the early morning sun cast long shadows on the tracks and outbuildings of what had been known for a century as Victoria Terminus but was now the Chatarapati Shivaji Station in a city that Indians called Mumbai but that the rest of the world would always refer to as Bombay.

'And I slept so good,' Rachel said, rummaging through her backpack as she spoke. 'The train was rocking nice and easy and when we went through a town I could hear the train's horn in my dreams. It made it easy to sleep.' She pulled out a toothbrush case and a tube of toothpaste. 'That and those pain pills the doctor gave you.' She pushed her hair away from her face and looked into his eyes. 'This is why I came to India, for train rides like this. And it wouldn't have happened if it wasn't for you. Thanks.'

Jason shrugged, not sure how to answer since all he had done was bleed. The stationmaster had insisted they get the private accommodations, his way of apologizing for 'a most unusual and unfortunate incident that in no way should influence your opinion of this fine railway system or of the people of India on a whole.' His arm ached under the bandage, and blood seeped through the gauze in several spots. He flexed his left hand — it was stiff but otherwise seemed normal, the site of the tetanus shot causing the most pain, and his chin hurt where the doctor had pulled through a few quick stitches, no extra charge.

But it wasn't the pain that had kept him awake. Despite a double dose of the pills that had knocked Rachel out, Jason had spent the night staring at the patches of light that raced along the blue-gray ceiling of the cabin.

He could see the man's face, a look somewhere between terror and embarrassment as he made his awkward stumble into the path of the train. It had slowed to pass through the station but it had struck with enough force to rip the man's head off his shoulders, knocking it down the track like an errant soccer ball before it rolled under the steel wheels. Three times that night the smell of the man's cheap cologne wafted into his memory and three times that night he hurried down the passageway to the communal restroom, dry heaving into the piss-covered black hole that opened to the tracks.

And the man had known his name.

They had asked him directly did he say anything to you and he had said no, nothing he could understand. He didn't know why he had lied but at the time it felt right, and as he lay awake in the cabin, Rachel's deep, measured breathing in sync with the clatter of the tracks, the lie still felt right.

Tell them what they want to hear. It makes them happy and it doesn't cost you a thing.

Alone in the darkness he thought about what he carried in his backpack. He knew it was the reason why he needed to get to Bangalore, the reason why he kept going when all he wanted to do was stop. An economy-class, return ticket to the States. It was the only reason he needed.

'I'm going to freshen up as they say,' Rachel said, tugging her Blue Jays cap tight on her head. 'We'll be in the station soon, so pack up.' She opened the door, apologizing to the porter who slid past their cabin with a tray of hot tea. 'Oh yeah,' she said over her shoulder. 'I took that red blanket out of your pack last night when you went to the bathroom. That air conditioning got frickin' cold. I think it fell under my bed. Don't forget it.'

'Look over there,' Rachel said, pointing across his body towards the crowd at the gate. 'Isn't that your name?'

Standing under the ornate Victorian clock and dressed in a black suit and tie, a copper-colored man held a computer printed sign on legal-sized paper that read MR JASON TALLEY.

'Go ask him what he wants,' Rachel said, giving Jason's good arm a tug. Jason didn't move.

'What are you, nuts? The last guy I ran into at a train station tries to cut my throat and you want me to go up and ask this guy what the sign's for?'

'Oh, get over it,' she said. 'It's not like that guy knew your name or something.'

Jason shuddered. 'I'm not that curious.'

'Well, I am,' she said and before he could stop her she cut through the crowd to where the man was standing.

'Hi, I'm Rachel Talley and this is my husband, Jason.' She held her hand out as Jason caught up to her, Jason watching the man's gloved hands on the sign.

The man stepped to the side and gave a slight bow. 'Please. Your car is this way.'

'You must mean another Jason Talley. I

didn't order a car.'

'Shut up,' Rachel whispered through clenched teeth. 'It's a free ride.'

'There is no mistake,' the man said, pretending he didn't hear Rachel's comments. 'The car is courtesy of Mr Kumar. I have been instructed to take you to his home where you are to be his guests.'

'I don't know a Mr Kumar.'

The driver bowed again. 'Mr Kumar said you might know him as SFX Wizard at India Gate Films dot com.'

'Oh yeah,' Rachel said, hitching her backpack higher on her shoulders. 'Good old SFX. Let's go.' The driver took her cue and led them through the station and out the arch-shaped wooden doors.

'I have no idea who this Kumar guy is,' Jason said, trying to keep up to Rachel as she weaved around the clumps of baggage-heavy travelers who swam upstream to the station's entrance. Ahead the driver held open the door of a black, American-sized SUV, the words *Tata Safari* emblazoned on the metal spare tire case. 'He could be another lunatic.'

'If he is, at least he's a rich lunatic. Come on, Jason,' she said, handing her backpack to the driver. 'What's the worst that could happen?'

# 11

'Now *this* is a vacation.' Jason sipped his gin and tonic, the frosted glass cold on his fingertips. He closed his eyes behind his sunglasses and listened to the ornamental waterfall that splashed into one of the concrete coves of the pool that wound through the palm trees, rock formations, and tropical plants that covered the terrace. Above, a white-hot sun inched across the cloudless blue sky.

He peeked out of the corner of his eye at the cedar chaise lounge at his side. The coconut sunscreen glistened on Rachel's flat stomach and smooth, toned, and already tanned legs. The straps of her bikini top were pulled off her shoulders and he watched as a lucky rivulet of sweat and lotion disappeared between her round breasts. Behind them a blender whirled as a silver-haired servant in a white coat and bow tie blended another banana daiquiri. 'You gotta admit this beats riding around in a train all day.'

'I'll admit that it's nice,' Rachel said, 'but that's as far as I'll go.'

After picking them up at the station, it had

taken the driver over an hour to negotiate the morning rush-hour traffic. It seemed that every one of the city's sixteen million residents was on the road, all of them directly in front of the high-riding SUV.

The city was as crowded as Delhi and Jaipur combined, yet it seemed as if the drivers were making a valiant attempt to follow many of the traffic rules. Most waited a respectable amount of time at red lights before cutting through the wave of cars with the right of way. There were no rickshaws in Mumbai — either bicycle or auto — and drivers limited themselves to just a few ear-numbing horn blasts a minute. Even the pedestrians appeared willing to play along, and Jason saw more than one wait for the okay from the crosswalk signal before venturing off the curb.

Jason was surprised by the neat, modern office buildings, each as well maintained as any in Corning, only taller and better designed, and when the driver eased the black Safari on to the palm tree-lined Marine Drive and he could see the city's skyline and the sandy beach and the blue horizon of the Arabian Sea, he was reminded of picturesque drives along the Florida coast. Rachel's guidebook had said that half of the population of the city lived in slums, some

123

that sprawled on for miles, but on this one stretch of road in this one corner of town, Mumbai was a beautiful city.

On a lush, tree-filled lane on Malabar Hill, an electronic gate opened at the side of the road. The driver gave the horn a discreet toot. Silhouetted by a bank of blue monitors, a uniformed and armed security guard waved back from his air-conditioned sentry box. The house was hidden behind banks of trees and shrubs, but through the branches Jason could see portions of white stucco walls and red-tiled roofs that jutted out from the core of the building. With a slight nod of his head the driver passed his charges off to a smiling house servant in a tailor-made black suit.

Inside, the main hall reminded Jason of the lobbies of the five-star hotels in New York that he frequented, pretending to be a guest but just looking for the men's room. The floors were tiled in multicolored marble and above, chrome and glass chandeliers seemed to float below the vaulted ceiling, dating the room from sometime in the near future. Paintings of abstract landscapes hung on the walls while on an oriental rug, antique chairs with wispy-thin legs formed a sitting area around a matching table. A pair of small fountains bracketed a glass elevator and door-less passageways led off to other sections of the home.

In their two-bedroom suite they found new bathing suits laid out on the bed along with a note inviting them to make themselves at home, signed with a flourish, *Narvin Kumar*.

Now, as he took another sip of his drink, the ice already half-melted in his glass, Jason stopped thinking about knife-wielding attackers and kleptomaniacal monkeys, murdered friends, and a sari wadded up in a backpack. It allowed him to focus on thinking about the half-naked woman at his side. The distant sound of a man laughing broke into his fantasy before it went too far.

'I think our host has arrived,' Jason said, tilting down his sunglasses to see into the shadows near the sliding glass doors. The man walked slowly, still laughing as he held a tiny cell phone to his ear, giving Jason and Rachel time to watch his approach.

What with his fellow passengers, the mobs at the train stations, and the endless streams of pedestrians, Jason felt as if he'd seen every male in India. But as he watched the man pause to listen intently to his phone, one arm resting against the open doorframe, Jason knew he had hadn't seen a man like this before.

It wasn't just his height, several inches over six feet, or his olympian physique, his hundred-dollar haircut, or the way his smile outshone his blindingly white shirt. Maybe it was the way he ruffled his thick black hair, confident it would fall back in place, or the way he gave a wink to the barman, who grinned back and started mixing the man a martini. It could have been his voice, strong and deep, or the honesty in his laugh or how, when he flicked the phone shut and crossed the patio to their chairs, hand outstretched and smiling, his attention made them feel like they were the most important people in the world.

'Oh. My. God.' Rachel said and fumbled her bikini straps back in place.

'Hi, I'm Narvin Kumar. You must be Jason Talley.'

'That's me,' Jason said, standing, wiping his palm dry on his swim trunks before shaking the man's hand. 'And this is my . . . '

'Sister,' Rachel said, cutting him off and leaning forward as she reached out for his hand. 'I'm his sister. Rachel.' Narvin took her hand, his smile wider as he held the handshake an extra beat.

'I'm sorry I couldn't meet you at the station,' Narvin said, lifting Rachel's daiquiri off the barman's tray and handing it to her, waiting until she took a sip before taking up his martini. 'I'm in the middle of doing four movies right now, all of them with temperamental producers and scripts that are written on the fly. I'm lucky I got away at all. Cheers.' He sipped his drink, dismissing the barman with another wink, pulling up a chair to join them. 'I heard from the driver there was some trouble in Ahmadabad. How's your arm?' He pointed to the fresh bandages.

'Okay I guess. It's a bit stiff from the tetanus shot though.'

'If you'd like I can have a doctor come by and take a look.'

'Thanks, but I think it'll be fine. It's a hell of a place you got here,' Jason said, waving at the house with his drink.

'Absolutely amazing,' Rachel said, staring at the man's hazel eyes.

Narvin gave a modest nod. 'I've been lucky. The film industry has been very good to me. No, I'm not an actor,' he said, guessing the next question. 'I've done some bit parts, a lot of walk-ons when they need an extra, but I work behind the camera. Post production. Computer enhancement, special effects, that sort of thing.'

'Computers. So that's how you knew Sriram.'

'We were friends since freshman year of high school. Our desks were side by side in every class for years. We roomed together at university.' Narvin chuckled, 'I even introduced him to Vidya.'

'Vidya and Sriram were friends of mine in Corning,' Jason said to Rachel and stopped, not knowing how to explain their deaths.

'I hope it was an arranged marriage,' Rachel said, still smiling at Narvin. 'I hear that those love marriages don't tend to last.'

Jason and Narvin exchanged an uncomfortable glance, Narvin turning to Rachel, his smile back in place. 'Theirs was definitely a love marriage. I never knew two people more in love.'

'The happiest people I ever met,' Jason added, his doubts falling away, and again met Narvin's eyes, this time to exchange silent memories of their dead friends.

'It was Sriram who got me interested in the movie industry here in Mumbai,' Narvin said, breaking the silence.

'Weren't you in on that business Sriram and some others started?'

'Bangalore Worldwide Systems,' Narvin said in a booming, heroic voice, his hand showing the placement of the words in the open, blue sky. 'Oh yeah. What pretentiousness. A handful of semi-talented programmers, hunched over a bunch of bashed-together computer terminals in a rented garage on the outskirts of Bangalore. But we were going to change the world.' He held up a forefinger to punctuate the line, laughing his baritone

128

laugh. 'Sriram was the only one with any real talent. The others were just hanging on, hoping to make it rich. Myself included, I guess.'

'Were you upset when he . . . ' Jason paused, trying to think of the best way to say it.

'When he left us for the States?' Narvin said, sensing his guest's discomfort. 'It was the best thing that ever happened to me. I would have waited around for BWS to take off, but when he departed and BWS collapsed I finally did what Sriram had been telling me to do for years. I came here to Mumbai and got myself into the tech side of the film industry. Of course I thought it was my talent that had gotten me noticed, but I later learned that it was Sriram — some ancient family connections that he could have called in for himself but instead used to get me started in Bollywood.'

'Bollywood?' Rachel said, finding a way into the conversation. 'Don't you mean Hollywood?'

'India's film industry is located here in Mumbai, which of course used to be Bombay. Hence, Bollywood.'

Rachel smirked. 'What were you saying about pretentiousness?'

'It's hard to be humble in Bollywood these

days. Look at it this way,' Narvin said. 'Each year Hollywood puts out about seven hundred movies. Bollywood averages close to eleven hundred. Most are made for less than four million, but three of the films I'm working on now will end up costing over thirty million. Each. And that's dollars, not rupees. It's a billion-dollar industry and, unlike Hollywood, it's growing. But please don't think I'm offended,' he said, sensing Rachel's embarrassment. 'It's just that when it comes to movies I'm afraid I'm a rabid patriot.'

'We don't get too many Hindi movies in Corning,' Rachel said, turning to Jason, who nodded, verifying her assumption.

'Well, don't tell that to any of the people you meet tonight. There's a première party on Madh Island.'

'Oh, how exciting,' Rachel said, beaming.

'Horribly dull, I'm afraid. Industry types, film people, the press. It will be boring as hell, but thanks to you, I won't have to suffer alone.'

# 12

The last time he had had champagne it had been mixed with orange juice and served in soft-sided plastic cups, part of Vidya's New Year's Day brunch in their drafty Corning apartment. It was over-fizzy and sickeningly sweet and he had felt a headache coming on after the third glass, Vidya and Sriram downing two bottles and a quart of o.j. between them. Now the champagne was buttery smooth and served in long-stemmed crystal flutes, a taste — and a style — Jason knew he could come to enjoy.

Behind him, the Retreat Hotel rose out of a garden of exotic trees and flowering bushes into the dark night sky. He could hear the clatter of china plates and polished silver echoing from the patio restaurants along with the mumble of a hundred dinner conversations, punctuated by the high-pitched laughs of women who had had one too many. Tiny strings of lights sparkled from the tops of towering palm trees, and along the twisting footpaths, half-hidden lights led down the stairs to the lagoon-shaped pool where, on an island bar, a Hawaiian-shirted Bengali waiter was ready in case any of the partygoers should end up in the water in need of a drink.

Ringing the pool and scattered about on the lower patio in random pockets, Bollywood's elite celebrated the release of the week's latest blockbuster. The men were all in suits, Savile Row or tailored Italian, with many wearing long, brightly colored Nehru coats, a centuries-old Indian style that was clearly still in fashion. Jason pushed out his chest, trying to fill Narvin's light gray Armani, and flexed the fingers of his left hand. His arm was stiff and warm, the fresh bandages filling the baggy sleeve like a well-developed forearm. The pants felt loose and long, but Narvin had insisted he looked great. 'Besides,' he said by way of consolation. 'they'll all be drunk anyway.'

They had ridden to the party in yet another chauffeur-driven, limousine-sized SUV, Narvin mixing drinks, pointing out the Rajera Victorian buildings and the wide-screen vistas, both frequent backdrops in Hindi films.

'We were filming on that beach there a couple months back,' Narvin said, tapping his swizzle stick on the tinted glass. 'Four in the morning and fifteen thousand people lining the street to watch. It was insane. You can't film a Bollywood film in Bollywood anymore.'

Jason stretched his legs out and swirled the

ice in his drink. 'You said that Bollywood movies are popular . . . '

'No. I said they were the most popular movies in the world.'

'Then how come I've never seen one?'

Narvin laughed. 'I'm afraid that says more about you than it says about Bollywood. Listen, who's the most famous actor in the world?'

'I don't know,' Jason said pausing. 'Tom Hanks. John Travolta maybe.'

'First would be Sean Connery, but not now. Back in his early Bond days,' Rachel said. 'Next would be Johnny Depp in that pirate movie, then Samuel L. Jackson. In anything.'

'That sounds like a different kind of list.'

'A girl can dream.'

'Careful,' Narvin said, looking into Rachel's eyes as he raised his glass to his lips. 'You're in the city where dreams come true.' Jason couldn't be sure — the light was dim and he wasn't watching that closely — but it looked like Narvin had winked as he said it.

'So anyway,' Jason said. 'The most famous actor in the world.'

'Shah Rukh Khan.'

'Never heard of him.'

'Well, *billions* have. Not just here in India or over in Pakistan, but in China, all throughout the Middle East, Europe, the Caribbean . . . everywhere Indians have gone — and brother, we've gone everywhere — we've brought Bollywood with us. And it's the locals — the Chinese, the Arabs, the French, whatever — they love these movies. They know the actors, the plots, the songs. It's far more global than Hollywood.'

'I've seen a few Hindi movies,' Rachel said. 'Like they say, seen one . . . ' She let her voice trail off, the cliché complete without the words.

Narvin nodded. 'It's a genre, I'll grant you that. Star-crossed lovers, cruel fate, loving families, lots of dance numbers, and catchy songs. No sex — not even a kiss — but bet on a clingy, wet-sari-in-the-rain scene. But even that formula is changing. Sure, there's a lot of crap, but that's true for Hollywood as well, yet Bollywood films are getting more popular. They give the people something they're not getting from the West. I'm telling you, Jason, there's some great filmmaking going on in Bollywood,' Narvin said as the Retreat Hotel loomed on the horizon. 'And it's coming to a theater near you.'

Inside, among the movie heartthrobs and music stars, Narvin lost some of his glamour, appearing simply average in this above-average crowd of men. Although he had never seen a Hindi film, Jason could spot the celebrities by their square jaws and confident smiles and by the way others stood gawking when they walked past, how they waved and gestured, knowing someone was always watching.

The women wore their dark hair long and straight, and when they tossed it back, laughing just so at a clever remark or turning on cue to catch the greetings of a male co-star, it glowed as if lit from within. In form-fitting gowns and black cocktail dresses, headline-grabbing chests strained clasps and straps while million-dollar legs teetered on ice-pick heels. At first they seemed inter-changeable, the almond-shaped eyes and the bee-stung lips, but Jason began to notice the subtle differences that separated the names-before-the-titles stars from the comic sidekicks' kid sisters — noses that wrinkled too much when they smiled, chins that came to too sharp a point, breasts that were a half-a-cup size too small. Some wore pinpoint diamond studs in their button noses, others opted for armfuls of gold bangles, and on their foreheads, between thin, arching eye-brows, many wore bejeweled bindis, the cut stone or colored plastic complementing their outfits.

Jason stayed on the edge of the crowd, just

inside the cordon of hotel security officers and sunglass-wearing bodyguards, never quite entering the circles of insiders that formed and grew and dispersed and reformed around the empty pool. After an hour of A-list overload, he began to notice that there were others at the party — overweight, out of style, unattractive, old — and Jason knew that these were the producers and directors and the moneymen that controlled the destiny of every flawless face at the party.

Narvin materialized at his side. He wore a pale blue, collarless jacket that stretched down to his knees, a complementing silk scarf hanging around his neck. He gave a low, deep hum. 'I still think you should have someone look at it, but it's your arm. So tell me,' he tilted his glass towards the pool, 'who do you recognize?'

Jason scanned the crowd, tapping along with the American pop tune that the DJ worked into the mix. 'Besides you and Rachel and that one waiter that I almost knocked over coming in, no one. Who should I know?'

'It's no fun dropping names if you don't know who I'm talking about.'

'I promise to be impressed.'

Narvin laughed. 'All right then. The gentleman in the black suit and no tie . . . '

'With all the women around him?'

'Yes. That is Salman Khan, sort of the Indian Brad Pitt.'

'Ohhh. And the Sylvester Stallone-looking guy?'

'That's Sanjay Dutt. Same type of Rambo movies. You see that woman by the edge of the pool, the one in the green sari?'

'The gorgeous one? Yeah, I sort of spotted her earlier.'

'That's one of the Shetty sisters, I can never remember which.' Narvin took a sip of his champagne and gazed out over the crowd. 'Amrish Sharma.'

'Is that the guy in the tux?'

'No, that was the man that you killed in Ahmadabad.'

Jason felt the crystal flute slip in his hand, gripping it tight before it fell, the champagne rippling as his hand began to shake.

'We called him Taco — it's funny, I don't recall why.' Narvin continued to look over the heads of the guests and out to the ocean, the white line of the surf just visible in the darkness.

'He came at me. I didn't even touch him. He stumbled and fell, I never . . . '

'It was his idea to call it Bangalore World Systems. Taco and Sriram and Ravi and Ketan, Attar, Manny and old Piyush, we'd sit for hours — days — in front of those

137

computer screens. He came from a poor family and he put everything his family had into BWS.' Narvin turned his head and looked at Jason, his eyes clear and dark. 'Sriram was like a brother to us. That's why it hurt so much.'

'Having fun?' Rachel stepped off the stairs behind them, an equally beautiful woman walking beside her. 'This is Laxmi. I met her in the women's room.' Rachel tilted her head in the direction of the hotel. 'She says she knows you, Narvin.'

'Never saw her before in my life,' Narvin said, turning to face them. He slipped an arm around the woman's sari-clad waist and kissed her golden cheek. 'Hello, darling. About time you got here.'

Laxmi smiled. 'Traffic was mad,' she said, her accent more England than India. 'You should be thankful I got here at all.'

Narvin pointed with his now empty glass of champagne. 'This is Rachel's brother, Jason.'

'Pleased to meet you,' Jason said, shaking the offered tips of her slender hand.

'Jason and I were just discussing mutual friends.'

'Well, Rachel and I were discussing shoes,' Laxmi said, 'and for a woman it's pretty much the same thing. I was telling her about the shops in Bandra.'

'You'll have to excuse my fiancée,' Narvin said to Jason. 'She plans on making me destitute in my old age, which, given her spending, must be closer than I thought.'

'If I had known he was such a miser I would have never agreed to marry him.'

'Fiancée, huh?' Rachel said, forcing a smile. 'So. Is it an arranged marriage or a love marriage?'

Narvin and Laxmi looked at each other and laughed. 'Our friends in London set us up on a blind date last year,' Narvin said. 'Technically you could say it's an arranged marriage.'

'The love part was just an afterthought,' Laxmi added with a dismissive wave.

'Well, isn't that nice,' Rachel said, smile still in place. 'From what I hear love marriages don't last.'

'A guy on the train,' Jason said. 'He was telling us about the low divorce rate for arranged marriages.'

Laxmi's smile leveled. 'That's because a divorce is more expensive than a box of matches.'

Narvin sighed and closed his eyes as he spoke. 'Laxmi, darling. You always pick the most interesting times to go political.'

'I'm sorry, Narvin, but it's an issue I care strongly about.' She turned and spoke to

Rachel. 'When marriages are arranged there is often a crushingly large dowry demanded from the bride's family. Money, electronic goods, cattle if you're in the countryside, maybe a car in the cities. For some families it represents the single largest increase in their wealth for a lifetime.'

'Doesn't it go to the newlyweds?'

'Some yes, but it is expected that most will go to the groom's parents. Now jump ahead four, five, ten years. The young bride isn't so young anymore. Maybe she's had three beautiful children who all unfortunately happen to be girls, maybe she's put on a few pounds in the wrong places. A divorce is difficult to get but not impossible. However, the groom's family would be required to pay back the dowry. But if something should happen to the wife — say an unfortunate cooking accident — well then, a divorce is not necessary.'

'So the men just set their wives on fire?' Rachel said, eyes wide.

'No,' Laxmi said, drawing the word out in contrived disgust. 'That would *never* happen. But a sari is such a flammable garment and cooking oil spills so easily and the flame from the gas stove, well, it can be difficult to adjust. By the time the ambulance arrives all that is left is a grieving widower and his still-wealthy parents.'

'Now Laxmi, you know this isn't as common as you make it sound,' Narvin said.

'One is one too many, darling. Last year there were close to three thousand cases of accidents,' she said, adding quotation marks in the air. 'Or at least that was how many were reported. Look, I'm not saying arranged marriages are bad. You can have a great love marriage and you can have a great arranged marriage, but abuse goes on in both. Divorce rates don't mean unhappiness,' Laxmi said, smiling at Rachel. 'They mean freedom.'

★ ★ ★

'After I won the talent contest at my high school I really started taking my acting seriously, but there were few opportunities in Chandvad so I moved in with an auntie here in Mumbai.'

With one hand on the steering wheel of the new Mercedes, Yashila Phatak reached back to flip her hair out from behind her collar. The brake lights of the cars ahead gave her long, brown hair a reddish tint that, for a moment, made Jason think of Rachel.

'I was always drawn to the theater,' Yashila continued. 'I feel the muse here, in my heart.' She placed her hand on her ample chest and risked a quick glance at Jason, holding it there until he returned a nervous smile. She gave her head a faint shake and half-puckered her lips before focusing back on the speeding traffic.

He had been standing with Narvin, watching as Rachel and Laxmi strolled off to find the bar, when Yashila approached, pretending to trip on the top step in front of them. Both men reached out obligatory hands to catch her feigned fall, the young woman giving a well-rehearsed gasp that slid into an I'm-*so*-embarrassed laugh, *amazed* that she bumped into *Narvin Kumar* since *Stardust Magazine* had reported he was wintering in the States, and hadn't she *just* been telling *Salman Khan* that she'd *love* to work on one of his films. In the time that it took Jason to flag down a passing waiter and exchange glasses, Narvin had sped through the introductions, explaining that Jason was a close associate visiting from the States, noting that it was truly a shame that Jason had never seen a proper Hindi film, insisting that Yashila come to his aid, insisting just as firmly that Jason take up her kind offer. Twenty blurry minutes later, Jason found himself wedged in the seat of the speeding Mercedes, the actress careening them towards the mid-city theater that was showing her first film.

'My agent and I felt it was important that I

start my film career with a small role,' she said, swerving the car into the valet parking line of the five-star hotel. 'He's been so kind to me, loaning me his car and paying me in advance for films they haven't even written.' She stepped out of the car, pulling the hemline of her short, black dress down a quarter of an inch in a feigned attempt to cover her long, smooth legs. 'Honestly, I don't know how I could ever repay him,' she said before handing the keys to the gawking valet.

'Oh, and if anyone should ask,' she said to Jason, adjusting her purse so that it hung between them, 'you're from Paramount.'

A short walk — the sidewalks still alive an hour before midnight — brought them to the front of the Palace Theater. Standing shoulder to shoulder, the movie's stars towered over the street. Two muscled men, arms crossed over tight, white tee shirts, grinned while between them the raven-haired female lead rested her elbows on their rocky biceps. The colors were several shades too bright and their legs seemed out of proportion with the rest of their bodies as if, halfway though the billboard, the artist realized that his initial vision was far too grand for his canvas.

Under the flashing marquee two clumps formed near the ticket windows. The first was filled with men — auto-rickshaw drivers, porters, day laborers, and the unemployed — pressing forward while reaching a twenty-rupee note through the pack, shouting at the men ahead of them and thrusting an elbow into the ribs of those behind, a few waving to their wives and sisters who waited near the gilded doors. Inside the ticket window the teller moved in slow motion, holding each note up to the light before poking tickets out under the glass.

At the other end of the entrance a smaller crowd waited, the hundred-rupee ticket price ensuring more dignity. Husbands and wives stood together and groups of single women, giggling into the scarves of their *shalwar kamiz*, eyed pockets of single men on their best behavior. None of the young people appeared to be on dates, but by the way glances were being exchanged up and down the line it was clear that, in the darkness of the theater, the rigid norms relaxed.

Inside, they were directed up the sweeping staircase to the special lobby for balcony patrons, their tickets checked twice en route by club-toting security guards. Going to the movies in Corning meant driving to the nearby town of Painted Post where a twin-plex cinema featured a two-hundred-seat theater for block-busters and a fifty-five seater for second runs. As he stepped out on to the balcony Jason realized that movies were a bit more important in Mumbai.

There were three sections to choose from, each with over a hundred seats. Single men filed into the one on the left, single women to the right, and couples in the center. Over the railing Jason watched as hundreds of people filed into the cheap seats, climbing over the backs of chairs to claim choice spots, sneaking a cigarette before the lights went down. Below the screen he could see mounds of spilled popcorn and paper cups, swept to the front of the theater between shows and, after looking at the acre of red fabric that hung in front of the screen, he made a mental note of the closest fire exits.

Yashila tugged on his shirt and led him to a row of seats towards the front of the balcony. She sat down and flipped open her cell phone to check her messages.

'I can't believe the size of this place,' Jason said, squinting to see the ceiling in the theater's half-light.

Yashila gave an embarrassed grin. 'My agent says many hit movies start off in smaller venues like this, until they catch on. This one is going to be a smash, I just know it.'

The theater darkened and a whistle-filled cheer rose up from the main floor. He flinched at the sudden movement on his left, lone single men cutting through the couples' section for secret back-row rendezvous. Ahead the red curtain parted to reveal a drive-in-movie sized screen while concert speakers trumpeted the coming attractions. Ten minutes later, with the patrons still streaming in, shouting into cell phones or yelling across aisles to friends who stood on their seats to wave, the movie began.

'*Mera Bhai, Meri Jaan*. My Brother, My Life,' Yashila explained as the title splashed across the screen in a huge, curlicue script.

'What's it about?' Jason tried to whisper, the people around him talking and laughing so loud he said it again in a normal voice.

Yashila opened her mouth, holding it open as her eyes looked to the ceiling and her tongue ran along her bottom lip. 'It's about a lot of things,' she said finally. 'I play the younger brother's friend's classmate's sister. I'm after the fourth song.' The first chords of *Ode to Joy* reverberated from her lap and she flipped her phone back open, the pale blue light illuminating her face. He half-turned in his seat to mime an apology to the people nearby but they ignored him, busy in loud conversations of their own or on the phone with their hard-of-hearing friends.

Jason settled in and watched the movie.

With an armload of architectural drawings and a pair of briefcases, and dressed in a blue suit and tie, one of the male leads was trying to negotiate a rush-hour sidewalk. The crowd howled as first one, then a second, then all of the rolled-up plans slipped from his grasp and cartwheeled down the long set of stairs he had just climbed. Predictably the briefcases followed and, as he scrambled to pick it all back up, he knocked over a woman too beautiful not to be the lead.

'Boy meets girl,' Yashila said as she punched in a new number.

For a half hour Jason tried to follow the plot, leaning over to whisper questions to Yashila that she would sometimes answer, sometimes ignore, giving up after a second lip-synched, high-pitched solo by the female lead left him confused about which brother the heroine really liked. Besides, musicals made him uncomfortable — a guy walking down the street, all of a sudden bursting into song? In public, with strangers looking? For an instant he was back in fourth grade, a packed auditorium waiting for him to start the grand finale of the Christmas concert, eight tiny classmates dressed as reindeer pawing at the stage floor, the jingling-bells intro starting up for the third time. No way.

He focused his attention on the background details from each shot — the expensive furnishings in the million-dollar homes and the modern glass and steel skylines from the sweeping outdoor dance numbers. Jason wondered how the cameraman managed to miss the run-down buildings and the beggars, the dented cars and the whirlwinds of litter that was kicked up with every gust. Like Disney World's America, Bollywood's India was a place where everybody visited and nobody lived.

In the dark, feet up on the back of the empty seat in front of him, Jason watched the action on the screen while he thought about his so-called vacation.

He had two weeks this year and he had spent it all on a favor for a friend who neither asked for his help nor, he feared, deserved it.

He missed the Sriram he thought he knew, missed his sense of humor, the way his face lit up when his wife walked into the room, the way he always handed Jason a cold Odenbach, the cap twisted off, the way he had left for work early every morning that winter just so he had time to brush the snow off Jason's car, how he called computers magic and had Jason believing it, how he handed out fat handfuls of candy on

Halloween and delivered twenty frozen turkeys to the food bank at Thanksgiving.

It was hard to like the Sriram he was meeting now.

Next to him, Yashila pulled out a second cell phone, text messaging with the tip of her long, painted nails while she babbled on in a mix of English and Hindi, the small phone lost in her thick hair.

He watched her out of the corner of his eye. She was beautiful and sexy and easy to flatter and he thought about how simple it would be to find a way into her bed — no isolating blanket maneuvers, no bench seats on a moving train — and he was surprised at how disappointed that made him feel.

It was all Rachel's fault. The tour group, the hours on the train, the throbbing in his left arm where the knife had dug in. It all came back to her. She liked to lie and she was good at it, more believable than the actresses in the movie, never confusing her stories, selling it all straight and earnest. He wondered if anything he knew about her was true. For some reason he knew it didn't matter. He liked to watch her as she stood in the open doorways of the trains, when the sun caught her hair just right, and when she slept, curled up and quiet on the wide railway window seat.

Tell the people what they want to hear, she had said. But was that a lie, too? He was still waiting.

On the screen the heavy had been shouting at the two brothers, tossing their blueprints around in their Euro-style office, but was now leading a chorus of twenty men in multicolored jumpsuits in a complex dance number near a public fountain, everyone waving giant, blueprint banners. As they rippled past in choreographed unison, Jason's eyes widened.

They were there on the banner. The right-angled lines and cryptic symbols of a technical drawing, the mechanical precision of a well-planed schematic.

Just like a real blueprint.

Just like the pattern on the sari he carried for Sriram.

# 13

'Out of all the cultural influences India has absorbed from the west,' Laxmi said, holding her fork above her plate, 'none is as important as the American Style Breakfast.'

Narvin stabbed at his pile of hash browns. 'More important than representative democracy?'

Laxmi curled her nose at the suggestion.

'More important than freedom of speech?' Jason said, pouring himself a second glass of orange juice.

'Overrated,' she said with a wave of bacon strip.

'More important than Elvis?' Rachel said.

Laxmi considered the idea then shook her head. 'Close. But no. To quote the seventeenth-century Mughal emperor Shah Jehangir, 'If there be heaven on earth, it is this, it is this, it is this,'' she said, gesturing with both hands at the morning meal.

'He was talking about his palace in Delhi, my sweet,' Narvin said. 'Not a ham and cheese omelet.'

'He misspoke,' Laxmi said, an eyebrow raised.

After ten songs, a thirty-minute intermission, and an hour ride through the frantic late-night traffic, Jason had arrived back at Narvin's home, Yashila tooting the horn as she drove off to another party, surprised that he didn't even try for a kiss. The security guard buzzed Jason through, matching his face to the image on the computer screen. The house was dark, but enough light filtered through the room-sized windows to show the way to the guest suite. Inside he expected to find the door to Rachel's room shut but it stood open, the bed still made. He nodded off on the couch watching a pre-recorded cricket match on the plasma screen TV, not hearing Rachel when she came in or waking up when she covered him with a blanket from her bed.

It was well past noon when they met for breakfast.

Across the dining room table, Rachel watched as Laxmi finished off the last of the bacon. 'I remember reading somewhere that people in India were vegetarians.'

'Depends on which India you mean,' Laxmi said between crunches. 'Do you mean the Hindu, Muslim, or Christian India?'

'Or perhaps the Sikh, Jain, or Buddhist India?' Narvin added.

'Don't forget the Jewish Indians. Or the Zoroastrians.'

'I guess I thought I meant the Hindu one.'

'Fine,' Laxmi said. 'Now which version? There are eight hundred thousand to pick from.'

'Okay, now *I'm* confused,' Jason said, setting down his buttered whole-wheat toast.

Laxmi dabbed at her mouth with the linen napkin. 'In Hinduism you are free to develop your own relationship with God . . . '

'Or gods,' Narvin cut in.

' . . . choosing the form of expression and set of beliefs that you determine is true for you. You want to worship Lord Vishnu? Go right ahead — and hundreds of millions will join you. You prefer to seek the assistance of a black-skinned goddess with a necklace of skulls? Have at it, friend. Are your spiritual needs best met by an elephant-headed man with four arms? Ganesh awaits. And when it comes to forms of worship, well then the options really open up. In a temple, on a mountain, in a river, alone, with a thousand others, wearing your richest finery or hanging around with the lads, nude but for a fresh coat of dust — you name it and I guarantee someone in India does it.'

'As usual, my dear fiancée oversimplifies everything, but essentially what she says is true. There is no centralized authority that says do this, don't do that. The word

153

Hinduism implies an orthodoxy that just does not exist. But curiously, the way that the word was originally used thousands of years ago is still quite accurate — the beliefs of the people on this side of the Indus River. And as for eating meat,' Narvin said, snatching the last sausage link off of Laxmi's plate, 'to each his own.'

Rachel picked up her fork and returned to her meal. 'Well then, they really need to update all those videos we had to watch in high school. Remember the ones Mr Ray used to show grade nine?' she said to Jason, who nodded as if they had been classmates. 'They're not at all like the India we're seeing.'

'Again, which India do you want? The world seems most comfortable with the poverty-stricken, dhoti-wearing, non-violence spouting Indian, happy as a clam behind his spinning wheel. They are not as comfortable with high-tech Indian millionaires and nuclear weapons. For some reason they can grasp the concept of three hundred million people earning less than a dollar a day but can't fathom the idea of a hundred million middle-class Indians.'

'Or the seventy thousand millionaires,' Laxmi said, pointing her fork at Narvin.

'Look, I'm not saying India doesn't have its problems — half our population can't even read about our space program in the papers, our drug manufacturing plants ship world-wide while people die from the same diseases not fifty meters from the factory gates. It's a crazy, chaotic madhouse, but it works. We spend far too much energy trying to define India and not enough just accepting it.'

'And the best way for you to accept it,' Laxmi said, winking at Rachel, 'is by doing some serious shopping.'

'Her forte,' Narvin said, adding a shrug.

'I want to get a sari,' Rachel said. 'What size do you think I am?' She stood and held her arms out to her sides, giving a quick turn, Jason and Narvin taking the opportunity to stare.

'One size fits all,' Laxmi said. 'Some better than others. But with saris, size is not the issue. It is all style — the color you choose, how you wear it, *when* you wear it. No article of clothing says as much about a woman as a sari. Her status, her history, her role in the family — see it all with one peek in her wardrobe.'

'They all look the same to me,' Jason said.

'If you know how to read it, a sari speaks volumes. Start with the color. Bright colors for the young, somber, rich tones for women of a certain age, white for widows. The wrong shade and you send the wrong message. You also have to consider the pallu, the end piece with the design. Is your pallu too ornate, too plain, too short, too long? Don't leave home if it isn't just right. And it's not just the folds and where the pallu is draped but the *way* you wear the sari. Not like in the west. You throw on a pair of jeans and a blouse and forget it,' Laxmi said, waving her hands to take in her own tailored outfit.

'And it still takes her an hour to get ready,' Narvin whispered to Jason.

'No one is raised wearing a sari. It is something you grow up to wear, a sign that you are a woman. But don't be fooled. A sari has a mind of its own. You move left, it slides right, you tilt, it turns. And it is all held together, all five meters of slippery silk or quick-wrinkling cotton, by nothing more than a few folds and tuck here and there. No zippers, no snaps. A sari must be tamed and the wearer must exert her will or she can quite literally be undone. If you look awkward, battling with your sari to keep it in place or too nervous to move, people will notice, a social *faux pas* that your peers will never forget.'

'Sort of a rite of passage,' Rachel said. 'Like high heels. The things we do for fashion.'

Laxmi straightened and drew in a long breath.

'Oh boy,' Narvin whispered. 'Here it comes.'

'Fashion is simply a clever means of control. Society dictates what a woman will wear to reinforce her social position. Spiked heels in the west, foot binding in China, kimonos in Japan, abayas in the Middle East, saris in India. It's all the same. Control a woman's sense of fashion and you can control her movements. *And* her status. Would a woman design a miniskirt or a push-up brassiere? Every item of clothing you buy says where you stand in this struggle against male-dominated oppression.'

'Weren't you wearing a sari and heels last night?' Jason said.

'By choice,' Laxmi said, her manicured finger wagging. 'The strong woman owns her fashion decisions. Come, Rachel,' she said, standing up. 'The stores are open. It is time for us to charge our way to victory.'

★ ★ ★

'I wanted to talk before the women got back,' Narvin said, and shut the solid oak door of his study behind him. Behind Jason a bay window overlooked the pool and gardens, concealed spotlights illuminating the thick stand of palm trees that screened the patio

157

from the surrounding homes. Crowded bookcases lined the walls and, centered on a kidney-shaped desk, a flat-screen monitor glowed.

'Narvin, I told you, I didn't know he was your friend, besides I was just standing there . . . ' Narvin raised his hand and Jason fell silent.

'There are some things you need to know before you continue your trip.' He took a seat behind the broad desk and gestured to the matching chair that sat off to the side, leaning back to pull two bottles of water from a dorm-sized fridge built into the wall. He tossed a bottle to Jason before kicking his feet up on to his desk.

'Do you know much about computer programming? Well, it doesn't make a difference. This is not about computers.' Narvin's smile looked sad and he took a deep breath before continuing.

'We were developing a business-to-business program . . . niche market stuff. We were getting ready to run all these complex simulations, really test the program. All of a sudden Sriram says he's found a problem, something with the security protocols. Nothing to worry about, he said.'

He cracked the seal on his water bottle and took a long drink.

'Now at this point we're all exhausted — we'd been working nonstop for the better part of a year. Some of the guys were ready to . . . well let's just say that tempers flared a bit. Naturally we all wanted to dig in and solve the problem but it was security related issues, Sriram's department. He said he'd be better off without our help.'

'Was it true?' Jason said.

'Depends. Some security systems are extremely complicated — layers on layers, blind alleys, false trap doors, firewalls. Others? I've been hacking in since elementary school. But the only person who could get around our system was the one who designed it. In hindsight, of course, we should have been more involved.' Narvin shrugged. 'He said give me a weekend to fix it. We gave him a weekend. He said trust me. We trusted him.' He shook his head and downed the rest of the bottle.

'A few days later we start the trials. Sriram seemed different, nervous. We knew he had been on the phone a lot with Ravi and we assumed he was on edge because he was hoping to land a job in the States. But it was hard to tell with Sriram. He could talk all night but if something was bothering him he kept it to himself. Bottled it in.'

The story in the newspaper had told of a

rambling, angry suicide note and for the first time Jason wondered if Sheriff Neville had been right after all.

'One day Sriram and Vidya are gone. Off to America. It was only a week later that our computers all crashed.'

'Did you ask him about it?'

Narvin gave the same sad smile. 'He said it was coincidental. He offered to help fix it but I told him he had done enough already. That was the last time I talked to him.'

Jason thought about the last time he had seen his friend and the strange package that brought him to this place.

'All the evidence points to Sriram,' Narvin said. 'The breach of the computer system, the sudden running off to the States, the total system collapse, him selling us out. But you know something, Jason? I still don't believe it.'

'Maybe you just don't want to believe it,' Jason said, surprised by the words he heard himself say.

Narvin shook his head. 'You didn't know him like we knew him.' He turned his head to look out the window. 'Most days I don't think about it at all. Then all of a sudden I'll see something or hear some song on the radio and that's all I can think about.'

'You seemed to do all right anyway.'

'You're missing the point. Anyway, I wanted to show you something,' Narvin said, swinging his legs off the desk. He typed a few words on the keyboard and the computer hummed to life. 'You met Attar Singh up in Jaipur, right?'

'We spent some time together,' Jason said, remembering now how the man smiled as the monkey leapt over the balcony with the backpack.

'I got a call from him today. He told me to check out this chat room.' Narvin entered a coded password on a website then scrolled down the long list of entries, dancing icons and thumbnail pictures shooting past. 'Most of the guys we went to school with hang out here. That would include the Bangalore World Systems team. Here, read this.' Jason leaned across the desk and Narvin angled the flat screen to cut off the glare. He had placed the blinking cursor in front of a short paragraph, the only one not bracketed by multicolored graphics. The time stamp said the entry was posted at two that morning from Mumbai.

'I'm hoping someone in this chat room can help me out,' the entry read. 'I'm trying to get in touch with an American traveling in India. His name is Jason Talley and he was a friend of Sriram Sundaram. It's very important and I'll pay $100 US for accurate information.

161

But do me a favor, don't tell him I'm looking for him. I want it to be a surprise.' There was no name, but a phone number followed the entry.

'I checked with the phone company. It's one of those pre-paid mobiles.'

'Jesus,' Jason whispered as he read between the lines of the entry.

'Oh, it gets better.' Narvin tapped the down arrow on the keyboard. Line by line a picture rose into view. 'If I'm not mistaken,' he said, 'that's the Holiday Inn in Delhi, near Connaught Place. And I think you recognize this guy.'

Jason blinked several times as he looked at the screen but the picture remained the same. It was his first day in India and he stood waiting in line behind old Mr Froman as the members of the Freedom Tours group filed on to the bus.

'Seems like you've got yourself a stalker,' Narvin said, and Jason felt the hairs on the back of his neck rise.

'I wanted to call the number, find out who it was, what they wanted.' Narvin leaned back in his chair again as he spoke, leaving Jason to stare into the screen. 'But I figure that would only pull me in and I don't want to get involved in your business.'

'My business?' Jason said, turning away

from the monitor. 'It's not my business.'

Narvin smiled. 'Unfortunately for you, someone doesn't see it that way.'

'But what are the odds someone is going to see me here in Mumbai *and* see this entry.' He pointed a limp finger at the screen.

'I saw it,' Narvin said. 'So did Attar, way up in Jaipur. In a city of sixteen million the odds probably aren't as long as you'd wish. Then you add in the reward . . . '

Jason swallowed hard. 'What do you think I should do?'

'If I were you,' Narvin said, running the wireless mouse across the desktop, clicking on the small box that closed the screen, 'I'd watch my back.'

# 14

'Unfortunately my research has been focused on the effects of advanced transportation methods on traditional market patterns,' Rachel told the two men sitting on the bench seat across from their own. 'But Dr Talley here is the economics expert.'

The two men looked over at Jason, who squinted out from under the sweat-soaked towel that balanced on his head. He forced a weak smile before closing his eyes, the sweat burning as it seeped under his lashes.

It was sometime after midnight and most of the other benches in the second-class rail car had been converted into beds, thin blue curtains offering a limited degree of privacy and darkness. Unlike the first-class car, where the compartments consisted of two bench seats that opened to create a pair of bunk beds, Indian Rail engineers managed to squeeze in a third pair of beds that hung two feet from the car's ceiling, suspended by thin chains wrapped in the same blue vinyl that covered the seats. Without checking their seat assignments Jason knew that that was where they would be spending the night.

'I'm afraid your friend doesn't look well,' one of the berth's other passengers said to Rachel, who turned sideways to see for herself. Jason pried open an eyelid and watched as she did a quick assessment. She noticed the dark sweat stains on his collar and the waxy sheen on his cheeks, but the light in the alcove was too dim for her to see the glazed look in his eyes. He was surprised that she didn't notice that his left arm, which was right in front of her, was on fire, the stitches straining to contain what had to be molten lava that churned just under his skin.

After his chat with Narvin, Jason had lost interest in lounging by the pool and spent the rest of the evening packing and repacking the sari among his freshly laundered clothes. The banner-waving dance number in the movie had forced him to see the sari for what it really was, an elaborate scheme to smuggle computer secrets out of the U.S.

He had spread all six yards of the sari out on the king-sized bed in his room, the patternless portion trailing across the floor. The embroidery was limited to a yard-long section of the fabric, and Jason had noticed that for most women, this was the part of the sari that was draped over the left shoulder to hang at waist level. The pattern was far more intricate than he had recalled, with strand-thin lines jutting back and forth, all right angles in Etch-A-Sketch patterns. At random points the lines doubled back or stopped or shot across the fabric. Gold wire knots appeared sprinkled atop the silver embroidery, and here and there glass beads were worked in with asymmetrical care.

It would be easy to mistake the complex design for the traditional needlework that appeared on the more elaborate saris he had seen, easy to bring it out through customs without a single question asked. An Indian guy with a sari for his mother. What else could it be?

He knew what he was looking at, but he still didn't know what it meant.

By the time Rachel came back from her shopping trip — hands filled with tiny bags of who knew what — Jason had finished with his packing. Head pounding, he slumped in a deep chair in the sitting room, his appetite gone and a queasy feeling settling in his stomach, certain it had nothing to do with his arm and everything to do with Narvin's warnings. He perked up for the goodbye at Narvin's front door but felt weak as the driver raced them back to Victoria Terminus. Inside the station, Rachel had left him propped up against a neo-gothic stone arch as she

166

scurried about the tracks, taking pictures and gawking at grimy diesel engines caked with black grease and dirt. He guzzled down bottles of water but it took three cups of masala chai, served steamy hot in red clay cups, to quell the nausea. His arm was stiff and he was sure he heard it creak as they carried their bags aboard the second-class car of the Konkan Kanya Express that would run through the night to the seaside resort city of Goa.

It was more crowded here than it had been in first class but, even with his head swimming, Jason sensed that there was a camaraderie here that had been missing in the more expensive car. People laughed more, made room for each other in the tight passageway, treated strangers to more cups of tea or instant coffee. White-jacketed vendors squeezed past travelers crowding the aisle, stretching their legs before retiring for the evening. He smiled and nodded as people introduced themselves, but left the conversations to Rachel, who spun tales of foundation grants and doctoral theses.

It took five minutes and the help of his compartment mates for Jason to climb on to the shelf that was his assigned berth. A dim light burned in the passageway and in the half-darkness Jason could see Rachel in her bunk, her eyes wide as she chewed on her lower lip.

'We need a plan,' he thought he whispered.

'Shhh. It's okay. You don't have to yell, I can hear you fine.' She held her hand out across the compartment. He wanted to reach out to her, to touch her, hold her hand, maybe tell her the things he'd wanted to tell her for days, but the hot lava shot up his arm and his elbow refused to unbend.

'We need a plan,' he said again, not sure if he had heard the words himself.

Rachel leaned out of her bunk, her fingers brushing his cheek. 'How you feeling?'

'We don't have a plan. We gotta have a plan.'

He watched as Rachel sniffed and rubbed her eyes, the dust probably getting to her, he thought. 'I've never had a plan and things have always worked out,' she said.

'You need a plan. Always have a plan. Plans are . . . ' He paused and waited for the words to catch up. 'Plans keep you from doing stupid things.'

From the bunk below he could hear the nasal snoring of a heavy sleeper, and down the passageway a tea vendor made one last silent pass. Rachel touched his cheek again, her fingers so cold he wanted to hold them to his lips to warm them. She drew her arm back and pushed her palms against her eyes.

'Sorry,' he heard her say, the words falling between the rhythmic clacks of the tracks.

'Yeah,' he mumbled. 'All 'cause of a damn sari.' He patted his backpack and pulled the makeshift pillow tight against his head.

# 15

Keeping his eyes closed behind his sunglasses, Jason felt around in his backpack until he found the plastic tube. He flipped open the top with his thumb and poured the sun block directly on his nose, rubbing it in with his fingers before snapping the container shut. He wiped the excess off on the back of his neck then patted his hand dry on the soft cotton bandage that covered his left forearm. Behind him, just above the sound of the waves, Bob Marley sang about redemption.

He tanned easily, a genetic flaw that meant he ended up spending more time in the sun than he really should. After three days on the beach, one and a half if you only counted the time he could remember, he had the dark tan of a winter-long German tourist. His arm still ached, but not as much as the spot where they had jammed in the needle, his knees tended to buckle a bit when he stood up and he needed a shave, but as he sat in the rented beach chair, his feet buried in the sand and a half-gallon jug of pineapple juice at his side, he knew he hadn't felt this good in months.

He cracked open an eyelid, checking to

make sure the view had stayed the same. Ahead of him, twenty yards of open beach ended where the low waves petered out at the shore. To his left, over the heads of the vacationers lined up in rented beach chairs, he could just make out a double-trunked palm tree that angled towards the sea. To his right and a few feet behind, a row of dark-haired European women sat topless reading paperbacks, their pointed breasts baking in the equatorial sun. Except for the cows that wore garlands of marigolds and lounged like royalty under the largest umbrellas, it could be a resort beach anywhere in the world.

Out in the water, too far out really, Rachel rode the waves on a Styrofoam boogie-board.

He closed his eyes again and tried to piece together the last hundred hours of his life. There were things he remembered with a clarity that frightened him — the early morning auto-rickshaw ride from the station to the beachfront hotel, the sight of his arm when Rachel removed the bandage, the wide-eyed look the little boy gave him when he collapsed on the roadside, the bat that fluttered against the window screen late at night, the tall blonde woman, her hair in fat dreadlocks, who came in to use their shower, toweling off at the end of his bed, knowing that he was watching.

And there were things he half remembered, images pulled from a dream that may never have happened. A bus ride somewhere, the passengers all staring at him, the smell of marijuana in a dark room, thick accents and Rachel giggling, another ride, this one flat on his back, Rachel again, shouting now, I'm telling you I'm a doctor, more rides, Rachel holding a sari up to the sun that slanted through an open window, tinting her face red, then on a cell phone, looking at him, cupping her hand over the mouthpiece as she spoke, the hot flashes and tearing off his clothes, the ice-cold sweats, shaking the covers off, Rachel crawling up tight behind him, her naked body warm against his, that magical moment when the sweating stopped and his muscles unwound and he felt himself drifting off to sleep, Rachel's face next to his, wet with tears.

And there were things he'd never forget. Like how they made love that morning as the sun broke over the horizon.

He took a long swig of the pineapple juice, crushed fresh at the reggae bar behind him. His strength was rushing back and he felt that convalescent's urge to get out and do something. Rachel hadn't mentioned any plans as they walked down the beach, hadn't really said much at all before grabbing a rental board and heading out to the Arabian Sea. It had been a while since he had shared his bed with a woman, if only for an hour, but Jason recognized the sullen silences and the way Rachel avoided looking at him when she spoke. Guys weren't allowed to feel guilty the next morning, a biological nonchalance that helped populate the planet, but women were . . . different. He hadn't had a long-term relationship since his teens but he worked in an office of chatty women and had seen enough episodes of *Friends* to have an idea what was going on in her head. Either she wanted to be held and told how special she was and that he wanted to stay by her side forever or she wanted to be left the hell alone, it was just sex and the last thing she needed was for him to get all clingy.

The hard part was guessing which one.

He opened his eyes to see Rachel walking out of the surf, shaking the water out of her ears. She wore a black bikini she had bought on her shopping expedition in Mumbai, all strings and small patches of fabric. She walked with the easy athletic grace of a gymnast and Jason knew that every guy on the beach was watching her approach. The beat picked up behind him and after a couple of measures Toots and the Maytals sang about true love being hard to find.

'How was your swim?' Jason asked as she stood next to his chair, seawater dripping off her hair and into his pineapple juice.

Rachel picked up her towel and wiped her face dry before wrapping it around her waist, the men at the bar turning back around to watch the post-goal celebration on the bar's TV. 'We're gonna need to get moving if we're going to catch the train to Mangalore. It's going to take us a half hour to get to the station and I have to make a stop along the way.' She looked over his shoulder at a bare patch of sand as she spoke.

So it was going to be like that, he thought. 'Another night train? You're going to miss all the scenery.'

'I hope you didn't get anything from the bar.' She shifted the towel and rolled down the edge of her bikini bottoms to reveal a tiny pocket, pulling out a soggy hundred-rupee note. 'We're going to need this to eat on the train.'

'Why are you in such a rush to go?' Jason said, patting the open seat next to him. 'This is beautiful. It's like we're not even in India.'

She sighed and rolled her eyes before looking at him for the first time since they had made love. 'One, we're low on cash. It's a resort town so all the prices are higher and we can't afford to stay here another night. Two, I have to meet someone in Mangalore tomorrow. Three, you made me promise I'd get you to Bangalore on time so you can catch your precious flight back to the States. Four . . . '

'When did I say *that*?' Jason said, careful to keep a laugh in his voice.

Rachel kept her eyes fixed on his sunglasses. 'The other night. You said a lot of things.'

'Really? Like what?' He tilted his sunglasses back and gave her his best smile.

'Come on,' she said, pulling her Blue Jays cap tight on her head, 'we're going to be late.'

* * *

Twenty minutes later they sat in the back of a full-sized cab, looking out opposite windows. Plots of farmland jutted up against dense tropical forests and roadside waterfalls cascaded down the moss-covered rocks. The landscape leveled off and there were more farms and more wandering cows. The driver slowed and turned off the main road, taking them down a winding, rutted trail, the highway disappearing behind stands of palms and broad-leafed ferns.

Jason was surprised when Rachel climbed into the cab that had pulled up near the hotel, ignoring the offers from a dozen cut-rate auto-rickshaw drivers. He didn't hear her tell the driver where to go and noticed the driver never dropped the metal arm of his taxi meter, a blatant notice that he was planning on overcharging them.

Other than a few grunts about luggage and room keys, they hadn't spoken since the beach.

The cab bottomed out every fifty yards on the dirt road but the driver kept up the same dust-raising speed. Ahead, a rundown farm-house — sun-baked red brick with a corrugated tin roof — rose into view and he noticed Rachel shifting in her seat as they got closer.

'Listen,' she said, turning to face him, her hand light on his arm. 'Don't say anything when we get inside. No matter what. And don't freak out on me. Promise?'

'What's this about . . .'

'Just promise me this. Nobody's gonna get hurt. It's gonna be all right. I swear I'll get you on that train and you'll be in Bangalore before you know it. Now promise me.'

'What's going on? I think . . . '

She looked into his eyes and he saw they were soft and sad. 'Jason. Please.'

He sighed as the cab pulled up in front of the shack, the dust cloud enveloping the car as it rocked to a halt. 'All right,' he said and he saw the corners of her mouth twitch upward.

The driver kept his seat as they climbed out of the car. The farmhouse sat in a field of crops — something tall and bushy and green — the field bordered by a wall of palm trees and rainforest. His backpack hanging off his shoulder, the pink Hello Kitty strap even brighter in the sun, he walked around the front of the cab to join Rachel. She slung on her backpack and gripped the straps in front of her chest. He heard her take a deep breath before she stepped on to the path that led to the house.

Jason had thought the building was abandoned, a farmer forced off his land by high debt or bad luck, but as they got closer he saw homemade rakes and hoes propped against the crumbly wall, and a new plastic cooler sat on a wood bench near the door. Inside he could hear the faint strains of music, sounding much like the big blueprint-banner waving dance number he remembered from Yashila's debut movie. He could also hear the deep rumble of men's voices and a hacking smoker's cough.

'Remember,' Rachel said, stopping at the door, 'don't say a thing,' the look in her eyes underlining every word. She reached out a knuckle but before she could knock the door was pulled open.

'Grab a Pepsi if you want one,' a voice shouted out from the darkness. 'In the cooler.'

'What? No beer?' Rachel said, standing taller than Jason remembered as she swaggered into the room. She swung off her backpack and tossed her hair around in the same move. 'Hold this,' she said, flipping the light bag to Jason, then turned to face the four men who sat around the table.

Two of the men were Indian. Small and wiry, they grinned blinding white grins at Rachel, their dark skin and black hair intensifying the effect. They wore tee shirts tucked into dress pants and brown leather sandals on their brown, leathery feet. The other two men wore their dirty blonde hair short but were in need of a trim, the younger one sporting a weak beard that was more red than blonde. He kept his lips tight together as he smiled, sitting shirtless in the dark room.

At the head of the table the older man balanced a cigarette on his lower lip but still managed to give them a welcoming smile. His shirt was unbuttoned and he wore the white sleeves rolled loosely on his forearms. A black string dangled a small gold cross around his neck.

'I heard it is offensive not to offer a Canadian a beer,' the man said to Rachel, 'but you'll have to make do with what we have, I'm afraid.' There was a halting rhythm to his words, and his accent and sky-blue eyes reminded Jason of a Nordic hockey player. 'Is this your brother?'

Rachel chuckled, a sound that surprised Jason. 'No. He's just some guy. You want to get this over or what?' She walked up to the table and pulled out the last empty chair with her foot. It was then that Jason noticed the two men who sat on the bed behind him, pistols held across their laps.

The older man looked at Rachel, leaning back in his chair as he drew on his cigarette. Despite the tin roof it was cool, the open windows channeling a breeze through the room. The man blew out a plume of smoke and it drifted into the face of his shirtless companion, who coughed into his hand. He took the cigarette out of his mouth, turned and yelled something over his shoulder, Hindi with a Swedish cadence. A door opened in a dark corner and a chocolate-skinned Indian brought out a cardboard box big enough to store the cooler. He set it down on the table and the older man stood up and opened the flaps.

'A man will meet you in Bangalore. He will

say his name is Sarosh Mehta and offer you a cab to the gardens at Lal Bagh.' The man looked up from the box. 'What do you have to carry this in?'

Rachel half-turned to Jason. 'Take everything out of my backpack and put it in yours. Leave the towel out.'

Jason paused for a moment, then, sensing her impatience, he stooped down and unzipped their backpacks. He noticed that half of her clothes and her thick guidebook were missing.

'You ride in the cab until he pulls over,' the man said. 'Get out and leave your bag.'

'Then what?' Rachel said.

The man shrugged and stuck the cigarette back in his mouth. 'As you wish.'

Jason was checking the last side pouch when he looked up to see the man lift two flour bag-size packages from the box. Wrapped in tan packing tape, the packages bulged unevenly, thudding on the wooden table as he set them down. Rachel turned again to Jason, snapping her fingers for the bag, which he tossed to her without standing, his hands blindly stuffing toothpaste and underwear into his full backpack.

Rachel stood up and set the empty bag on the table. 'So that's it?'

'It's enough,' the man said, which made his

companion laugh and the other men smile.

'I know you are not a stupid woman,' the man said as Rachel placed the packages in her backpack, 'but people sometimes do stupid things. There will be a man on the train, maybe two. They will watch to be sure that you are not tempted.'

Rachel shook her head as she shifted the tan bags in the backpack, stepping back to pick up the towel from the floor. 'You don't have to worry.' She stuffed the towel in around the packages and zippered the bag shut.

'But I must worry. You are a determined woman,' the man said to Rachel. 'A strong woman. A resourceful woman.' He waited until she looked up at him before continuing. 'A *passionate* woman.'

The men at the table exchanged dark grins, the shirtless European displaying a row of chipped and tobacco-stained teeth. The way they looked at him as he crouched on the floor made Jason's chest tighten, and he could feel his face grow hot.

'Really? That's sweet, thanks,' Rachel said, her voice carefree and light. 'By the way, I'm also one hell of an actress.'

The older man's smile held for a moment before leveling out, the men in the room, heads bowed, smirking in the darkness. 'Do not fuck this up,' the man said and flicked his fingers towards the door.

Two minutes later they were in the waiting cab, bouncing back down the rutted road.

'Hold it,' Rachel said when he opened his mouth to speak. 'Don't say a word.' She nodded at the driver and Jason was left to sort out his emotions, the anger that made his clenched fists shake and the fear that tore apart his stomach.

The driver gunned the engine to get the cab up on to the paved road, turning the car back in the direction they had come. They drove in silence for ten minutes before the driver slowed down to let them off by the side of the road. '*Atcha*. Twenty minute. Train station,' the man said through the open window, pointing down the road, his head weaving side to side in the hypnotic gesture that Jason had come to realize meant everything from a definite yes to one chance in a million. He sped off without mentioning the fare. Jason waited until the car was a mile down the road before he spoke.

'That's drugs in there, isn't it?' He pointed at her backpack, his hand as shaky as his voice, and fought to keep from yelling.

Rachel shifted the pack on her back, yanking her Blue Jays cap out of her back pocket. She slapped it open on her thigh and set it on her head, pulling her auburn hair through the opening in the back. She turned away to look down the road. 'I have no idea what it is. All I know is that we've got to get it to Bangalore.'

'We?' Jason said, his voice cracking, the shouting ready to start. '*We*? Where'd you get *that* idea from? I didn't ask to be dragged into some drug deal . . . '

'You don't know it's drugs.'

'Well, it sure as hell isn't somebody's laundry. Those men back there had guns, they all but said they'd kill us if you screw this up.'

'We're not going to screw it up,' she said, her voice soft but confident.

'Oh, that's right,' Jason said, high-pitched, leaning in as he shouted. 'Because there's no 'we' in it.'

'Fine,' she said. 'I'll go alone.'

'Damn straight. Whatever it is you've got in there it could get me thrown in some prison for the rest of my life, which given the fact that we're in India would probably only be a few days anyway. What were you thinking?'

'We needed money,' she said, turning around to look at him. 'We're broke.'

Jason felt his jaw drop open as he thought about her words, then reached back and tore his wallet out of his khaki Dockers. 'There was over five hundred dollars in here,' he said, fanning open the empty wallet. 'Where are my credit cards? The airline tickets?'

'They got those, too. But I got the passports back,' she said, patting the security purse she wore under her shirt.

Jason stood with his mouth open, dizziness mixing in with the nausea. 'Who?'

'The people in Goa.'

'Who?' he repeated, shouting again.

'Jason, I don't know, okay? We got ripped off. Deal with it.' She turned back around and started walking towards the distant station.

'What do you mean 'deal with it'? I had five hundred dollars in here.'

'Well, if it's any consolation I lost everything I had, too.'

Jason ran a few steps to keep up but stayed behind her on the narrow path on the side of the road. Inches away, an overcrowded bus and a pair of beeping passenger cars raced by, three abreast.

'And now you're carrying forty pounds of something that can get us thrown in jail or worse. What the hell, Rachel, what did you *do*? How could you be so damn stupid?'

Rachel spun around fast and Jason stumbled to keep from running into her. 'You're right. I *don't* know what I was doing,

184

I *don't* know how I could have been so damn stupid. I had no *fucking* clue what to do, is that what you want to hear? That I screwed up? Fine. It's all my fault. I screwed up. But tell me this, Mr Perfect.' She jammed a finger into his chest, tapping it in with every syllable, the rapid-fire words hotter than the steaming blacktop. 'You have any idea how easy it is to rip off a hysterical woman dragging a delirious, ungrateful bastard down the street, how much she will believe anything — *anything* — people tell her, especially people who look like her and swear they can help, swear they can get a doctor to look at a friend's bloody arm, swear that they know a guy who knows a guy who can get his hands on some brand-name antibiotics, no questions asked? How she'll let them talk her into doing crazy shit just to save this stupid-ass so-called friend? And then leave her with nothing and the guy still dying on the street? And then when you're crying so hard you can't fucking breathe somebody all of a sudden comes to the rescue, takes care of everything, gets your friend in to see a real doctor, gets you your passports back and loans you fifty bucks. And all you've got to do is deliver a package. You tell me Jason, what would *you* do?'

She stared at him, her finger pressed white

against his ribs. 'I . . . I . . . ' he stammered.

Rachel smirked and blew a half-breath out from her dry lips. 'Yeah, that's what I figured.' She turned back around and started down the road.

She was twenty yards away before he moved.

'Rachel, wait up.' He ran towards her, his backpack swinging him off balance with the extra weight. 'Hold on a second, we gotta talk.'

'There's no 'we,' remember?' she said, walking backwards as she spoke.

'I didn't know,' he shouted, a passing truck blasting apart his words with its air horn. 'I didn't know,' he shouted again.

'Well, now you do. So leave me alone. I can do this myself.' She turned her back to him and started walking faster.

'For cryin' out loud, hold on a second,' he said and grabbed a swaying strap of her backpack.

'Let *go*,' she said, twisting around far enough to swing a quick right at his head. He leaned back and she missed but followed through with a kick to his shins. 'Just leave me alone,' she shouted, yanking the strap from his grip. She reached down the front of her shirt and pulled out the black travel wallet that hung around her neck. She ripped open the Velcro and removed her blue Canadian passport before throwing the wallet at his feet. '*Here*. Now leave me alone.'

He watched her for five minutes, until she disappeared around a bend in the road, before he picked up his passport and started walking.

# 16

If Victoria Terminus was a picture-book example of late nineteenth-century excess, the station at Goa stood for the bland, utilitarian construction of the nineteen-eighties. Other than the flashing lights of a weight & fortune machine by the entrance and the chalkboard listing of the day's specials at the Veg/Non-Veg Restaurant, the flat, lead-paint white walls were bare. A quarter mile of poured concrete platform stretched out equally in both directions, and overhead steel rafters supported a football field of corrugated tin and dangling fluorescent lights. A cast-iron bridge took travelers across the rail lines for the northbound trains while below, a half-dozen dogs sniffed around the trash-strewn tracks, their sense of smell deadened by generations of over-stimulation.

Jason had arrived at the station just as the setting sun was touching the tops of the palm trees that lined the entrance for a train that was scheduled to depart at seven minutes after midnight. According to the schedule taped up by the ticket window, this was where the Konkan Kanya Express had dropped them off a few days ago, but when he looked around the open-air, tropical station, he didn't remember any of it. It had taken the man behind the desk only a few moments to call up the schedules of the various trains that would pass through that night, punch in Jason's rail pass numbers and print out his berth assignment. It had taken the man's assistant five minutes to transcribe the laser-printed ticket information into the yard-wide station master's log in a graceful Palmer-perfect cursive, a bureaucratic tradition computers were not about to change.

Jason had set up camp parallel to Rachel's position, just in front of the book vendor's stand. From where he was now standing he could see Rachel, still slouched down against a support beam, her backpack still hanging around her arms. Her eyes seemed fixed on some point miles away, straight across the tracks, the same position she had held for the past two hours.

He filled the first hour thinking about the stupid, stupid, stupid things he had said, playing them back again and again, amazed at what an asshole he was. He took a break for twenty minutes and tried blaming everything on Rachel, but when that line of reasoning collapsed he returned to his original theme with a renewed sense of certainty. He'd glance down the long platform at the tiny form, growing dim in the early evening light, and think about what was in her backpack and what was in her heart.

Whatever it was she was carrying — it didn't have to be drugs but he knew that it was — it was clear from the way the European man spoke it was worth a lot of money and that people would be willing to kill for it. Just like whatever it was he was carrying in his own backpack.

He wanted to eat something, the smells from the kitchen making his stomach growl with desire, but then he'd think about Rachel and how she had given him the last of the money — money that she had somehow earned when they were broke — and he didn't feel quite as hungry anymore.

Walking back from a trip to the men's room — two rupees to piss down a hole in the cement floor — Jason spotted the Beachfront Internet Café tucked in a dark recess of the station wall, just five miles from the ocean. It was hot and muggy, the room smelling of the herbal shampoos and hemp, the glowing computer stations filled with dreadlock-wearing Europeans and mousy Japanese college students. The boy in charge — fifteen, twenty or thirty-five, depending on how the light hit him — pointed Jason to an open seat. The creeping dial-up connection gave him time to memorize every message in his email account, waiting as each page cleared before the next was called up.

There were ten real messages and one hundred and fifty pieces of electronic junk. Six of the ten messages were from women he worked with, each one asking when he'd be back, each one telling him how Marcy was fired for stealing money from the coffee kitty, each one swearing him to secrecy.

Two messages were from people he didn't know, the first from a man in Mumbai asking Jason to call when he arrived. Since Mumbai was hundreds of kilometers and many days behind them, he deleted the message. The second unknown sender identified himself as Ketan Jani, the chief computer systems manager for Al Call Center Services.

'Our mutual friend in Jaipur, Mr Attar Singh, has forwarded your itinerary and updated me on your journey. Contact me when you arrive here in Bangalore. I can recommend several pleasant accommodations that you and your lovely wife will most enjoy.' Jason printed out the man's letter and contact information but doubted that he would call. It would be too difficult to explain his lovely wife's absence.

Two messages remained, the first from Ravi Murty.

'I trust your trip is going well and that you don't find India to be too overwhelming. When I first arrived in India to attend college I was stunned. I had never seen so many people in my life. And the poverty! It was too much for this Sooner! Well, as long as you keep your sense of humor intact, you'll do fine.'

Around the small room, touch typists and hunt-and-peckers rapped out emails to all points of the world, the clicking keyboards reminding Jason of the clacking rails of his journey. He thought about his first day in India, sitting on a bus filled with geriatric tourists, with Danny, the fast-talking tour director, assuring everyone that the tour's minute-by-minute itinerary made India completely hassle-free. He knew that if he had stayed with the tour he wouldn't be where he was now, waiting for a late-night train out of Goa, a short chain of evidence connecting him to a backpack of drugs and a shit-load of trouble.

No hassles.

No delays.

And no Rachel.

He laughed to himself as he thought about his choice.

'Drop me a line now and then to let me know that you are safe,' Ravi's email continued. 'And be sure to contact my representatives in Bangalore. They know the city inside and out and can save you a lot of headaches. I'm in the midst of finalizing an outsourcing deal with a company there and it's a nightmare trying to navigate that bureaucracy. I hope to avoid a trip to India, something I'm sure you'll agree is a good idea!'

When the monkey had swung across the Jaipur streets with his backpack or as he stood on the platform in Ahmadabad, blood spurting on to the dusty concrete, Jason was sure he would have agreed with Ravi. But it wasn't all thieving fleabags and homicidal attacks, and avoiding India would mean avoiding the other things as well — the sweet taste of masala chai, the faces of the children as they looked up at the tall, white man, Attar, Narvin, Laxmi and the someday-starlet Yashila, the unexpected landscape that flew past the train window, the unimaginable poverty, the unimaginable wealth, the way that, no matter where he was, he saw things he had never seen before and knew he'd never see again. This wasn't Spring Break in Daytona, and for the first time Jason realized that he was glad. He clicked the little arrow and waited as Ravi's message inched closed and the next message scrolled open on the screen.

'I trust that you and Rachel enjoyed Goa,' Narvin Kumar's email began. 'It's a good place to flush the glitzy bullshit of Bollywood out of your system. For your sake I hope she didn't keep up that silly 'I'm his sister' routine. That could make for some tough nights. Tell Rachel that when Laxmi finally runs off to marry some rich Indian ex-pat, I'll be giving her a call.' There was no little typed symbol but Jason could picture Narvin's playful wink.

'Drop me a line when you get to Bangalore. I've got a project starting there this week and might drop in to see you.'

Under his computer-generated signature and the three-color logo for his company, Narvin added a postscript and Jason felt his stomach roll as he read.

'I called that number the night you left. I figured you might as well get it over with. Lucky for you I was in my car and the call didn't go through. The next day I saw this on that website and figured you had enough going on without me making it worse. Good luck.' Jason clicked on the small icon and waited fifteen minutes for the attachment to open.

It was a simple Word document, cut and pasted from the chat room Narvin had showed him that afternoon in Mumbai.

'I'm looking for Mr Jason Talley, traveling through India with female companion named Rachel Moore. I need to find him. I will pay $500 US for valid information and I will honor any requests to remain anonymous.' There was no return email address and no signature, just the phone number that was already burned into his memory.

'It is the time of the closing,' the boy manager of the Beachfront Internet Café said. Jason looked up and noticed that he was the last person in the room, the others slipping past, his attention focused on the screen. Jason signed off and walked to the desk.

'How much?'

'Eight hundred and ten rupees,' the boy said, holding up the calculator as proof.

'The sign says twenty rupees for thirty minutes. I was on, what, an hour?' Jason said, pointing to the list of rates posted above the first terminal.

The boy's head started swaying. '*Ahcha.* Just fifty minutes.'

'So it should only be forty rupees.'

'It is thirty-five rupees for the Internet,' the boy said, 'and seven hundred seventy-five rupees for the printings.' He hefted an inch-thick stack of papers out of the wire basket next to the printer.

'I didn't print those. Okay, maybe a few, but not all that.'

'You are the last one here. The columns must balance at the end of my shift.' He ran his finger down a long list of numbers in the ancient register book.

Jason shrugged his shoulders. 'That's not my problem, pal. I'll pay for mine but . . . '

'The rules are most clear on this point,' the boy said and flipped open a three-ring binder on the desk to reveal a single typed sheet encased in plastic. He spun the book around, his index finger pointing to the relevant bullet.

'Look, I don't care what it says. I didn't print these out.'

The boy gave a sympathetic smile. 'These must be paid for.'

Jason pulled a paper from the bottom of the pile. 'Here,' he said, holding the sheet out for the boy to see. 'This says it was printed at fourteen hundred hours. That's what? Two in the afternoon? And how long did you say I was here?'

'Fifty minutes.'

'Right. So how can I have printed these?'

'But the rules . . . '

'The hell with the rules,' Jason said, his voice rising above the hum of the worthless ceiling fans. 'The rules are just stupid. And I'm not paying. What does your rule say about that?'

The boy gave his head another side-to-side waggle. 'The rules must be followed. As such, the rules state that I must now report you to the station master who will then notify the local police . . . '

'The police?' Jason said as he thought about all it meant.

'This is the rule.' The boy tapped the laminated sheet as proof.

Jason paused long enough to sigh before handing over the money. He scooped up the papers and headed for the door.

'No sir,' the boy said, blocking the door with his arm. 'You can not yet go.'

'But I paid. You can't call the police now.'

'You must wait for your receipt. It is the rule.'

★   ★   ★

It was eleven-thirty when the police arrived at the station.

Jason had been sitting alone on a wooden bench reading and grouping the papers he had bought. A third were in French or

197

German or Spanish or some other language that used the same alphabet, none of which he could read. Another third were printed in a font he had never seen before, tiny circles and boxes and dashes that gave him a headache to look at. He made separate piles for each assumed language, tapping even the edges of the stacks on the back of the bench before tossing them in the trash.

The printouts in English were mostly hardcopies of email letters — important reminders of the things people had come to Goa to forget. Updates on family members in Helsinki, reminders about college registration deadlines and syrupy notes from pining lovers, counting the days till this 'finding yourself' bullshit was over. There were papers that Jason was certain someone would be tearing backpacks apart later to find — an invitation to a full-moon party on Ko Samui, complete with a detailed map and stock drawings of pot leaves, a list of phone numbers of reputable escort services in Athens, the address of an Australian abortionist in Madras who took credit cards, names of pawn shops in Calcutta that didn't ask a lot of questions. He subdivided the money-from-home letters into three piles — ones that promised to wire funds to a Western Union office, ones that said they would not, and ones that said that this was absolutely the last and final time money would be sent, noting in capital letters or italicized type or both that they meant it this time.

There were a handful of 'hilarious' forwards that 'you *have* to read' — fifty reasons why a beer is better than a woman, fifty reasons why a cucumber is better than a man, two pages of light bulb jokes, ten pages of lawyer jokes, a list of stupid laws in Texas and the same list of laws, this time from Alberta. He was re-reading a piece downloaded from a London comedy club's website — a 'wafty crank of a monologue' that took on the way Americans 'try' to speak and write in English — when he thought about Mrs Maxwell.

Every student agreed that Mrs Maxwell was the best teacher at West Corning High School. Her classes watched whole episodes of *Cheers* so they could learn about character development, they could rap out their evaluations of stories instead of writing essays, they read the comic book version of *Mice and Men*, they did collages, they held parties, they played Pictionary. You can't cage the learner, she liked to say. Jason was never late for her class, never jerked around and, as the ninth grade standardized test at the end of the year proved, never learned a thing.

Every student agreed that Mr Switzer was the worst teacher at West Corning High School. His classes were painful, nothing but sheet after sheet of equations and questions, the word problems lacking so much as a single damn train leaving a station. Correct answers on wrinkled papers were marked wrong, stray marks lowered test scores, and don't even think about cheating. A disciplined mind starts with a disciplined desk, he said. No one was late, no one misbehaved, and no one scored less than a ninety on the standardized test.

In the four years that he took his classes, Jason learned a lot from Mr Switzer.

He was thinking about the things he didn't learn from Mrs Maxwell when he saw the police out of the corner of his eye.

All three were dressed in starched khaki uniforms, spit-shined shoes and gleaming belts. Their brass buttons glowed in the fluorescent light. Two were tall and thin, their arms swinging free in their stiff short sleeves, like clackers in a church bell, the shorter man — still taller than Jason — walking just ahead. Their waist bands dipped an inch on the right, pulled down by heavy holstered revolvers. They didn't twirl their billy clubs by leather straps or slap them into their open palm, using them instead as an extension of their arm, pushing open the station doors and prodding sleeping beggars out of their way, the official version of a ten-foot pole.

They moved with an easy grace — the last train was still a half an hour away and they could take their time, no one was going anywhere. They started with a small group of blond Rastafarians from Sweden who knew the drill. They stood when the policemen spoke, they smiled as clubs poked into bedrolls, turned torn pockets inside out and even helped spill open tattered backpacks. They didn't complain when a Walkman dropped from a bag and shattered in half. If they were hiding something it was small and not worth the officers' time and they gathered up their ratty possessions as the police moved down the line.

Rachel was still sitting, her back against an iron support. She had seen enough to understand what was going on and Jason watched as she turned back to face the tracks, her elbows on her knees, her hands hanging loose above her feet.

The Japanese girls giggled nervously as the policemen asked them questions, their embarrassed blushes misinterpreted as exotic flirtations. There was a great deal of smiling and head bobbing and *ahcha* head swaying, but other than glancing at their passports while pretending they weren't looking down their baggy tee shirts, the police left them alone.

Sprawled out next to a chai vendor's stove, two guys, college-aged, glared up at the police who stood over them. Jason didn't hear what the one said but the other laughed and he saw the officer's jaw tighten, the billy club coming around fast and sharp and catching the laughing student on the knee. He yelped and rolled back, his friend standing halfway up before a second club rapped on his wrist and he fell back down hard. The one clutching his knee was shouting in English, a heavy Teutonic accent adding the attitude, when the smallest officer stepped forward and set the tip of his club on the man's stomach, leaning on it as he explained the situation in a low, calm voice. Whether it was the words or the club or something else Jason couldn't see, the man was soon nodding and, flat on his back, dumping the contents of his pack on to the concrete by his head. The officer waited, still leaning, as his partners sifted through the pile with their clubs, and, finding nothing, tipping his hat as they walked away.

Rachel had tilted her head back, the bill of her Blue Jays cap pointing into the night sky. She curled her lower lip between her teeth and he watched as her shoulders rose and fell in jerky bursts.

After their chat with the two young Germans, the three policemen regrouped for a moment at the edge of the platform, the tallest knocking a discarded clay chai cup off the platform to break on the tracks three feet below. For a moment Jason thought that they would turn away and wander down to the far end of the track where dark shadows waited on dark benches, but they turned back to scan the crowd for the usual suspects. The shortest, silver tabs on his epaulets denoting his rank, rocked back on his heels, sniffed the humid night air and stepped towards the woman in the baseball hat who sat crying against an iron column.

They were four feet away when the singing started.

'*jingle bells, jingle bells, jingle all the way . . .* '

He was off key, off beat and his voice was cracking, but Jason was loud enough to attract the attention of every person at the open-air station.

' *. . . oh what fun it is to ride a something horse open sleigh, HEY!*'

The police officers, like everyone but the crying girl, stared at the singing man, the tallest bringing a hand up to conceal a bright, white smile. The officer in charge smiled too, but they hadn't moved towards him, still towering above the crying girl.

Jason looked at the police, drew in a deep breath that came out as a desperate sigh, held imaginary reins in his hands and broke into a prancing gallop.

'*Dashing through the snow, in something something sleigh, over the hills we go, laughing all the way, ha, ha, ha* . . . '

It was the laughing that got the police moving. They walked over slowly, billy clubs now behind their backs, surrounding him. Jason stopped singing but held tight on his reins. 'Oh, hello,' he said, with a polite, I'm-not-dangerous smile.

'What are you doing?' the officer in charge said, his partners looking away to keep from laughing.

Jason raised his eyebrows, the answer obvious. 'I'm taking a sleigh ride,' he said, and held up his hands to show the invisible reins.

The officer nodded. 'Where are you from?'

Jason was tempted to say something about over the river and through the woods but he sensed that he'd already gone far enough. 'The U.S. I'm an American.'

The officer nodded again. 'American,' he said to the taller men, as if that explained everything. 'Is that your bag?' He pointed with his club.

'*Ahcha*,' Jason said, and gave his head a slight bob.

'Pick it up. You will come with us,' the officer said. 'And leave your horse here.'

# 17

Despite the impressive brass nameplate on the door, the stationmaster's office was small and cardboard boxes filled with old station logs and office supplies lined the walls. The two taller guards stood with their backs to the closed door, their billy clubs held diagonally across their chests, the shorter man motioning to a chair against the wall as he stepped behind the room's only desk and took a seat.

For five minutes no one said a word as the officer flipped through Jason's passport, the sound of the turning pages slow and deliberate. By the door, one of the policemen sneezed and rubbed the end of his nose with the back of his hand that held the black club. Jason tried to think of what he would do if they started beating him, realizing then that he could do nothing at all. The officer set the passport on the desk, and said something to the tallest policeman, who took Jason's backpack, placed it on the desk and began the inspection, starting with a long, critical look at the bright pink Hello Kitty shoulder strap with its trendy Japanese cartoon cat logo.

The first thing the policeman pulled out was a handful of Rachel's underwear.

'A souvenir,' Jason said, forcing himself to smile as the man held up a wispy red thong. The police officers exchanged glances before conversing in Hindi, the meaning evident in their disgusted tone. He was waiting for them to pull a bra from the backpack when he remembered that Rachel seldom wore one.

They went through the pack, pocket by pocket, pouring the shampoo down the floor drain in the center of the room, breaking open his disposable camera, squeezing toothpaste into the wastepaper basket. There was no malicious bullying, no leering grins, just a quiet efficiency that Jason found frightening. They unfurled all six yards of the red sari, the two taller men holding up sections and examining the silver embroidery with its circuit board pattern, tugging on the button, holding the fabric up to their nose, the smell of the cologne still strong, the officer first looking at the sari then at Jason, then back at the sari, saying nothing.

He knew it was coming but he still flinched when the officer told him to undress. They turned his clothes inside out, yanked the padded instep from his Nikes and removed the laces. He stood naked, not knowing where

207

to put his hands, shaking even though it was hot in the windowless room, and listened as the Matsayagandha Express pulled into the station.

The man behind the desk picked up Jason's green rail pass and printed ticket from the pile of papers he had built next to a pair of Rachel's jeans.

'You have a ticket for this train.' It wasn't a question but Jason still said yes. The man said something to the others, which made them laugh, but he kept the same flat, cryptic look.

'Do you always sing in public?'

'No sir, th-this was the first time I ever did anything like that,' Jason stammered and he realized as he said it that it was the truth.

The officer looked back at the pile of papers and thumbed through his passport for the tenth time. 'I have one last question for you, Mr Jason Talley,' he said, looking right into Jason's eyes. 'What did you do with the money?'

Streams of cold sweat ran down his sides and his stomach muscles cramped. He held his hands tight against his crotch to keep them from shaking. 'Money?' he said, his voice dry, and he thought about the packages in Rachel's bag, small bundles that could be anything.

'Yes. The money.'

Jason swallowed and focused on his words. 'What money?'

'The money your mother gave you for singing lessons,' the officer said as he stood up and placed his cap on his head. 'You had better hurry if you are going to make your train.'

Through the closed door he could hear the three men laughing as they left the station.

★ ★ ★

The train was already moving when Jason sprinted out of the stationmaster's office, jumping through the door of the last passenger car with ten feet of platform to spare, his swinging backpack pinballing him into the narrow passage. An old man stood looking out the opposite door. He gave a friendly nod as Jason, panting, leaned against the wall by the restroom door.

His rail pass guaranteed him a berth in a first-class sleeper. If the Matsayagandha Express was like the other trains he had seen in India, he would have to pass through twenty third-class cars and cut through the kitchen car before he reached the air-conditioned portion of the train, three or four cars with cushioned seats and reading lights and hefty price tags. Unlike the first-class cars, there was no heavy, soundproof door separating this entrance area from the wooden benches that served as seats and, now, as beds. He took his pack off, held it by the good strap, and started down the aisle.

The seating arrangement was the same in third class as it was in first, the car subdivided into a dozen alcoves, each with forward and rear-facing benches. In first class the thick, padded backrest swung up to create a second tier bed — in third the hard beds were bolted into place, three tiers high. Each alcove in first class offered dark blue privacy curtains, third class making do with saris knotted to support poles or nothing at all. People slept three to a berth, their luggage chained to the bench frame to deter on-board thieves or crammed in the corner, serving as rough pillows. There had been close to a hundred people waiting for the train at Goa station and he spotted a few who were trying to settle in among the passengers, most of whom had been aboard for hours. They smiled and stepped out of the way as he passed, the train's movement adding some strange steps to the dance.

The car ended in an entrance area that was the mirror image of the one he had climbed aboard, complete with two restrooms, a child-sized sink and twin doors that stood open to let in the cool night air, the roar of the train a small price to pay. Two long steps took him through the passage that linked the cars, and he was glad that it was too dark to see the tracks that raced below.

The pattern repeated for the next twenty-four cars — dark passageway, entrance area, crowded benches, entrance area, dark passageway. Sometimes there were men standing in the open doorways, watching the night go by, smoking little joint-like cigarettes under the No Smoking signs, sometimes he bumped into people going in or coming out of the restroom, a single-seater that lacked a seat, just an aluminum basin low on the floor that flushed on to the tracks. In every car there were snores that drowned out the train, a crying baby that drowned out the snores, and someone in the middle of the aisle, bags open, driven by an insomniac urge to repack his luggage.

The white-coated chai vendors and the teeshirt-wearing cooks were enjoying a late-night snack in the kitchen when Jason walked through. One of the cooks held out a wrapped sandwich and motioned for Jason to take it, shrugging his shoulders to say it wasn't a big deal, another setting a cup of milky chai on the box that served as their makeshift table. Jason thanked him and took a seat, not realizing how hungry he was until he held the sandwich in his hands.

From a metal kitchen drawer one of the cooks pulled a boom box, setting it on the floor by his feet as he hit the play button. He skipped the first few tracks on the CD to reach a slow ballad, the woman singing in an impossibly high voice. The men around the tabled bobbed their heads in time with the music, and although he didn't know the words, Jason sensed she sang of lost love and missed opportunities. When the song ended the man skipped back to play it again.

The sandwich was good, chicken maybe, or some deep-fried vegetable. One of the chai vendors, a sleepy-eyed adolescent working the midnight shift, pointed to Jason's sneakers and laughed, and Jason held up a leg for the others to see the missed eyelets and huge bows of a ten-second lace-up, laughing along with the boy. One of the chai vendors tapped Jason on the arm. 'Policeman?' he asked, pointing back down the tracks, and Jason nodded, drawing sympathetic grunts around the table.

The CD moved on to a bouncy number built around a call and response refrain. By the second verse they were all clapping and singing along. He'd had enough singing for the night, but Jason kept the beat on the bottom of an overturned plastic bucket. The third time through the song, Jason added polyrhythmic flourishes to the backbeat, finishing up with a double-handed drum roll and a geographically incorrect *Olé*. He left the kitchen a half-hour later, the cook handing him two more sandwiches, adding the same no-big-deal shrug.

Although it had the same basic layout as its third-class cousins, the entrance area of the first-class car was cleaner and, with a fifteen-watt bulb in the ceiling-mounted fixture, better lit. The parallel restrooms — one featuring the aluminum hole, the other a chipped and stained porcelain toilet — jogged out of the walls, narrowing the passage further. The car's doors stood open, held in place by the train's momentum, and through the doors the lights of distant villages and the more distant stars stood out against the black night. Jason opened the heavy, soundproof door to first class and shook as a blast of mechanically chilled air swept down his shirt. The door closed with a muffled thump behind him and he started down the passage, looking for his assigned berth. He was halfway down the car when a hand reached out from behind a blue

213

curtain and caught his pant leg.

'So, Santa,' Rachel's voice said in the darkness, 'am I back on your nice list?'

Jason pulled back the curtain. She was sitting alone on the cushioned bench, the backrest still in place. On the two bunks across from her he could see the sprawled-out bodies of a pair of travelers, mouths open, drooling, decorum lost to sleep. She slid over and patted the seat next to her. He sat down and fished the sandwiches out of his pack, handing her both. 'I think it's chicken,' he said.

Rachel peeled back the corner of the white paper and nibbled at the bread. 'You eat?' she asked.

'Back in the kitchen,' Jason said, his thumb pointing the direction.

Rachel nodded and re-wrapped the sandwich. 'I'm not hungry,' she said and handed it back.

He leaned over and lowered his voice. 'Listen, Rachel, what I said back there on the road . . . well, what I *didn't* say . . . hell, I'm sorry.'

'Sorry?' she said, just as soft. 'Jason, you're not sorry. You're fucking amazing.' In the darkness he felt her reach over and squeeze his hand. 'But I'm still not hungry.'

'You haven't eaten all day.'

'I know. I should be starved, but I'm not. Maybe it's nerves.'

Jason chuckled. 'Nerves? What do you have to be nervous about?'

'I'm afraid,' she said, cuddling up next to him, resting her head on his sloping shoulder, 'you might start singing again.'

# 18

The train made three different sounds as it headed south towards Mangalore.

There was the low rumbling sound of hard earth beneath the thick foundation of crushed stone and cement sleepers, half buried in the red clay, a never-ending roll of thunder that boomed up through the open door. When they blew through a village station or over an improved roadway the rumble jumped an octave, the sound thinner as it echoed off the concrete runners, there and gone as fast as a speeding train through a no-name town.

But it was when they crossed over a trestle bridge and sound dropped off to a whisper that the train was most frightening. The first time it happened Jason felt his grip tighten on the vertical handrails that ran outside the train's east-facing door, a split-second of terror as he imagined the car flying off the tracks and hurtling down into the sliver of moon reflected in the wide, shallow river. It was a silence that hinted at long drops and pointed rocks.

Jason tried standing like Rachel had stood on that first train trip to Jaipur, one hand on the rail, the other in his pants' pocket, but the darkness and the unfamiliar sensation of leaning out an open doorway of a speeding train compelled both hands into place.

He had left Rachel asleep in the berth, wrapped in a thick blanket the purser had set on the end of the bed when he saw how she was shaking. She had made a quick dash back to the restrooms, then a second trip, not so rushed, before falling asleep. Jason had sat by the aisle, Rachel's feet against his leg, and eaten one of the sandwiches, the caffeine from all that chai holding open his eyes. Other than the rumbling thunder of the train, it was quiet when he eased down the length of the car and passed through the sound-proof door to stand with his toes hanging out into the warm, black Indian night, a giddy charge running up his spine.

On the ground by the tracks he could see his shadow cast from the weak bulb that lit the entrance area, jumping up to face him as they cut through an embankment, stretching flat again when they hit the open plains, falling away when they flew across a bridge, nothing but air between him and whatever lay below. Lights a mile away stayed in view for minutes while trackside images blurred past. Men with kerosene lamps leading elephant-drawn carts, a mob of late-night bicyclists lined up at an unguarded crossing, a lean-to convenience store with a flickering Coca-Cola sign, miles and miles and miles of farmland or forest, he couldn't tell which, and in the distance, hills that rose and rolled like those around Corning, his mind suddenly filled with images of his hometown, his job, his street, his apartment, his dead neighbors.

There was no reason why it couldn't have been a murder-suicide. It seemed that the news was filled with stories of husbands or boyfriends or brothers unloading their anger into a loved one before taking their own lives. To the victims' families it always came as a shock, no one seeing it coming, the couple appearing so happy, so in love. The psychologists explained to the viewers at home that the men who committed these acts — it was always men — had suppressed their true emotions for so long that they were — again always — 'ticking time bombs.' But the authorities were quick to reassure the public that these incidences were 'rare,' saying the same comforting lines the next time it happened. Men snapped, Jason reasoned, it happened. But not Sriram.

Sriram loved to talk about computers, about technology and the 'magic' that was this *frickin'* close to being commonplace, his eyes sparkling as he threw out acronym-laced examples and Asimovian applications. Sure, there were complaints about the job, but it was all the usual crap — co-workers who didn't pull their weight, supervisors who didn't know heads from holes in the ground, copiers that jammed in sync with deadlines, all for a paycheck that wasn't worth the trouble. But Jason knew that Sriram had loved it. He never complained about the long hours or the stress and Jason never heard a bad word about Raj-Tech's owner.

'It must be nice to work for a friend,' Jason said one night as they sipped beers on the front porch of the apartment building, and he remembered how Sriram had sighed.

'I can never forget what Ravi did,' Sriram had said. 'Someday I hope to pay him back.' Jason sighed now as he recalled the line, wondering how many things he would leave undone if he died.

Not a hell of a lot.

His work at the mortgage company had been divvied up before he left — if he never returned they'd either hire someone to fill his cubicle or, more likely, tell the others the increased workload was now the norm. His parents lived less than ten miles away, but it was different now. No traumatic blowups for the Talleys, just a steady, comfortable slide apart, a neat and predictable relationship,

219

uncomplicated by any real emotions. They were willing to watch Bindi — his cat by default — but he knew enough not to ask for more.

He had a few friends in town, none as close as Mike Myles, his best friend since fourth grade. Mike who showed him how to talk to girls, Mike who helped him get a fake ID, Mike who got him to skip school once in their senior year, Mike who made a special late-night trip to drop him off at the Syracuse airport the first time he flew to Daytona, Mike who went and fell asleep as he drove back home. No one knew how to get in touch with Jason in Florida, and when his return flight landed and Mike was not at the airport as planned and he was forced to pay close to two hundred bucks to rent a car to get home, he had left a long and angry message on Mike's machine, Mike's mom calling him the next day to apologize for her dead son's irresponsibility. You only get so many best friends, Jason knew, and he'd used up his allotment, owing them both more than he ever gave.

He squeezed his eyes shut and forced his mind back into his office cubicle.

The gray fabric partition walls. The Far Side cartoons. A plastic Spiderman scaling the side of his monitor. The quarter-inch thick stack of pre-printed, gold-bordered certificates, thumb-tacked next to the phone extension list. Most Third-Quarter, Non-Government Loans Prepared Within Mandatory State Guidelines. Quickest Turnaround in Post-Closing Deviation to Correction. Fewest Errors in Calculating APR Rate (Final Copy). Most Festive Desk Decoration, Halloween. There was no aspect of his job he didn't know, no documentation process he hadn't mastered. He was twenty-seven years old and the thing he did better than anyone else was file forms.

You can be anything you want, the guidance counselors had said, paralyzing him with limitless options. He had fallen into his job, a vague position, difficult to explain, impossible to justify. He could walk away any time he wanted to, something that made him more depressed than the thought of staying.

The train sped on, fewer towns, no lights, the conductor sounding the horn now and then to keep him company, the train whistling in the dark. He was leaning back, legs crossed, one hand white on the handrail, when the man came out of the first-class car carrying his backpack.

For the five seconds it took the man to push the heavy door shut behind him, the chilled air from the car whooshing around the backpack dangling by the man's legs and out the open doors on both sides of the train, Jason tried to place where he had seen that backpack before. He could see where someone had stitched up a nasty tear on the top flap, the kind of tear a monkey might make as it searched for tasty toiletries, and there was a bit of red thong poking out of a side pocket that he thought he recognized. But it was the Hello Kitty pink padded replacement shoulder strap that made his brain snap awake.

The man was turning around, heading across the entrance area for the passageway that would lead down the train to third class, when Jason grabbed at his wrist, the green fabric of the man's wind-breaker bunching up under his fingers, Jason's hand wrapping around the bony forearm.

'What the hell are you doing with my bag?' Jason said, knowing the answer, knowing it was a stupid thing to say.

The man's eyes widened as connections were made and he jerked his arm free, pulling the backpack up and away as he swung a fist into Jason's jaw. Jason didn't notice the hit as he stepped forward and grabbed the black shoulder strap, yanking the bag and the man towards him. A second punch, hard on his cheek, made Jason wince but he held tight to the strap, opening his eyes, things now in slow-motion, watching as the man jerked a black pistol out of his waist band, fumbling to get his finger around the guard and on to the trigger, the roar of the train gone as they crossed a trestle bridge. With both hands on the strap, Jason pushed forward, the backpack crushed between them, the pistol, trapped, held flat against the man's stomach. The man's face was inches away, his breath smelling of ginger and tobacco, both men focused on the bag and their balance. Jason pushed, his sneakers slipping on the dusty linoleum floor, the man pushing back, somehow stronger, his arm rising as he worked the pistol free. Jason gripped the strap and gave one final push, his knee snapping up, slamming into the man's groin, the man gasping, holding tight to the pink strap as Jason rocked back and kicked, his heel thrust into the man's gut, launching the man backwards, the pack now suspended between them, the gun, free, leveling, the twin cracks as the pink snaps broke free, the man a foot above the cabin floor, the bright flash in his hands, a moment in midair, pink strap waving, the train's whistle covering any scream, then the dark Indian night, high above an unseen river.

With the flash and the faint pop, Jason doubled over, the pack in the way, a sharp jab catching him just below the ribs. He slumped, sliding down the wall, the backpack flopping against his legs. Eyes closed, his breath came in half-gasps and he ran a hand down the front of his shirt, feeling for the warm dampness. When his hand, still dry, reached the top of his jeans, he moved it back up to where it hurt and rubbed, feeling for the hole in his shirt. When he didn't find it, he opened his eyes and looked down.

The black backpack, minus a strap, sat on the floor between his legs. His right hand pressed against his stomach. He angled his hand back from his shirt, ready to slam it down to stem a gushing red stream, but saw nothing. With both hands he lifted his shirt to his chin and saw a baseball-sized red mark where he knew the bullet had hit him, a round welt where there should have been a bloody hole. He took a deep breath and checked again, rubbing both hands across his body, certain he'd find the wound. It was then that he noticed the small hole in the front of the backpack.

Grabbing the lone strap, Jason pulled the bag on to his lap. Synthetic fibers fused together, creating a ring of tiny black globs around the edge of the hole, too small to push a pencil through. He unzipped the top flap and felt along the inside of the bag, finding the hole with his fingertips, twisted his hand around and pulled a wadded pair of Rachel's jeans and some other clothes from the bag. The bullet had made seven holes as it tore through the folds of the jeans, two holes through his favorite polo shirt, four in his last pair of clean khakis. He reached back in the pack and lifted out the sari, a tight bundle with an easy-to-spot hole, a ragged black dot on a red background.

Resting the sari on the top of the backpack, Jason began to unravel the six yards of intricately patterned silk, the hole appearing anew with each turn of the fabric, his hands moving faster, racing to end the damage, when something small and hard dropped from the bundle and bounced on to the floor of the train, rolling under his outstretched leg. With a shaking thumb and forefinger, Jason retrieved the misshapen slug, holding it up to the light for a full minute before leaning his head out the open train door to throw up on the now roaring tracks.

# 19

'You really should eat something,' Jason said, digging his fork into his third masala dosa, the rolled, potato-filled crepe hanging off both ends of his plate. He tore off a three-inch piece and dunked it in the low metal dish of sambar, the spicy soup doubling as a dipping sauce. Rachel looked up under the bill of her cap, her nose wrinkling.

'I don't dare eat anything spicy,' she said.

Jason pointed to a neighboring table with a dripping hunk of dosa. 'Get a couple of idlis. They're just steamed rice cakes, not spicy at all.'

He wiped his fingers on a paper napkin and took a long drink of water from the metal cup the waiter had brought with his meal. Rachel watched as he downed half the cup, shaking her head, saying, 'You really should stick with bottled water.'

'I've been stabbed, shot, nearly died of an infection, and was robbed by a rabid monkey,' he said, raising the cup up to his lips as he spoke. 'You think I'm scared of a little microbe?'

Rachel's eyes narrowed. 'Be afraid,' she

said in a low growl. 'Be very afraid.'

Jason had sat in the doorway of the rail car until the horizon turned pink from the approaching dawn. Rachel was still asleep, her arms wrapped tight around her backpack, the blanket kicked off in her sleep. Jason had sat on the end of the bed, his head throbbing, too many thoughts crossing paths at the same time. Just before five, Rachel woke up with a start, grabbing a roll of toilet paper from her pack and heading to the restroom, returning forty minutes later, digging through her pack for a clear plastic cosmetic bag and a foil-backed card of shrink-wrapped pills.

A half hour outside the final station, the chai vendors made their last rounds, one stopping to shake Jason's hand, miming the song and dance from the night before. Jason bought chai for his section of the car, paying the tab with a lone five-dollar bill he had hidden in his wallet. With ten minutes to go, his fellow passengers started hauling their luggage into the aisle and out on to the entranceway where, as they had slept, one man was shot, saved by a balled-up sari, and another fell flailing to his death. When the Matsayagandha Express entered the station, a herd of red-coated porters climbed aboard, forcing their way down the crowded aisles, each man trying to secure the largest load of luggage, ignoring the light-traveling tourists and focusing on the baggage-heavy families, working out the multi-levy charge in their heads faster than he could have done with a calculator. A minute after the train came to a stop, the car was empty.

They were standing on the platform, shifting their backpacks and getting their bearings, when one of the porters dashed off the train and handed Jason a paperback, turning and running back before Jason could stop him. Inside the battered copy of *The Code of the Woosters*, Jason found a five-hundred-rupee note and two bus tickets to Bangalore, their names computer-printed in red.

The bus station was at the foot of a gently sloping hill, the two-lane street lined with shops and movie theaters, bold letters on one marquee advertising *Mera Bhai, Meri Jaan*. In a restaurant halfway down the hill, Jason filled in the blanks about Sriram and Vidya, the sari, the computer stalker and the two dead men.

'If you want me to go on alone,' he had said as they watched the waiter navigate through the breakfast crowd with his serving tray, 'I understand completely.'

'Sure,' she had said, 'trying to get rid of me just as it's getting interesting.'

Twenty minutes later they were sitting on a cement retaining wall outside the restaurant, watching the traffic go by, waiting to board the ten a.m. bus for the six-hour ride to Bangalore. Bicycle-rickshaws filled the street, the drivers joking with their passengers, coasting down the hill or, standing on the pedals, grunting, struggling back up to the train station. Waves of young school children, their blue uniforms clean and pressed, scurried past, while, lolling behind, their high school brothers and sisters exchanged copied homework papers and sticks of gum.

'I used to love going to school,' Rachel said, waving to a giggling pack of pre-teens who noticed the roll of toilet paper in her hand. 'Especially geography. I had an aunt — Helen — she was a missionary with our church. Lived for years in South Africa. Soweto. This was during apartheid. She had this Zulu spear, called an *umkhonto*,' she said, hefting the imaginary weapon to her shoulder. 'Anyway, I brought it to school, thought the teacher would love it.'

'I take it she didn't.'

'Oh, she loved it all right. It was the principal who had issues. He started ripping into the teacher right there in front of the class, telling her how stupid and irresponsible she was, and I could see she was starting to cry and that pissed me off, so I gave it to him.'

'The spear?'

'Just the point,' Rachel said. 'Right in the ass. You'd be surprised at all the blood. Anyway, that's when my mom started home schooling me.'

Ten yards away, a barber set up shop on the sidewalk, propping a rectangular mirror in a niche on the low wall, setting out his gleaming razors on a dull gray towel. 'That really happen, that thing with the spear?' he said.

'Depends. Do I look heroic or just crazy?'

Jason watched the barber as he passed the blade back and forth across the leather strop, testing the edge with his calloused thumb, rubbing the blood off on his trousers. 'More heroic I think.'

'Good,' Rachel said, jumping off the wall and slapping the dust off the seat of her baggy jeans. 'Then it really happened. Now let me see this infamous sari again.'

'Here? Out in the open?' Jason said, looking up and down the street.

Rachel stopped and looked at him. 'You think it makes a difference?'

He thought for a moment and gave a shrug, throwing open the top flap and pulling out the red and gold bundle.

'Jesus, it's a wreck,' Rachel said, taking it

from him, stuffing her toilet paper in her pocket. 'Here. Hold the end.'

Twisting and turning, the sari unrolled in clumps, drooping to the sidewalk. He knew there'd be holes, he had seen them that morning as he tried to figure out why he wasn't dead, but he didn't think there would be this many. Folded and doubled up against itself, the bullet hole multiplied symmetrically, leaving four holes across the yard-wide fabric. The four-hole pattern repeated every foot down the six yards of the fabric, with a four-foot space in the middle left intact. 'I guess that's where the bullet got stopped,' Jason said, rubbing the thin silk between his fingers.

'You sure you only got shot once?' Rachel said, poking her finger through one of the holes. 'There's gotta be fifty holes in this thing.'

'It's the way it was wrapped up. It's just one bullet.'

'Check it out,' she said, accordion-folding the hole-less middle section, pinching the fabric together until it was no thicker than a magazine. 'You were this close to being dead.'

Jason rolled up the sari from the far end, leaving the embroidered section draped along the wall. 'What's this look like to you?' he asked.

'You mean besides a bullet hole-ridden sari

that smells like cheap cologne?'

'It wasn't cheap, and yeah, what's this pattern, the embroidery, look like?'

Rachel stepped back to get a better look, her head tilting from side to side, squinting to focus on the pattern alone.

'Don't you think it looks like a circuit board?' Jason said. 'Like a computer program chip up close?'

Arms outstretched, Rachel examined the sari. 'No.'

'What do you mean no?'

'It's just a pattern.' She held the sari by the corner button as Jason rolled up the design.

'These lines, they could be circuits. And these rounded things, I don't know, they could be some other kind of computer thing.'

'You're reading way too much into it.'

'Well, there's something to this sari. That guy last night was going to shoot me to get it.'

Rachel tilted her head to the side, her ponytail swinging to the side through the opening in the back of her cap. 'Is that what you think? That he was after *this*?' She gave the fabric a final shake.

'My friend said it was really valuable.'

'Jason, look at it. The alcohol in the cologne made the colors run, there's these faded lines where it was folded, and now it's all full of holes. Even the embroidery is unraveling.'

'Still, that guy was . . . '

'That guy was looking for *my* backpack,' Rachel said, cutting him off. 'But he couldn't have known I was using it as a pillow. He saw yours — where you left it, on the edge of the bed — thought it was mine, and took it. I mean, what guy has a pink shoulder strap?'

'What about that man that's looking for me, the guy on the chat room pages. And there was that guy that gave me this,' he said, holding up his bandaged arm. 'That was a week before you even had that crap.' He gestured with his chin at her backpack.

'You don't know what he wants. He may just want to meet you. You say this Sriram guy had lots of friends. Okay, so maybe he's an old friend. You got the number. Call him.'

Jason shook his head. 'He also had a lot of enemies.'

'Oh god,' she said, rolling her eyes. 'You have something more important to worry about than some computer hacker.'

'You mean going with you to drop off those packages?'

'Worse,' she said, pulling the roll of toilet paper out of her baggy cargo pocket. 'You've got to explain to your friend's mother why you ruined her son's last gift. Now wish me luck. I'm going to try using that public bathroom.'

# 20

In a single, perfected move, Mukund Chaudhary checked his mirrors, downshifted to second gear, signalled his intention, and swung the fifty-passenger bus around the slow-moving flatbed that was itself overtaking an even slower tractor-trailer on the two-lane road that wound uphill into a blind curve. It was almost noon and he was ten minutes behind schedule, not that anyone at Mangalore Transport would care. He could pull his bus in four hours late and no one would say a word, but after five years driving the same route, hitting the target landmarks on time was a personal, if not professional, goal.

The engine revved hard and he felt the tires on his side of the bus slip off the paved highway and on to the hard-packed shoulder, a tactile signal that he was an inch or two from sliding along the metal guardrail. Fortunately, the guardrail on this section of the highway had been taken out a year ago by a doomed lorry driver from Madras as his flaming truck tumbled down the mountain side, so Mukund didn't have to worry about scratching the paint on the company-owned bus.

For a moment, the three vehicles ran abreast, spanning the entire width of National Highway Forty-Eight. Foot to the floor, the bus moved ahead of the flatbed that was struggling to pass the creeping tractor-trailer. After flicking on his directional, he cut in front of both vehicles, just in time to give the horn a friendly toot, waving hello to a rival bus company driver who came full-speed around the bend. Behind him, Mukund heard the two tourists suck in their breath and he could picture them, eyes-wide, gripping on to the arm rests or on to each other, certain they were about to die. Mukund made a mental note to cut it a little closer next time.

There wasn't a ten-meter stretch of the route that Mukund didn't know as well as he knew his own home. The crumbling pavement outside of Bantval, the traffic-choked area around Sakaleshpur with its busloads of pious Jain pilgrims, the constant road work between Hassan and Channarayaptna, the thousands of bends and twists of the blacktop as it snaked through the mountain passes — he could close his eyes and see all of it. The six-hour morning run to Bangalore he could do in his sleep. The run back to Mangalore — the last two dead-tired hours coming in the dark jungle foothills — well, that was different. He didn't just drive his bus, an air-conditioned Tata that wasn't even three years old yet, he controlled it, dominated it, like an expert rider controlling a fiery thoroughbred. And yet they gasped as if he didn't see the bus coming headlong at them. Damn tourists.

He kept his foot on the gas pedal, slowing down just as he came up to the back end of a truck hauling burlap bags of rice, the words *Horn Please* ornately painted on the tailgate. Mukund hit the horn twice as he shot by, staying in the wrong lane even after he was well past the truck. He glanced in his rearview mirror to make sure the tourist couple was watching.

The first thing he had noticed about the man when he climbed aboard the bus was the long gauze bandage on his left arm. He had been watching as the man had replaced an older, dirty bandage with a smaller one, doing the whole thing one-handed, easy, biting the white medical tape from the roll with his teeth like he'd been wearing the thing his whole life. From where he had been sitting, Mukund didn't think it was much of a cut, but he knew that it was the small cuts that were most trouble. The man needed a shave and his clothes looked like he'd slept in them, but overall he didn't look like the typical scruffy western tourists that took the bus, anyone with money hiring a car, cutting an hour at least from the trip.

Mukund tried not to stare too much at the woman. Her hair was dark but when the light caught it right it seemed red — not a henna-based red, something richer, more natural — but for some reason she bunched it all up under a grimy, long-billed cap. She smiled at him when she had climbed aboard the bus, asking if the bus had a restroom, him pretending he didn't understand just to draw out the conversation, captivated by her bright eyes and beautiful smile, that lean, hard build. She had to be the one from the note.

In the mirror, Mukund watched as the man closed his eyes and looked away from the front window. It was that kind of disrespect, that open lack of confidence in his driving ability, that questioning of his skills, that Mukund hated most. He yanked the bus back in his lane, waving to the cement truck driver who didn't wave back, too busy screaming as he stood on his brakes, long, smoking black lines appearing under his locked-up rear tires.

The other passengers rode in proper silence, eyes glued to the TV monitors, Shah Rukh Khan lip-synching the title track to a tear-jerker film. Two movies, a clean toilet on board, reclining seats and a fifteen-minute rest stop at the halfway point — what more could you ask for?

But Mukund knew what they were asking for. A rail line. For decades there had been talk about connecting the two cities, politicians proclaiming that, if elected, they would drive the final stake themselves, one more promise forgotten the day after the voting, the geography blamed for the delay. It was all hills and sharp bends and swamps. Maybe — someday — a narrow gauge line like the one they had up in Simla, a toy train that would take three times as long as the bus. But a proper rail line? Not possible.

Then the computer boom. Bangalore — sleepy little garden-city Bangalore — suddenly the Silicon Valley of the East, whatever the hell that meant, everybody moving there, all those high-tech companies starting up, failing, starting up again, money everywhere, pensioners forced out of their hometown by the high rents, those young guppies or puppies, whatever you call them, driving brand-new cars, not content with Ambassadors, no, demanding Toyotas and Hondas and Mercedes. Demanding a rail line, a real one, getting it from a New Delhi government cowed by their success. The line would be complete in a year, maybe two. The smaller bus companies were selling out already, the bigger ones scaling back. He had four years at most before he would be out of a job, already thinking about the money he'd be missing. A thousand rupees to see that the backpack stays on the bus? Easy money.

Ahead, an overturned truck, its lights still on, its wheels still spinning, had dumped a load of stone in the street. He downshifted and stopped, waiting for his turn to move around the wreck, the dazed truck driver clearing a path with a broken-handled shovel. Mukund looked back into his mirror, wondering what the hell they were doing now, the cute girl holding up part of a ratty old sari, sticking her fingers through little round holes, holding the fabric up to her nose and laughing, punching the man in his shoulder, the man rubbing the spot like it actually hurt, the girl leaning over, kissing him on the cheek, then the mouth, again, right in public, the guy making a veil out of the fabric, covering their faces, probably kissing under the red sari.

Mukund looked back at the road and waited for an opening in the traffic. He didn't care what they did. Just as long as that backpack stayed on the bus until Bangalore.

# 21

The Mangalore Transport Company's morning bus pulled into its assigned parking space
at four-forty in the afternoon, ten minutes
ahead of schedule. The driver wore a toothy
grin as he eased the blunt nose of the bus
under the corrugated tin awning, the air
brakes hissing as the bus came to a stop.
Unlike the airlines that kept their passengers
in their seats until the captain gave the
two-bell signal, the aisle of the bus had been
packed for the last five miles, the travelers
eager to abandon the air-conditioned comfort
for the sweltering humidity of their hometown. Jason and Rachel were the last two off,
the driver, happy, saying something that
sounded like thank you as they passed.

There was more hustle to the crowd at the
bus terminal, a greater sense of urgency
brought on by the unpredictable schedules
of the privately owned transports. Unlike
the train stations, with their chai vendors
and porters, their distinctive architecture and
their panoramic rail-side views, the bus
terminal was a stripped-down transportation
hub, all revving engines and blue clouds of

diesel exhaust, no one waiting, everyone rushing, dodging the buses that didn't even pretend to slow down. They were making their way out the front gates to the pack of auto-rickshaw drivers and cabbies when the man approached.

'My name is Sarosh Mehta,' the man said. 'May I offer you a ride to the lovely gardens at Lal Bagh?'

He was just taller than Rachel, heavy but not yet fat, pushing fifty, with a high forehead, wispy black hair covering a growing bald spot. He had a thick salt-and-pepper mustache, wide, round glasses, and a kind, cherubic face, the corners of his eyes wrinkling as he smiled.

'You are the couple looking for the ride to Lal Bagh, yes?' Sarosh Mehta said, and when they nodded the man nodded too, waving to a tall, beefy, dark-eyed man who pushed his way towards them. 'Please. This way,' he said, and stepped aside to let Jason and Rachel pass, the three of them falling in behind the big man as he forged a way out.

They cut across the small parking lot where a white Ambassador waited with the doors open, the driver smoking a scrawny home-made cigarette as he leaned against the hood. 'Please,' the man said, guiding them into the back seat of the car, the big man climbing in

241

to sit between them. As the driver pulled the car out into traffic, the round-faced man turned in the passenger seat to face them. 'How do you like your trip so far?' he asked.

Rachel gave a slight shrug. 'It's been okay,' she said, a nervous crack in her voice.

'You will enjoy the gardens at Lal Bagh. They are quite beautiful this time of the year.' Sarosh's smile widened as he spoke. 'Did you begin your vacation in Goa?'

'No,' she said. 'Up in Delhi.'

'Then you must have gone to Agra. What did you make of the Taj Mahal? Isn't it magnificent?'

When Rachel didn't answer, Jason leaned around the big man to look at her, busy untying and retying a pull cord on her pack, ignoring the man's questions.

'We didn't get there,' Jason said, sitting back. 'Maybe next trip.'

Sarosh straightened and his smile dropped. 'Oh, but you must not leave India without seeing the Taj. It's bad luck.'

'Thanks, but I think we've had our fill of bad luck,' Jason said. In the front seat, the driver gave the wheel a violent yank, swerving around a swarm of auto-rickshaws, cutting down a side street lined with thick-trunked trees.

Sarosh said something short and fast in

Hindi to the driver, repeating it for the big man, who stretched his arms up and around the shoulders of his fellow back seat passengers, his flowery deodorant as overpowering as his cologne. Sarosh pushed his round-rimmed glasses up the bridge of his nose with a pudgy finger. 'Now my friends, I believe you have something for me.'

Jason heard Rachel swallow hard and saw her hand shaking as she tugged open the zipper on her backpack, her hand slipping off the short metal tab. 'Here,' she said, thrusting the bag at Jason. 'I can't do it.'

Jason reached out and took the bag by the straps, his hands caressing hers as she slowly let go, her lips moving, the words inaudible above the engine's whine.

'Is there a problem?' the man said, his eyebrows arching.

'No problem,' Jason said, unzipping the bag and lifting out one of the bundles from the pack, the tan wrapping paper crinkling under his light grip. 'We're not very good at this drug-running thing.'

The round-man's mouth snapped shut, his smile replaced by a tight-lipped scowl, the veins on his neck rising as he drew in a sharp breath through his nose. 'Who told you it was drugs?' Sarosh said through clenched teeth. Jason stared into the man's hooded eyes but said nothing. 'I asked you a question,' the man said, almost shouting, his teeth still held tight. 'Who said it was drugs?'

Jason felt the big man's forearm flinch and out of the corner of his eye saw the man's long fingers curl into a fist. 'No one told us,' Jason said, the words bunching up. 'I just figured . . . '

'That I am a drug dealer? Is this what you are saying?' His face was flushed, his nostrils flared, a double-edged knife appearing now between the front seats, slashing out at Jason, catching the bundle near the top, cutting through the tan paper and shipping tape. Rachel gasped as Jason pushed back against the seat, trapped, waiting for the knife to slash again.

The round-faced man pointed the knife at the bundle, holding it steady until he was sure they were listening. 'Open it,' he said, his voice calm, almost soft.

It was several moments before Jason moved. He balanced the bundle on Rachel's open backpack, his sweaty hands leaving dark prints on the thin paper. He started where the knife had made its cut, pulling the paper down the side, tugging loose the shipping tape. Freed from the wrapping, layers of cotton batting puffed up, the bundle seeming to grow as he unraveled it. He pulled the fabric away to reveal a block of machined parts bound in a layer of bubble wrap and rubber bands, not much bigger than a forty-ounce can of Odenbach beer. He held it out in front of the big man so Rachel could see.

'It's part of a multi-directional joint for a robotic arm,' Sarosh said, tossing the knife back in the glove box. 'A prototype. The other bundle contains the rest.'

'A *machine part*?' Rachel said, her voice rising as she spoke. 'I did all of that for a stupid *machine part*?'

'I wanted you to know that I am not a drug dealer,' Sarosh said, his cheerful voice and smile returning. 'Drugs are a terrible thing.'

'I'll tell you what's terrible,' Rachel said, slapping the big guy's chest for emphasis. 'What's terrible is everything I went through — *we* went through — to deliver a stupid damn part.' She leaned over and waited for Jason's support.

'I'm glad it's not drugs, Sarosh, but come on. A machine part? What's going on?'

'As I said, it's a prototype of a very expensive piece of equipment. Potentially it could be worth billions of rupees. Things have changed in India. The computer industry is on the rise. So is industrial crime. These parts came from a plant in Germany and tomorrow they'll be delivered to an Indian robotics research firm here in Bangalore. Six weeks from now they'll introduce an Indian version — smarter, better, cheaper than the original.'

Jason looked down at the two bundles, a fortune on his lap. 'It's still against the law.'

'Of course,' Sarosh said, laughing. 'That is why you were paid to carry it.'

'But if we were caught?'

'You are tourists. The police seldom bother tourists. If you are stopped, all they look for is drugs. And if they did arrest you, what would you know? You couldn't tell a Tamil from a Rajasthani, let alone pick out the subtle differences in accent. Industrial secrets? What do they care? No, tourists make the perfect people to carry these type of goods.'

'So we just helped ruin some German company?' Jason said.

'You are helping to complete the circle. For two hundred years the West robbed every-thing from India — our resources, our wealth — and they still rob us today. Tell me, how many doctors and engineers and computer programmers in your country come from India?'

'That doesn't make it right,' Jason said, seeing Sriram, Vidya, and Ravi as he spoke.

'No,' Sarosh conceded. 'But it does make it quite profitable.'

246

'Well, we're outta here,' Jason said, dropping the plastic-wrapped parts, the padding, and the second bundle in the big man's lap. 'You can drop us off right here.'

'I'm afraid I can't do that,' Sarosh said, his smile bending as he spoke to the driver, the car picking up speed.

'But we delivered the packages,' Jason said. 'We kept our side of the deal.'

'I swear we won't say anything,' Rachel said, adding her attempt at an earnest *ahcha* head sway.

'I know this, but I can not let you out. You see,' Sarosh said, pointing at a series of road signs, 'this is a no-stopping zone. We must circle around this block. That is the rule.'

# 22

Propped up by three pillows, Jason leaned back against the headboard of the double bed and sipped a cold Kingfisher beer as he watched the Indian version of MTV's All-Request Live. On the screen, a dozen beautiful women danced in unison through a shopping mall, part of a video requested, the show's equally beautiful hostess explained in a mix of English and Hindi, by a loyal viewer in Mysore. Over the high-pitched singing and the rubbery thump of traditional Indian drums, Jason could still hear the shower, the steam curling up from under the door.

On the low dresser next to the television, the room service tray of fruit and croissants was picked clean, the last two beers of the sixpack sticking out of the copper ice bucket. The bouquet of tropical flowers that covered the table by the balcony doors filled the room with lush, green smells, and the rattan ceiling fan created the illusion of a warm, soft breeze. It was a bright and comfortable room, just like the woman at Raj-Tech had promised.

The driver had dropped them off near the

cricket stadium, Sarosh waving as the car pulled away, wishing them a wonderful stay in Bangalore. They had wandered through a nearby park for a half hour before Jason remembered Ravi's email.

'Mr Murty told us there was a chance you might ring,' the woman at Raj-Tech's Bangalore headquarters had said. 'So please, feel free to make any request. You are our most welcome guests.'

On a cell phone he had borrowed from a peanut vendor, Jason had told the woman about the stolen credit card, how they had no money and no place to stay, leaving out any mention of industrial spies and festering knife wounds. With a smile he could hear in her voice, the woman assured him that she would have a new card delivered to the Karnataka Hotel on Lavelle Road, a five-minute walk from their location, where he would find a room waiting, her assistant finalizing the details with the hotel as they spoke.

'Mr Murty has also asked me to apologize in advance,' the woman added. 'His schedule is filled with meetings here in Bangalore and it is doubtful he'll be able to get away.' Jason chuckled to himself as they walked to the hotel, picturing Ravi's face when he had learned he'd have to come back to India after all.

After devouring half the welcoming snacks and chugging a beer, Rachel declared herself fit and announced that she would attempt to use up all of the hotel's hot water in a scalding shower. Fifteen minutes later the shower was still running.

While the TV blared Shalini from Hyderabad's request — a sari-filled dance with a flashing number one in the corner of the screen — Jason thumbed through the folded printouts he had kept from the train station's Beachfront Internet Café, a half-dozen emails from potential contacts in Bangalore and the 'wafty crank of a monologue' downloaded from the London comedy club, the small hole punched through the stack hinting at the role they had played in saving his life. He ran his palm across each sheet, flattening out the wrinkles, and thought about his next move.

His Air India flight back to the States was scheduled to leave in four days. Jason's ticket was one of the things that had disappeared while he was blacked out in Goa, Rachel insisting that he was lucky that that was all they took, not sure what she meant since they had taken everything else as well.

According to his original itinerary, found crumpled at the bottom of his pack, the bus from Freedom Tours was scheduled to pull into Bangalore at noon tomorrow. He had paid extra for flight insurance, the travel agent in Corning frightening him into the pricey purchase with tales of lost tickets and bankrupt airlines. He'd contact fast-talking Danny and get it all straightened out. It would probably cost him a couple hundred bucks and there would be petty bureaucrats to suck up to and reams of redundant paperwork to endure, but those were the things, he realized with a sigh, that he did best. Sitting in the travel agent's office in Corning, everything had seemed so simple. Fly to India, track down Sriram's mother, give her the sari. But nothing was simple now — not India, not Sriram, not the sari.

Then there was Rachel.

In the melancholy week between Christmas and New Year's, Jason had spent his evenings surfing on-line dating sites, filling out the personality profiles and ticking the 'my perfect match' checklists, reading the computer-generated ads, closing out each website, careful not to hit the click-here-to-sign-up-now button. The questions were different but the results all sounded the same. Single white male, twenty-eight, average looks, average build, office worker, some college, good organizational skills, honest, responsible, punctual, no hobbies, likes to read magazines, stay-at-home kind of guy, non-smoking, no pets, seeks single beautiful woman with similar background.

She was beautiful, he'd give her that. Bright eyes that seemed to shift from brown to green, a toothpaste ad smile, that wild auburn hair, a tight body that was made to wear low-slung jeans and halfshirts. Standing in the road outside of the train station in Goa, fists clenched and jaw set, he knew she was the most beautiful woman he'd ever known.

But that was all he knew about her. She was reckless and unpredictable, making her life up as she went, creating a personality to fit the moment, telling people just what they wanted to hear. He had seen her passport, so the Canadian part was probably true, but the rest? Did she really win the trip? Did she honestly like trains? Did she expect him to believe that the pattern on the sari was not a stylized circuit board?

And did it really make a difference? He'd spend the next few days with her and maybe they'd fly back to North America together. There'd be promises to keep in touch, emails that first month, maybe a phone call or a lunch date in Niagara Falls, then they'd drift apart, him back to his gray-on-gray cubicle, her back to whatever it was she did. It was not the way he wanted it, but it was the way it was going to go. Her? With a guy like him? Too much even for a Hindi movie.

Jason could hear her in the shower now, her off-key version of *Jingle Bells* a half-beat off the dance moves on the request video. He tried not to think about her, focusing on all the things he needed to get done. Like delivering a sari.

★ ★ ★

'I'm gonna get the vegetarian thali, some prawns, a double stack of nan bread and a side of this coconut crab curry,' Rachel said from behind the restaurant's tall menu. 'Wanna split an order of chicken vindaloo?'

'I guess you got your appetite back,' Jason said, closing his menu, Rachel's order enough for the both of them.

'Nothing like a hot shower and a good romp in the hay to bring a girl back to life.'

Jason cupped his hand along his eyebrows, sneaking a glance out from under his fingers. 'Geeze, Rachel. Not so loud.'

Rachel waved off his complaint without looking up. 'It's not like anyone could hear me over the music,' she said, tilting the menu towards the tinny speaker that hung on the wall near their table. 'And besides, they shouldn't be listening in. Just like the people across the hall. I can't believe they called the front desk.'

'Well, you were a little . . . '

'Excited? It doesn't make a difference. Polite people ignore those things.'

After the second verse of *Jingle Bells* she had called him into the shower, telling him it was his last chance for hot water that day. He had tapped politely on the door, asking her to let him know when she was decent, Rachel laughing, telling him she was a hell of a lot better than just decent.

The hot water lasted another five minutes. They dove, dripping wet, under the covers, wrinkled emails flying, interrupted an hour later when the manager phoned and asked them to keep it down, Rachel saying that she was working on it. That evening, when Jason went down to the concierge's office to sign for the replacement Visa card, he endured the blushing grins of the women at the registration counter and the bellhop's knowing smirk.

'The way I see it,' Rachel said after placing her order, the waiter not correcting her pronunciation or pointing out she had ordered enough for four, 'your friend was a classic example of an unresolved Oedipus complex.'

A fresh pint of Kingfisher lager hung suspended in front of his lips as Jason looked across the white foam. 'A what?'

'Psychology 101, Jason, hello. Hates the father, wants to have sex with the mother. It's pretty obvious.'

Jason looked at his beer and thought about chugging it, settling for a healthy sip, motioning with his fingers for her to continue. Rachel clicked her tongue and looked up at the ceiling, letting him know how elementary it all was.

'How well do you know mythology?' she asked.

'It's all Greek to me.'

'Cute. Well, there was this king who went to a fortune teller and he found out that one day his son would grow up and kill him and then a whole bunch of things happened and then the kid, this Oedipus, he kills the father . . . '

'Before or after he slept with his mother?'

'Before I think. Or after. So anyway, Freud . . . '

'Sigmund Freud?'

'You know any others? Anyway, Freud comes up with this theory that all male children secretly want to kill their fathers and have sex with their mothers.'

Jason took another long pull on his beer. 'I don't believe it.'

'You just don't remember it,' Rachel said. 'You were like five years old, you dealt with it and moved on. But the memory is still there, locked away in a dark corner of your mind.'

'Where I plan to keep it, thank you,' Jason said, holding his beer up in mock salute.

'But your friend, Sriram? Obviously he didn't deal with it. It sat there, right on the surface, gnawing away at him for all those years. Kill dad, hook up with mom.'

'But his parents were here in India.'

'Exactly. He had to get away from them or he'd go nuts, but he still had issues.'

Jason set his chin in his hand. 'How do you know all this stuff?' he started to say, then changed his mind and waved off her answer, knowing she'd be making it up anyway. 'Go on, Herr Doctor.'

'His wife, what was her name? Vidya? Well, Vidya must have started to remind your friend of his father.'

'Trust me,' Jason said, recalling the tight black jeans and tee shirts Vidya had favored. 'There's no way she looked like anyone's father.'

'I don't mean physically, I mean the way she acted. Maybe she was domineering, maybe she put him down a lot, you don't know, you didn't live with them. It's all about resentment of parental authority and if he saw her as a parental figure . . . ' She let her voice trail off as she picked up her beer. 'You said yourself he didn't want his wife to know about the sari. That doesn't sound too normal. Maybe he felt she was coming between him and his mother, just like his father had done ever since he was a kid. The sari might represent that hate he felt for his father. Or better yet, maybe it was a symbol of the love he felt for his mother and that's why he wanted to get it to her, to declare his love.'

'I don't know, Rachel. It sounds so . . . '

'He shot himself in the head, right?'

'I suppose so,' Jason said, his voice dropping as he spoke.

She held her hands open in front of her. 'When Oedipus realizes he had sex with his mother and killed his father he puts his eyes out. The gun is the phallic symbol, the shot to the head the symbolic blinding. It all fits.'

'Except you didn't know Sriram and Vidya.'

Rachel shook her head. 'You're too close, Jason. You can't see it. The only thing special about that sari is that it saved your life. It was just this poor, demented guy's security blanket.'

'I think it's more than that.'

'No, you *want* it to be more than that. Because that way your friend didn't kill his wife and shoot himself.' She reached across the table and took his hand in hers. 'I know you want it to be a treasure map or a blueprint or something, but it's not.'

Jason looked down at her hand, her stubby thumbnail rubbing against his palm. It all made sense, but something inside kept him from admitting it. 'I still need to deliver it,' he said.

'Believe it or not, that sorta makes sense,' she said, leaning back in her seat as a team of waiters arrived. 'But I wouldn't plan on her being too happy.'

★ ★ ★

The man cracked open the service stairwell door with one finger. He set the toe of his shoe against the spring-loaded door and lowered his arm, his hand brushing against the pistol tucked in his waistband. He looked down at his shirt, checking again to be sure that the gun was covered. He wasn't used to carrying a gun and was surprised how easy it was to keep it hidden.

He could see him across the lobby, twenty yards away, printing out emails from the Internet kiosk that stood near the concierge's empty desk. He had watched them as they ate dinner, hidden in the shadows of the hotel bar, the couple's table angled so that he could only see the girl's face. Beautiful. He had watched her as she ate, her smile so infectious that, half a building away, he smiled, too.

They sat at their table till after midnight, downing pints of beer like college freshmen. He expected the girl to stumble each time she walked to the restroom, but she held her alcohol well. When they finally left — over-tipping by the look on the waiters' faces — she gave him a kiss on the cheek and headed to the bank of elevators while he had logged on to the Internet.

The man was thinner than his photo-graphs, but they had been taken on his first day in India, before the unfamiliar food and the predictable illness. And his clothes looked different, the color and shape beat out of them by a few Indian hand-washings. Yet despite the changes, there was no mistaking that this was Jason Talley, and the man wondered again why no one else had found him first.

The picture had been posted for over a week now and the reward for information was up to seven hundred US — more than a hotel maid would earn in a year. But hotel maids weren't logging on to that chat room, and the money might not have been enough to attract attention among the high-paid computer engineers and software designers who were the site's regulars. Whatever. It didn't make a difference now anyway.

It would be easy to follow him up to his room. He could knock on the door, smile up at the peephole, no doubt get invited right in. And he could end it there, everything cleaned up, that bastard Sriram paid back in full, these two atoning for their friend's sins.

But that would be messy. And loud. Too many people had seen him in the hotel, too many people who would have no trouble identifying him to the police. No. There were easier ways. And now that he knew where Jason Talley was, the man thought as he slid his foot back and let the door ease shut, he could take his time and do it right.

# 23

Jason stared past his reflection in the plate glass window of the second story Pizza Corner restaurant and watched the one-way traffic as it flowed down the slight slope of Brigade Road. On the sidewalks, people moved in every direction, darting across the street when they spotted a break in the traffic, while deliverymen, boxes piled four-high on their heads, worked their way through the crowds. He could see a few gray-haired women in color-muted saris and a handful of grandfather types in white shirts and ties, but overall the street was filled with fast-walking twenty-somethings and hyperactive teens, everyone on a cell phone or plugged into an iPod, free hands swinging plastic shopping bags or holding frosty frozen cappuccinos.

The Pizza Corner was as shiny and clean as any turn-key franchise in the States, the girl behind the counter displaying a mix of phony cheerleader enthusiasm and robotic efficiency that reminded him of home, the pepperoni pizza and Pepsi identical to countless Corning lunches. An hour ahead of the lunchtime crowd, he nibbled at the slice, not wanting to finish too quickly, unsure if his first contact in Bangalore would show.

He was awake before sunrise, taking his pile of emails down to the hotel's all-night café, letting Rachel get back the hours of sleep she had lost proving she could be just as passionate without making a sound. On the back of a paper placemat he had jotted down the email addresses and phone numbers of the strangers who had volunteered to help. He had started by writing the phone number from the web page Narvin had shown him back in Mumbai, the pre-paid mobile of his stalker, but halfway through he crossed it out. The number, and what it meant, was burned into his memory.

The offers of help from people outside of Bangalore he had written at the bottom of the sheet. Some were responding to the original email he had sent out from his cubicle back in Corning, the email that Ravi had told him he should have never sent. Some of the emails were responding to updates sent by Attar Singh, the information on Jason's travels hacked from India Rail and bus company computers, sent to everyone Attar knew. By things written in a few of these notes, Jason realized that news of Sriram's and Vidya's deaths had not reached everyone in their circle, news that they wouldn't be learning from him.

At the top of the page Jason had written the contact information for the three people in Bangalore.

Manoj 'call me Manny' Plakal said that he was thrilled and delighted to meet any of Sriram's American friends and that he would be thrilled and delighted to help Jason out in any way, insisting that Jason call as soon as he arrived in Bangalore, promising that he would have a thrilling and delightful time in the Garden City.

'I made the mistake of associating with Sriram Sundaram once before,' the 'reply all' email from Mr Piyush Ojha began. 'Live or dead, I have no desire whatsoever to renew that association. Please do not contact me again.' Whether by habit or a preset computer command, the address of a Bangalore bank appeared under his typed name, along with his office and mobile phone number. Despite the man's directions, Jason wrote down the information.

The email from Ketan Jani started like most of the others.

'You did not respond to my first email but my offer to help you in Bangalore remains. Please call me upon your arrival.' The note went on to list phone and fax numbers and possible places they could meet. It was the final line that prompted Jason to move Ketan to the top of the list.

'I have spoken to a few others and I must warn you that there are a couple people you would be wise to avoid while here in India. To this point I suggest you stop sending out emails announcing your location as this may prove dangerous.'

Ketan did not sound surprised when Jason called his office at eight a.m., suggesting that they meet at eleven at the Pizza Corner. 'It is a good place to meet, but for your own safety,' he had said, slowing his words as he spoke, 'don't let them put hot peppers on your slice.'

Jason had the plastic top off his empty cup, crunching a mouthful of ice when Ketan Jani arrived.

'You are a brave man, Jason Talley,' Ketan said as he pulled out a chair and sat down. 'Most tourists avoid the ice in India.'

'I like living on the edge,' Jason said, extending his arm across the table to shake the man's hand. Ketan was tall and lean, his pointed chin capped with a close-cropped goatee. There was a natural curl to his hair that he had gelled into submission, his kohl-black eyes intense even when he smiled, and an expression that didn't seem to match the rest of his face.

'I suppose I should start with some pleasantries. The how-do-you-like-India sort of thing,' Ketan said, waving a uniformed counter girl over to the table. Jason listened as he ordered his lunch in English, his voice reminding Jason of Sriram, Attar, and every other Indian male he had met.

'I have to admit,' Jason said after the girl skipped back to the counter, 'I didn't expect India to be so modern. I mean, just look down this street.' He turned sideways, his hand sweeping to take in the second-story view of European boutique stores, glass and neon computer shops, and western restaurant chains. 'It's better than anything in my hometown. And everyplace is hooked up to the Internet — even my auto-rickshaw driver had a cell phone.'

Ketan shook his head and smiled his happy, demonic smile. 'Don't confuse the parts with the whole. You've seen a handful of big cities in one section of India. It would be like spending a day or two in New York, D.C., Daytona Beach, and Orlando and saying you *know* America. Half of everyone who lives in India lives in a small village, none of which I'm sure you saw.'

'I saw a lot of farm land from the train.'

'A sliver, what, mile-wide? All right, you

265

saw India — a hell of a lot more than most people will ever see, including Indians. But you saw a special, tourist-friendly version.' He paused and looked up at the ceiling. 'Listen to me,' Ketan said. 'You come all the way to India and I sit here telling you it's not enough. Forgive me, I'm a boorish ass.' He brought his hands together in front of his chest, giving his head a quick nod. 'So, is this where I say, how about them Red Sox?'

Jason laughed. 'I'm a Yankees man myself.'

'Ah, just like Sriram. I don't know what he saw in the game. He was such a cricket fanatic in university. I guess he made do with baseball when he left the civilized world behind.'

'What was he like back then?' Jason said.

Ketan shrugged. 'Funny. Obsessive when it came to computers. Good with the complex stuff, the minutia. And he loved learning new things. He was always after Ravi to teach him more.'

'Did he get upset easily, throw things around?'

'No, he was more apt to sit and stew. He'd get frustrated, sure, we all did. Some of the guys would wing keyboards out the back door or punch the wall — only once, it was concrete — but Sriram wasn't like that. He'd shout a while but that was it. But let me tell

266

you, the guy could hold a grudge.'

'Against you?' Jason asked.

'Not that I know of, but then if he did he would have never let on. There was this guy in one of our first-year classes, this is before Sriram became the quote-unquote security expert, well this guy, he hacks into Sriram's computer and copies a paper Sriram was writing, some elective course. Anyway, Sriram turns in his paper and a week later the professor calls them in.'

'And fails them both.'

'No, that's the funny thing,' Ketan said. 'He congratulated them for their collaborative spirit, gave them both As. Of course the guy tells Sriram all about how he hacked in and they had a good laugh. Two years later, the guy's applying for a fellowship. He walks into a faculty committee review of some project he's working on — his data's all wrong, the references are made up, huge plagiarized sections. The guy swears that it's not his real paper, somebody's fucking with him. The poor guy spent a semester trying to clear his name. In the end he just washed out.'

'You think Sriram was behind it?'

'I didn't at first. A couple years later we're at this party, everybody pretty smashed. This guy's name comes up. Well, you know what it's like, those things are funny when you're drunk. So we're all laughing. But not Sriram. So I said something like, what, you got no sense of humor, I mean he's the one always cracking us up. But he just looks at me and says that bastard's lucky I let him off so easy.'

'Hot stuff, coming through,' the uniformed waitress said, resting her tray on the top of the napkin dispenser, naming each item as she set them on the table just like the training manual prescribed. Jason transferred his straw to a fresh Pepsi and waited as Ketan cradled his slice of vegetarian pizza with three fingers.

'I'm doing it again,' Ketan said, biting the tip off the drooping slice. 'I'm focusing on the negative. My apologies. Sriram was a good man. Better than the rest of us.'

'You mean the guys involved with Bangalore World Systems?'

Ketan nodded as he chewed, wiping his lips with a transparently thin paper napkin. 'We were arrogant, greedy little shits and to this day I make it a habit to avoid them all. We thought we had all the answers, that everyone else was wrong. People tried to warn us, the failure rate for computer companies was running close to a hundred percent back then, but no, not us, we were different. The world *owed* us something.'

'So you don't see any of them? Get together to reminisce about the old days?'

'No thank you,' Ketan said. 'Someday we will. Maybe one of us will get the crazy idea to start it all up again. BW freakin' S.' He laughed. 'Knowing us we'd all be stupid enough to come back. But right now? No. Probably for the best.'

Jason poked at the ice in the drink with his straw. 'Do you still blame him?'

Ketan took a second bite and washed it down with a long swig before answering. 'At this point, I don't know who to blame.'

★ ★ ★

Jason was leaning against a parked Ambassador outside the Ivory Tower Hotel, twisting open his second bottle of Thumbs Up cola when he remembered her name. Mary Bacca. She sat in front of him every year, from fourth grade through middle school. She had neat handwriting and was fast with her multiplication tables, but it was her taste buds that made her a schoolyard legend.

Eyes closed, Mary could identify the brand of gum in just ten chews, could name the color marker with one tap on her tongue, and with a single sip she could tell the Cokes from the Pepsis, the R.C.s, and the grocery store pretenders.

Jason had been there the day Ronnie Wolf, known paste-eater, challenged her to an old Coke, New Coke, and Coke Classic tasteoff.

It was over in three sips.

'They changed it, you know,' Mary said later as they took their seats in science class. 'The Coca-cola we grew up with? You'll never taste it again.' First sex-ed, then that bombshell. It was the year Jason knew his childhood was over.

Mary had moved on, too. Cigarettes, beers, fortified wines, nickel bags of weed — with a puff or a chug, she could name them all, brand, mix or country. In high school there were rumors of wild parties, picking out boys in dark rooms from other things she put in her mouth. 'I can't help it,' she had told Jason once as they sat sipping beers at an outlaw senior class party. 'It's how I make sense of the world.'

She got married and moved away, a pastry chef somewhere upstate. He'd found his niche in Corning, dotting i's, crossing t's, buttoning up the details of other people's lives with a manila folder and a rubber stamp. Making sense of the world.

He took a long pull on the Thumbs Up, with its heavy syrup flavor and teeth-rattling

270

sugar content, and thought about his next move.

The concierge at the Karnataka Hotel didn't laugh when Jason had asked for a Bangalore telephone directory — he was far too professional for that — but by the way the others behind the desk reacted to his early morning request, Jason realized finding Sriram's family wasn't going to be as easy as it looked back in Corning. He had told them that he knew the family name and was planning on spending an hour calling the Sundarams listed, betting that he'd either find his friend's family or find someone who knew of them. Here the concierge did allow the corners of his mouth to twitch, explaining, as he would to a small, slow child, that Sundaram was a common family name, that in a city of over six million there would be thousands of Sundarams, and if such a fantastic book did exist, it would not list those who only used mobile phones, something which, he assured Jason, was quite very common in this day and age.

So much for Plan A.

What he needed now was a Plan B.

Jason tapped the plastic cola bottle against the bumper of the Ambassador, burning off the nervous energy that was half caffeine, half that gnawing desire to put things in order. It was the same anxious feeling that came at the end of every month, with files due and forms still missing, knowing that million-dollar deals hinged on everything being right where it was supposed to be. And, with his files, everything always was.

He needed more time to put it all together — Sriram and Vidya, the attacks, that damn sari. But as the Freedom Tours' bus pulled in from its half-day trip to the spice merchants' emporium, he was hoping he'd have less.

Dayama 'Danny' Satyanarayan was the first off the bus, sucking in a deep breath of air and rubbing the scowl off his face before he turned, beaming, to help each passenger as they stepped down from the coach.

Jason strolled over to the entrance of the hotel, nodding to the worn-out travelers as they shuffled past. A few waved back, trying to place where they had seen that young man before. He waited as Danny climbed back aboard, checking for items left behind and pointing out the cramped space where the driver was expected to squeeze the bus. When he spotted Jason, Danny's stock smile widened a bit and he held his hand out as he crossed the hotel's driveway.

'Mr Talley, what a pleasure it is to see you again,' he said, pumping Jason's arm. 'I trust you had a most excellent time.'

'So far, so good,' Jason said, remembering now how Danny's clear voice and reassuring, if feigned, smile had made him feel so secure.

'No troubles at all for you and Miss Moore?'

It was Jason's turn to fake a smile 'No trouble at all.'

Danny looked at the six-inch ridge of skin and sutures that ran down Jason's forearm. 'I hope you had that looked at.'

'This?' Jason said, holding up his arm. 'Just a scratch.' He rested his hand on Danny's back. 'I know you're a busy man, but I was wondering if you could help us out arranging the flight back to the U.S.'

Danny's smile disappeared and his eyes widened. 'You have not made arrangements already? Oh, Mr Talley, this is not good, not good at all. I'm afraid that you will find every flight completely booked for the next few weeks. That at a minimum.'

Jason's shoulders drooped and a fist-sized knot started forming in his stomach.

'I was quite clear with Miss Moore. You needed to plan ahead if you were looking to fly on the same date as the tour group.'

'We had tickets,' Jason said. 'But they were stolen when we were in Goa. Can't you just get us replacements?'

'No, Mr Talley. We paid Miss Moore for the tickets when you left the tour in Delhi.

273

Your tickets are invalid. You have no tickets.'

Jason felt himself rocking back on his heels and he squeezed the fabric of Danny's shirt between his fingers to steady himself.

'Miss Moore assured us that she had your permission to act in your behalf,' Danny said, covering for any breaches in company policy. 'If you have any complaints I suggest you bring them up with her first . . . '

'No, there's no problem. I'm sure I told her it was okay,' he said, not sure now of anything where Rachel was involved. 'Still, any chance you can help us out?'

Danny shook his head slowly, as if Jason was having a hard time understanding. 'No, sir. There are scores of reasons. Business, vacations. It does not help matters that both Air France and British Airways are coping with strike-related slowdowns. Travelers have flocked to the other airlines and there are just not enough seats to go around.'

'What about stand-by or taking a flight with more layovers?'

There was no ambiguous *ahcha* in Danny's headshake. 'There simply are no flights available. However . . . '

Jason leaned forward as Danny paused for effect.

'A seat did open up on the Freedom Tours flight back to the U.S. One of our patrons was

. . . well, something happened in Calcutta.'

'Was someone hurt? No one died on you, did they?'

'No,' Danny said, dragging the word out as he thought of the best way to explain. 'Let us just say that Mr Froman desired to participate in certain . . . activities, and did not show the discretion one would hope to find in a man of his years.'

Jason remembered waking up his first night in India to find the old man watching him as he slept and decided he didn't want to know the details.

'I'm afraid the authorities have severed our connections with this traveler and his seat will go unfilled,' Danny said.

'But?' Jason prompted.

'There is a chance — slight — that I can persuade a cousin at India Airlines to change the name on the reservations. It may be difficult . . . '

'How difficult?'

'Oh, two, three hundred dollars difficult . . . '

'But it's only one ticket.'

'That is most accurate.'

'But I need two.'

'I have one.'

'Damn.'

The doorman watched as the two men

stood facing each other in front of the entrance to the Ivory Tower Hotel. Slowly, imperceptibly, a smile moved across Danny's lips and he swung an arm up across Jason's shoulders. 'Come,' he said. 'I have a small office inside. Let us conclude our business there.'

# 24

Sarosh Mehta, dealer in smuggled machine parts and unofficial Bangalore tour guide, had been right, the gardens at Lal Bagh were indeed gorgeous this time of the year.

Acres of manicured grounds rolled under an impenetrable canopy of palm fronds and tent-sized leaves, the dark green grass butting tight against miles of red brick walkways that meandered through the park. Formal gardens and Victorian fountains provided a sense of order among the bright, tropical flowers and lush vegetation leading the way to the centerpiece of the park, a five-story glass and wrought iron pavilion surrounded by symmetrically arranged benches and reflecting pools.

Although it was mid-afternoon on a weekday, the park was still filled with patrons — sari-clad mothers pushing baby carriages, uniformed kindergartners on a field trip, tied waist-to-waist in a class-long line by a length of bailing twine, old men in thick sweaters, chilly in the ninety-degree sun. Clustered together by a wireless Internet portal, a dozen white-shirted businessmen made desks out of their closed briefcases, racing to out-type the short-life batteries in their laptop computers, while in the shadows of the giant banyan trees, young lovers walked winding paths, hoping they would lead nowhere.

There were no beggars in the park, no sallow-faced toddlers digging through the ornate garbage cans, no squalid shanties thrown up along the high brick wall. The twenty-rupee entry fee and the armed guards made sure of that.

Eyes closed, Jason stretched his arms out along the back of the wooden bench and took a deep breath. The humid air was thick with the soft fragrance of plants he didn't recognize and school kids' songs he couldn't understand. It had been air-conditioned in the offices of the Hindustani First National Bank, but even as he felt the sweat rolling down the side of his face, Jason knew it was far more comfortable here in the park than it had been sitting in Mr Piyush Ojha's office.

'What part of my email did you fail to grasp?' Mr Ojha had shouted, pounding his fist on his metal desk as he spoke.

Jason had tried to explain that all he wanted was some information, a little help finding Sriram's family, maybe some thoughts about Bangalore World Systems, Mr Ojha, standing now, damning Sriram, damning

278

them all with a final metallic thump, asking, no *demanding*, that Jason get out of his bank *immediately*, assuring him the authorities would be summoned post haste.

It went pretty much the way Ketan had predicted.

'I wouldn't call Piyush if I were you,' Ketan had warned him as they sat in the Pizza Corner. 'He's not dangerous, just a bit hysterical when it comes to BWS.'

The advice had been good, he just didn't listen. As he sat in the park, Jason wondered how accurate the rest of Ketan's advice would prove to be.

'Everybody at BWS got screwed when Sriram ran off, some more than others. It's the core group that have the right to be the most pissed,' Ketan had said, running a paper napkin across his black goatee as he finished his pizza.

'Attar Singh you met up in Jaipur. His family invested a lot in BWS. When it failed they blamed him personally. Disowned him. Vowed they'd get even, ruin him like he had ruined them.'

'I don't know. When I talked to him it sounded like he had made peace with it all, moved on. Some Kirsna-merska religious thing.'

'Krishnamurti. A philosopher. And I don't

279

believe it. The rest of us just lost money. Attar lost his family.'

'What about Manoj Plakal?' Jason had asked, thinking about the upcoming Happy Hour meeting he had arranged that morning.

'Manny? Nice guy, wants to be everybody's friend. But he was just a bit player. He's not your problem.'

'Who is?'

Ketan had tossed the crumpled napkin on the table and looked straight into Jason's eyes. 'There're two people you need to watch out for in India. The first is a guy up in Rajasthan. Ahmadabad, I think. Name's Amrish Sharma.'

'Taco?' Jason had asked, knowing the answer. If he was surprised, Ketan hadn't shown it.

'When he lost his investment he bankrupted his family. Unlike Attar, Taco's family forgave him, but it did something to him, up here,' Ketan had said, tapping the side of his head with a hooked index finger. 'But unless you go looking for him, he's not likely to find you.'

With his eyes closed tight against the bright white sun, Jason's mind drifted away from his conversation with Ketan, back to the train station at Ahmadabad. He could still see the man's face, the look of hatred in his eyes as

280

he attacked, the look changing to terror as he hung in the air over the tracks. Between the pauses and the backtracking it had taken Jason ten minutes to explain the events of thirty seconds, Ketan nodding occasionally, Jason still not sure why.

When Jason was finished, Ketan had waited a few moments before continuing his warning.

'What did you think of Narvin Kumar?'

Jason just smiled.

'Listen, I know you stayed with him in Mumbai. He's a charming guy, but he's also very dangerous.'

'The man is worth millions, Ketan. If it wasn't for Sriram he might still be waiting for BWS to take off. And according to him, it was Sriram who got him into Bollywood. If anything he *owes* Sriram.'

Ketan shook his head. 'You don't understand. When Sriram left he took . . . '

'I know, I know, I heard all about it,' Jason had said, bored by the same accusations. 'He stole their dream. He stole their fortunes. He ruined them. Sorry, Ketan, but it just doesn't fit with Narvin.'

'I guess it depends on what you value,' Ketan had said, standing, pushing his chair in, ready to leave. 'Narvin was engaged at the time. A sweet girl, really beautiful. Her name

281

was Vidya.' An hour later Jason was still in the park, relaxing in the shade, writing the postcards he had promised to send to family and friends in Corning, half of whom he was certain couldn't find India on a map.

He had bought the postcards — a variety pack of fifteen — from a kiosk near the park entrance, paying the extra hundred rupees for a five-rupee pen. He flipped through the cards, organizing them, stacking them in order from ones he'd send to ones he'd leave on the bench.

The top card was a full-length shot of two barefoot women dressed in bright blue saris, backs to the camera, leading a small, naked toddler down a dusty trail. At first he thought about sending it to the women at the mortgage office, the kind of card that would get tacked up in the break room next to the postcards from Disney World and the typed reminder to keep the microwave clean. There'd be cold comments about the sweat-stained saris, a couple of jokes about future convenience store owners, and the longer he looked at the picture the less he wanted to send it. He'd get one of those peel-off magnetic strips and put it up on his refrigerator instead.

The second postcard showed the entire front façade of the Palace of Winds. Jason held the postcard close to his nose, his eyes squinting as he tried to spy a backpack-stealing monkey on one of the red sandstone balconies. Given the angle, Jason realized the picture could have only been taken on the rooftop near where the monkey had sat snacking on a tube of toothpaste. The pink Hello Kitty strap had served as a daily reminder of the encounter but that had disappeared, along with another thief, out the open door of the speeding train. He decided to keep the card.

Jason had seen hundreds of cows wandering the streets, but something about the cow on the third postcard seemed to capture the solemnity that the flower garlands and gold-painted horns inferred. So far he had done a good job avoiding the pervasive spirituality — he hadn't seen the inside of a single temple or mosque, nor had he been pulled into any discussions about religion or faith. Just like at home. For years his only connections to religion were restricted to prayers for completed passes and ninth-inning home runs. But he had almost died — twice — on this trip. The cow postcard would be his reminder to stop ignoring the big questions that crept in late at night.

There were trains in the background of the next two postcards.

He thought about Rachel's fictitious one-eyed grandfather and his dying wish that she keep the trains running, a neat, orderly explanation for her obsession. But there was little neat and nothing at all orderly about Rachel. Thanks to her, he'd never be able to look at a train the same way. He put the two postcards with the ones he knew he'd keep.

He had a postcard-sized frame for the shot of the sunrise at a beach near Goa, and the one of the chai vendor's stall would look good next to his coffee maker, the one of the autorickshaw perfect for the sun visor of his car.

He set aside the postcards of the places he hadn't seen — the Golden Temple at Amritsar, Victoria Monument in Calcutta, the Himalayas, the carved temples of Puri, the Ganges River at Varanasi, a leaping tiger on an unnamed game reserve — and was left with one final image.

The Taj Mahal.

Jason looked at the picture for a full minute. 'You'll see it someday,' he said to himself, putting the postcard on the bottom of the stack.

★ ★ ★

Tossing the stack of postcards on the table in the hotel room, Jason picked up the one-line note Rachel had left propped up by the telephone.

'Narvin made me an offer I couldn't refuse,' the note read, a sloping R filling the bottom half of the page.

His backpack had been dumped on to the center of the bed, the contents scattered. Rachel's backpack was gone. Along with the red sari.

# 25

Jason placed the yellow plastic sword between his teeth and drew back, dropping the gin-soaked olive on to his waiting tongue. It was the fifth swordful of olives he'd eaten since he sat down with Manoj 'Manny' Plakal and, after only a minute of focused thought, Jason deduced that feat called for another round.

When Jason had phoned him early that morning, Manny had suggested a late after-noon rendezvous at Nineteen Twelve, a former warehouse that had been converted into an upscale bar and restaurant around the corner from Jason's hotel. 'Don't worry,' Manny had said when Jason asked how they would know each other. 'You can't miss me.'

The tall, broad room was crowded when Jason arrived a half-hour late, the vaulted beams of the open rafters thirty feet up just darker shadows above the hanging lights. The rough-hewn stone block walls were unpainted, Pop Art prints and plasma screen TVs adding bright splashes of color. Burnished metal chairs and light oak tables gave the furnishings a contemporary, Euro feel while young execu-tives in designer suits stood in small circles, laughing confident laughs and joking in Middle-American English, a few words in Hindi sneaking in between shots. Dressed in bright polo shirts and loose-fitting Dockers, the hotshot computer programmers drank imported beers and conversed in their own acronym-laced language. There were a handful of women in the bar, none in saris or the two-piece *shalwar kamiz*, all of them wearing gray-skirted business suits and the same bored expression. Beneath the tables, feet tapped unconsciously to the ambient Indi-techno pop.

But even if there were twice as many people packed in the bar, he couldn't have missed Manny Plakal. He had seen plenty of pudgy people on this trip and more than a few beer bellies, but Manny was the first truly fat person Jason had seen in India. He wore a light cotton safari shirt, the choice of fashion conscious overweight men around the world, and a bushy mustache that hung over his top lip, giving him the appearance of a dark-skinned walrus with a rapidly receding hairline. When he saw Jason looking his way, he waved his hand over his head, the gesture rippling down his flabby arm.

'I knew it was you the moment I saw you,' Manny said, gripping Jason's hand in his meaty palm. 'You look just like the picture on the Internet.'

Jason winced. 'Oh, you saw that.'

Manny laughed as he continued to shake his hand. 'I wouldn't worry about it. It's obvious that whoever posted that note is up to no good. And who wants to get pulled into something like that?'

'But the reward is up to five hundred.'

'Believe me,' Manny said, releasing his hand, 'anyone who would be visiting that site is not impressed with five hundred rupees.'

'I think it was dollars.'

'Really?' Manny said, rolling his eyes like a silent film star. 'I'm afraid you're doomed now.' He laughed again, patting Jason on the back, turning to the bar to order the first round. While they waited for the drinks to arrive, Manny pulled a photograph from the wide pocket of his shirt, setting it on the bar between them. 'Which of these happy fellows do you recognize?'

Given what he knew about Sriram and BWS, he assumed the photo had to be less than ten years old, yet the washed-out colors and satin finish made it look much older. Six men, all in their late twenties, stood shoulder to shoulder, leaning back against a white-washed wall, the bottom half of the words *Bangalore World Systems* visible above their heads.

He spotted Sriram first. Taller than the

others, he stood towards the middle, one foot up against the wall, a club tie pulled loose to reveal a tee shirt under the white, short-sleeved shirt. He was smiling — Sriram was always smiling — gripping the edge of a clipboard with his right hand, his left resting on the shoulder of Attar Singh. In many ways the two men looked alike, both tall and thin, both with jet-black hair and a crisp right side part, but Attar's closed-mouthed grin wasn't as wide as Sriram's open smile, and his hooded eyes lacked Sriram's sparkle. It was a sadder, darker version of the man Jason had met in Jaipur. But then he remembered the anger that had flashed up as Attar described Sriram's betrayal, and Jason wondered which image was real.

'I didn't think he was part of BWS,' Jason said, pointing to Ravi Murty. The future owner of Raj-Tech stood with both hands in his pockets, looking off to the left of the camera.

'He wasn't,' Manny said. 'He was a couple years older than us, sort of Sriram's mentor. He'd stop in now and then, give us some pointers, help Sriram with the tricky stuff.' Manny sighed. 'I guess I hitched my wagon to the wrong star.'

Next to Ravi stood Ketan Jani, his devilish goatee and gelled-down hair looking the same in the picture as it had looked when they met that morning for pizza. Instead of the uniform white shirt and tie, Ketan wore a black Ramones tee shirt, the punk rock pose lost with the pleated dress pants.

'This is Ketan, right?'

Manny raised his eyes, clicking his tongue against his teeth. 'Mr Rock and Roll. Someday he'll grow up.'

'Who's this?' Jason said, pointing out the man to Sriram's right who wore his feather-cut, blow-dried hair parted in the middle and his long sleeves rolled halfway up his muscular forearms.

'Isn't it obvious?' Manny said, grinning, holding the picture alongside his glistening, round face.

'I didn't recognize you without your mustache.'

'A common mistake,' Manny said, setting the picture back on the bar. 'But I am sure you recognize Narvin Kumar.' A bulbous pinky tapped on the Bollywood millionaire's chest.

'Was he always so . . . '

'So damn good looking?' Manny said, lifting his gin and tonic from the cardboard coaster as soon as the bartender set it down. 'Oh yes. Captain of the rugby team, the cricket team, the debate team, top of his class academically, popular with the ladies, never at a loss for words, great singing voice. Yes, that was our Narvin.'

Jason looked at Narvin, then down the row to Sriram, then back to Narvin. 'Was this picture taken before Sriram met Vidya?'

'I think what you are politely asking is why did Vidya run off with Sriram, leaving behind her handsome fiancé. But in asking that you are also asking how the mind of a woman works and for that, I'm afraid, we are all at a loss.' He paused while Jason laughed in agreement.

'They were engaged for almost a year,' Manny said. 'I thought they were happy but again . . . ' He shrugged his round shoulders, the fat of his neck rolling up to touch his ears. 'I can say most definitely that Narvin took the news hard.'

'Would he have hurt Sriram?'

'If the girl you loved ran off with a guy you thought was your friend, what would you do?'

Jason took a deep sip of his martini. 'That's an interesting question.'

'But, as the cliché goes, time heals all wounds. Or wounds all heels. Either way,' he said, dismissing it with a chubby wave, 'that is all history.'

Jason was ready with another cliché, the one about history repeating itself, but instead

291

pointed to the short, wiry man at the end of the row that he had only seen once before.

'Why did you call him Taco?'

'I didn't,' Manny said, glancing at the photo. 'I called him Amrish. I think Narvin started it. Part of a joke, kind of cruel, really. Amrish dreamed of getting a job in the States, making big money, Narvin assuring him they were always hiring at this fast food restaurant.'

'Taco Bell.'

'Yes, that was it.' Manny paused, then shifted his bulky frame so that he could look straight at Jason as he spoke. 'Sriram was in charge of security and when that failed, Amrish needed someplace to direct his anger. But with Sriram gone . . . I guess he just took it out on you. I want you to know that no one blames you for what happened. He had been unstable for years and I guess it was only a matter of time before something like this happened, maybe not being killed by a train, but you know what I mean. I am sorry he hurt you,' he said, nodding down at the scar on Jason's arm. 'The Amrish I knew, he would be sorry too.'

Both men finished their drinks in silence, Manny waving over the waiter to order another round. A Hindi version of a Madonna song blared overhead, the tune the same, the words lost in the translation. When the drinks arrived, Jason bit the olives off the sword-shaped swizzle stick.

'I stopped by the bank today to see Piyush Ojha.'

Manny's laugh was so loud and unexpected that Jason felt himself flinch along with the other patrons at that end of the bar. 'Good old Piyush. I am sure he was absolutely *thrilled* to see you.'

'That reminds me of a time,' Manny said, launching into a string of BWS stories, all ending with an inside joke and a 'you just had to be there' refrain. The story of dripping light fixtures led to the one about the upside-down monitors, followed by the thrilling details behind the chapatti eating contest and the office chair races, Manny pausing between tales to catch his breath and gulp his drink. While he knew some of the names and had to struggle to follow the long-winded accounts, Manny's accent thicker with every gin and tonic, Jason kept drifting off to his own memories, of trains and saris and a beautiful auburn-haired liar.

It took the better part of two hours, but as Jason aligned the five plastic swords on his napkin, Manny ran out of stories. As the bartender shook up a fresh double martini, Jason remembered why he was there.

'Manny,' he said, louder than he had meant. 'Manny, my friend. I need a favor. Can you do me a favor, Manny?'

At first Manny's head nod was slow and deliberate but as the seconds dragged out he picked up steam, taking on a side-to-side *ahcha* waggle, reminding Jason of an obese bobble-head doll. 'It's like this,' Jason said, pausing, trying to recall what it was like, starting again. 'It's like this. I have something — had something — that I want, no I *wanted* to deliver. It's a surprise so I can't tell you it's a sari.'

'Not a word,' Manny said, pulling an invisible zipper closed across his lips.

'It's really nice. Well, it was when I started. It got shot and a monkey poured my best aftershave on it.'

'Damn monkey,' Manny mumbled, his head rolling from side to side.

'So I had it and then I go and screwed up the only thing Sriram ever asked me to do.' Jason felt his chest tighten and took a deep, choppy breath, holding it, letting it out in a long, slow airy whistle.

'But I'm gonna make it up to him. I'm going to explain to his mom what a great guy he was. He was a great guy, Manny, you know that?'

'Great guy.'

'That's what I'm gonna say. I'm gonna say Mrs Shumb . . . Suhunderrunder . . . '

'Sundaram.'

'Mrs Sundaram, your son was a great guy.' Manny blinked several times to focus his eyes. 'These are the words any mother longs to hear.'

'I need her address because I wanna tell her how Sriram brushed off my car and he gave away candy and made poor people eat frozen turkeys.'

'This was a good man.'

'So, do you have it?' Jason said, tapping Manny's bloated arm with the back of his hand.

'The frozen turkey or the address?'

Jason took a sip of his drink and considered the question. 'Just the address,' he said.

'I do not know the exact address but I can get you close enough. It is in a small hill station, very beautiful this time of the year but chilly.'

'Chilly is not a problem.'

'It is south of here, a place called Uthagamanadalam.'

Jason raised an eyebrow.

'It is also called Ooty.'

'Ah, Ooty,' Jason said, nodding his head. 'Can we go there tomorrow?'

'Not tomorrow. A week. Maybe ten days.

But, yes, I can take you.'

'No, that's not good, Manny,' Jason said, easing his drink down on to the bar. 'I gotta go right away.'

'Getting to Ooty requires several days and I would need to make many arrangements. A week is good. Not much more.'

'That's not good. I've got a job to get back to. An *important* job. I don't have time for Ooty. And I've got a gift for Sriram's mom.'

'A sari,' Manny said.

'Yeah. How did you know?'

Manny shrugged. 'A lucky guess.'

'I promised Sriram I'd deliver it myself,' Jason said, realizing as he spoke that he had never promised a thing. 'That big sari holiday coming up. The one where sons give their mothers new saris.'

'Ah yes. One of our most cherished traditions.'

'But the problem is I can't get the sari to Sriram's mom.'

Manny cleared his throat. 'This is not a problem. I will deliver the special gift for you and relay your message.'

Jason propped his elbow on a wet spot on the bar, dropping his chin into his open palm. 'You'd do that for me, Manny?'

Eyes closed, Manny gave his head a quick bob, letting Jason know that it was as good as done. Jason sighed. 'I don't know what to say.'

'Then say nothing.'

For five minutes they stood at the bar and listened to the pounding dance music and the static wash of a dozen conversations.

'You know, Manny, I feel like a complete idiot.'

'This is understandable.'

'The one thing I came here to do I gotta pass on to someone else.'

'Please,' Manny said, lightly touching his own chest. 'It is my privilege.'

'No, what I mean is I came here to deliver that sari and now I'm not even going to do that. I went through all this,' Jason said, arching his arm overhead, 'all this for *nothing*.'

'It may not be Corning, New York,' Manny said, tilting his head down, looking out from under his heavy brows. 'But I would hardly call India nothing.'

'That's not what I meant. I really like India. I mean, I didn't at the start — it's just kinda hard to get used to. The things that happened to me, the stuff that Rachel dragged me into — the drugs that were really a robot and the monkey and getting shot and me almost dying and having to sing for the police and standing there naked . . . '

Manny set a heavy hand on Jason's shoulder. 'I think it is best you stop now before you say something truly embarrassing.'

'I just thought there'd be a reason, some point of me being here.'

Manny smiled. 'There is a reason. And it is in here.' He prodded Jason's chest with his finger. 'You did not come to India for Sriram Sundaram. You came for Jason Talley. Something inside here made you buy that ticket. Look in here for the answer.'

'Is that it?' Jason asked, rocking back on his heels with every tap on his chest. 'That's why I'm here?'

'That and the party I am throwing for you tomorrow night. A little get together at the old BWS site.'

'You didn't have to do that, Manny.'

'Oh yes I did. The others, they all insisted. It will be a nice little reunion. We shall have a cookout. But, my friend, I must warn you of one thing.'

Jason swallowed down the lump that sprung up in his throat. 'What's that?'

'When they come in the room, be sure to jump,' he said, his voice just above a thick-lipped whisper. 'It is supposed to be a surprise.'

# 26

Ringed by small stacks of emails and printouts, Jason sat cross-legged in the center of the king-size bed. It was just after five in the morning and he'd been awake for over an hour, the bed spinning too much for him to lie down.

It was the same thing every time he drank — eyes popping open at sunrise, a shot of adrenaline firing up his system, sputtering out long before noon, resetting his internal clock like liquid jetlag. There was never any nausea or dry heaves, just a blinding headache that shrugged off aspirin and ibuprofen, responding only to a double dose of daytime sinus pills and a sugar-heavy cola. The breakfast of champions.

The hotel was quiet, a few auto-rickshaws beeping a greeting to the day. He didn't remember walking home from Nineteen Twelve or riding up in the elevator or who paid the bill, if they paid it at all, and he tried not to remember how it felt when, lights off, he had sat on the end of the empty bed, knowing she wasn't coming back.

While he waited for the antihistamine and

caffeine speedball to kick in, Jason read through his expensive stack of emails yet again.

Most were wrinkled and water damaged, a reminder of his post-shower afternoon with Rachel, and all but the most recent bore a hole just large enough to pass a twenty-two slug. The dozen pages of linguistic study — that wafty crank of a monologue — lay fanned out on the bed, after ten readings no longer quite as wafty but he found it more interesting each time he read it. There was a steady, practiced efficiency to the way he worked, picking up each email, reading it through, underlining words with a stubby hotel pencil, shifting emails from pile to pile to pile, stacking and restacking, organizing the chaos, separating the darkness from the light.

Jason knew that Manny had been right. There was a reason he had come to India. It wasn't about Sriram. It wasn't about Vidya or the sari and it wasn't about him either. It was about a moment. The split-second flash of a moment just before Sheriff Neville spoke. The last moment things were in order, the last moment the universe made sense.

He leaned back and stretched, the spinning not as bad now, but he could feel his heart picking up the pace and he knew that sleep would be impossible. He tossed the pencil on the bed and thought about the red sari. He didn't remember thinking much about it that night that Sriram handed it to him in the laundry room of his apartment, didn't see it as special, didn't know what it meant. A dozen weeks and thousands of miles later, he still didn't know what it meant. But he knew he was close.

The schematic pattern looked so obvious when he saw it on the big screen. Now, as he tried to remember the geometric design wrought in silver threads and crisscross embroidery, he thought it looked too simplistic, more like the instructions to an old Tandy radio kit than a cutting-edge micro-chip. Maybe it was a case of relevance. The pattern didn't seem like much to him, but to a computer expert it might tell a different story. Sort of like the reams of papers and government forms that crossed his desk every day at the office — meaningless unless you knew what they meant. No, that wasn't true. Even if you knew what the forms meant, they were still meaningless.

Maybe he was being too literal — no surprise there, he thought as he remembered half the arguments he'd had with past girlfriends. Maybe the sari's meaning was more symbolic, something more complex

301

than a blueprint, more intricate than the most complex computer program. Sriram knew the meaning, knew that he had to get the sari to India, knew that he had to keep it from Vidya. His dark, Oedipal secret. Or evidence of something else.

The files that Ravi uncovered rambled on about Vidya's infidelity, real or imagined. Jason let his own imagination wander. A bored, underemployed substitute teacher. Long, sweaty workouts at the fitness center at the Radisson Hotel. An ex-lover, a former fiancé. A gift from Bollywood, a little memento of home, of an old life, found, crumpled and dirty, hidden under their bed. An unannounced flight to India never taken, a confrontation at the studio that never occurred. Or maybe a slow day at the office, sneaking out for a long lunch, Vidya in bed, naked, alone now, laughing at how long it took him to figure it out.

Jason shook the images from his head, forcing his imagination down another path, one that featured a jilted lover with everything in the world but the one thing he lost.

The key piece was there, and his sources — a B-grade movie actress and her infallible *Stardust Magazine* — were far enough removed to be believed. Narvin Kumar had spent the winter in the States. For a man like Kumar the States meant Los Angeles and New York City, the stuff in the middle beautiful from thirty thousand feet. It was an easy four-hour ride from Manhattan to Corning, five if you stuck to the scenic and seldom used back roads. A half-day road trip to settle things forever. Then, a month later, Sriram's lone friend shows up in India, dragging around a bolt from the past. Giving him the chance to run up the score.

There were other paths to explore. Attar, ruined, with family in Binghamton, spitting distance from Corning. Amrish 'Taco' Sharma, angry enough to kill a stranger, with a loving, forgiving, understanding family who might have been willing to help. Then there was the unknown stalker with the cell phone. What about Ketan Jani, the pizza-loving man with the long memory? The crazy banker Piyush Ojha? Manny Plakal, Ravi Murty, Sheriff Neville, Mrs Dettori in apartment B — maybe it was that loner guy, Jason, in the basement apartment, the one who everyone at the mortgage company would describe as 'really nice' and 'kind of quiet.'

There were a thousand possible answers. But only a few that made sense.

Jason swung his legs over the piles of paper and off the side of the bed. The clock on the

303

nightstand said ten-thirty. Time for a coffee break. He'd shower, get something to eat and, if this day went like any other post-drunken binge day, he'd lie down — just to rest his eyes — around one, waking up hours later. Manny wasn't picking him up until four. Plenty of time to practice looking surprised for the going-away party slash Bangalore World Systems reunion.

It'll be simple, he told himself as he thought about the questions they'd ask. I'll just tell them what they want to hear.

The phone was ringing when he stepped out of the shower.

'There is a gentleman here at the front desk who wishes to speak to you,' said the high-pitched, sing-song female voice. 'A Mr Piyush Ojha from the Hindustani First National Bank.'

★ ★ ★

As the elevator doors opened at the hotel lobby, Jason realized he should have taken the stairs. If there were armed bank guards or a special detachment from the police department waiting for him at least he had the chance to ease the stairwell door shut and creep back up the stairs, sneaking out a side exit or hiding under his bed. But other than the hotel staff and the gray-suited, gray-haired Piyush Ojha, the lobby was empty. When he saw Jason exiting the elevator, Piyush Ojha stood and held out his hand, letting Jason know before he crossed the lobby that this meeting would not be like the one at the bank.

'I am so glad you have agreed to meet me,' the man said as he shook Jason's hand, setting his left hand on Jason's wrist, a sign of sincerity that Jason knew was heartfelt. 'I can not apologize enough for how I treated you yesterday. The moment you left my office I felt ashamed. I am ashamed that I blamed you for my own lack of judgment years before our paths crossed.'

'Don't worry about it,' Jason said, touching the older man's shoulder. 'If I were you, I think I would have acted the same way.'

Piyush Ojha smiled a tight-lipped, embarrassed smile and gave Jason's hand a final squeeze. 'I know that you Americans are partial to your coffee,' he said, tilting his head towards the hotel's café.

'Actually, I could go for a masala chai,' Jason said, and led the way across the polished faux marble floor.

Ten minutes later, the awkward silence and talk of the weather fading away, Piyush Ojha stirred two lumps of sugar into his teacup.

'When you left my office yesterday I was so angry. At you, yes, and at Sriram, but mostly at my own stupidity. I have carried around this anger for years and it is only of late I realize the toll that it has taken on my soul.'

'I think it was Krishnamurti who said that anger was based on fear and to overcome that fear you had to forget the past and live in the moment.'

Piyush stopped stirring and looked up at Jason. 'You are a well-read man, Mr Talley. Yes, that is true. Anger has consumed far too much of my energy and each day is a struggle against my own negativity. It is a struggle that, as yesterday shows, I can easily lose. You had mentioned some questions about Bangalore World Systems?' His smile seemed hesitant and unnatural, but he stayed with it anyway.

Jason blew the steam off his milky chai. 'What can you tell me about Sriram and the others behind the company?'

'If you are talking to me then you must have talked to some of the others as well, Manoj Plakal for instance.'

'Manny.'

'Yes, Manny,' he said in a way that let Jason know that he preferred Manoj. 'Also, I believe that Ketan Jani still lives in Bangalore.'

'We did lunch.'

Piyush nodded a quick, jerky nod. 'I am sure that both men had less than kind things to say about me.'

'They just said that you took the whole BWS thing a bit hard.'

'You are being too kind, Mr Talley. I know what they say . . . what is the American term? . . . Is it nerd? Yes, well, I was the nerd of the group.'

Given that anyone associated with BWS was, by definition, a computer geek, Jason understood that it was a harsh admission. And he knew enough to respect his honesty. 'From what I understand, Sriram was also a bit of a nerd.'

Piyush looked down at his tea as he spoke. 'People use the word genius all of the time with no real concept of its meaning. A genius cricketer, a genius businessman, a genius actor, a genius game-show contestant.' He paused and stirred his tea again. 'When you are in the presence of a true genius it is something you never forget. There is an aura, a glow. You may smile but I tell you it is real. You feel it engulf you, pass right through you. The talent, the energy — the *magic*. It is overwhelming. And you know that, no matter how hard you work, how intently you struggle, the thoughts that pass through that mind will never pass through yours.' He

307

looked up at Jason, his eyes puffy and wet, and whispered, 'It is a horrible feeling.'

Jason thought back to the late nights at the Sundarams', Vidya lounging on the couch, Bindi on her lap, her purr louder than the stereo, Sriram, tossing back another Odenbach lager, running down the batting order for his fantasy baseball team or an imagined set list for a Beatles reunion. He didn't remember seeing a beatific glow or feeling engulfed in a shimmering aura of energy, recalling instead a sense of contentment and a warm buzz from the cold beer. Whenever Sriram got talking — lecturing, really — about the next big thing in computers or how science fiction led to science fact, Jason had tuned him out, unable to follow his friend's train of thought, happy just to see him so excited. Maybe Sriram was a genius — Ravi had seemed to think so and so did everyone involved with BWS. For the thousandth time since his trip started, Jason wished he had paid more attention to his friend.

'I am sure you know what happened with BWS,' Piyush continued. 'I will not bore you with my story — suffice it to say that it took me several years to reestablish myself financially.'

'Do you think Sriram really did it? That he

stole the program you were working on?'

Piyush drew in a deep breath and held it as he thought, his jaw tightening, and Jason braced for a gale-force tirade. But Piyush exhaled slowly, the tension slipping from his face. 'There was only one way to get at the information on our computers and that was through Sriram's security protocols, something I'm certain that only the person who designed them could do. I'm sorry, Mr Talley,' Piyush said. 'Sriram stole that program and sabotaged our computers.'

The men sat in silence as the waiter refilled their teacups, Piyush dropping in a pair of sugar cubes as the man poured, Jason thinking about computer security and theft.

'So what do you do at the bank?' Jason said, steering the conversation back to small talk and towards a close. He was surprised when Piyush seemed to perk up, edging forward on his seat and squaring his shoulders.

'It is most fascinating work,' he said. 'Quite fulfilling. Thankfully nothing to do with computers. Essentially it is the sorting and organization of forms and documents. It requires a close attention to detail and a *constant* vigilance. You see, unlike so many people, I like to have things planned out. I have found that it makes life much easier if you are aware of what is to come. If I am not properly organized, one step could be missed, nullifying the entire process. Large and important deals hinge on my ability to keep things organized.'

'I see,' Jason said, a cold chill cutting through his body, the ghost echo of words he was sure he had heard before.

'Yes, it is most fascinating and I must say that I have earned quite a reputation within the loans division of Hindustani First National Bank. Thrice named Employee of the Quarter. And,' he said, smiling his first real smile of the morning, 'I believe I will be nominated for a promotion soon.'

'I bet your family is quite proud,' Jason said, not bothering to shake the monotone from his voice.

'Oh, I had no time to start a family — my work requires far too much of my time. One could say I am married to my profession. *Happily* married, I might add.'

'You don't live with your parents, do you?' Jason said, his own fears rising to the surface.

Piyush shook his head. 'No, sadly they have both passed away. I live alone, a studio flat nearer the airport.' He sighed as he raised his teacup to his lips. 'This was one of the few things I shared with Sriram.'

'You shared a studio apartment with

Sriram?' Jason said, remembering his tall friend. 'That must have been crowded.'

'I am sorry,' Piyush said, setting his cup back down. 'I was not clear. I did not share an apartment with Sriram. What I meant was that we shared a similar background.'

'Studio apartments?'

'No. We both lost our parents at an early age.'

The teacup and saucer rattled in Jason's hands. 'What?'

'My father died in an auto accident when I was sixteen. Five years later my mother was diagnosed with cancer and passed away later that year.'

'Wow. That's rough,' Jason said, rushing through the words. 'What about Sriram?'

'It was his mother who died first, I don't know the cause. His father passed away during his last year at university. A heart attack, I believe.'

Jason set down his teacup and collapsed back in his chair. 'Are you sure? I mean about Sriram's mother being dead.'

'Coincidentally we both lost our mothers in the same year. I was twenty-one at the time, so Sriram would have been in primary school. Fourth, fifth grade perhaps. It came up quite accidentally one afternoon. Someone at BWS had recalled a football championship or some

311

nonsense and Sriram mentioned that it was the same date his mother had died. Later that day we shared a pot of tea and told sons' stories.' Piyush smiled again, a melancholy smile that seemed to fit.

'Did he have a sister? An aunt he was close to?'

'Here again we were alike. We were both only children, but where I had many aunties, Sriram often joked of a plague of bachelor uncles. He did have a wry sense of humor.'

'There has to be somebody. Sriram told me he was planning a trip to India for that holiday that's coming up, the one with the saris.'

Piyush tilted his head and gave a slight frown. 'Which holiday is this?'

'The one where sons give their mothers new saris. It's coming up soon.

'Sons give their mothers saris all the time, there is no set holiday for the gifting of saris.'

'So, as far as you know, there was no reason for Sriram to bring a sari to India?'

'Bringing a sari to India,' Piyush said, his slight smile returning, 'would be like bringing coals to Newcastle.'

'But it could happen, right?'

Piyush shrugged his narrow shoulders. 'There is no law forbidding it. But I must say it would be a rare sari indeed that would deserve such treatment.'

# 27

'Behold!' Manny said, pulling his Ambassador to the side of the road. 'The international headquarters of Bangalore World Systems.'

Jason looked out the passenger window at the building and waited for the punch line, Manny slapping his leg, laughing, saying he was only kidding, driving on as he made more cracks at the poor building's expense.

When he heard the engine cut off and then the ratcheting clicks of the parking brake, Jason realized it wasn't meant to be a joke.

Dropped down on the edge of a sprouting farm field and surrounded by bent poles that should have supported a missing chain-link fence, the slate-gray concrete and cinder block building sat — with a slight lean to the right — in the chunky red earth.

It was hard not to stare and Jason felt himself first lean out of the passenger window, as if drawn in by curiosity, then pulling back, an instinctual response he obeyed without fighting. Squinting, he tried to envision the architect's original concept.

He seemed to have started with a simple cube but, midway up the building's façade, the architect veered from his original plan, adding half-moon balconies and bay windows, tentatively at first, then with a reckless passion that mocked the petty dictates of aesthetics and physics. The main entrance — once a grand two-story portal, now a gaping black cave — was not as far off center as the odd-sized windows made it appear, with those on the bottom two floors either broken or hacked out of the wall, the windows on the top stories still in place but crusted over with a protective layer of grime, a few propped open with a piece of wood or busted bits of plastic pipe. On the flattish roof, stubby cement pillars, bristling with rusting lengths of steel rebar, hinted at a still bolder, never-to-be-realized dream, one that, given the ambitious start, might have included flying buttresses and pointed spires.

'That's a building,' Jason said without conviction. 'It must have been rather . . . '

'Hideous?' Manny said. 'Repugnant? An eyesore? An abomination?'

'I was going to say big,' Jason said, stepping out of the car, 'but those are good, too.'

'Ah, but you should have seen the plans,' Manny said, his voice breathy and wistful. 'They were far worse.'

Although Manny had driven most of the way with the gas pedal pressed to the frayed carpet, the ride from Bangalore had taken almost two hours, half the time spent in complex flanking maneuvers and back-tracking shortcuts that Manny insisted were the only way to avoid rush-hour gridlock. 'It was not always like this,' Manny had said as he clipped the bumper of an auto-rickshaw during an illegal u-turn. 'When I was a child, Bangalore was still a sleepy little place — we played cricket in the streets and on Sunday you could hear the bells of the Catholic church across town. Then the computer boom came and suddenly it seemed that the whole world was moving in. My father has not driven in years and has stopped going to the temple because the walk is too dangerous for a pedestrian.' He checked his rearview mirror as he crossed four lanes, his directional still blinking from two turns back. 'Then there is the pollution and the crime and beggars . . . I suppose there is a price to pay for progress.'

Twenty minutes outside the city limits, the price went up.

It started with a few scattered lean-tos — shipping crates roofed in blue plastic sheets, held in place with head-sized rocks and twisted car parts — propped up along both sides of the highway, the lean-tos growing, becoming shacks, the distance

315

between them closing as they drove on until there was no space left at all. Hard-packed dirt roads sloped up to the asphalt highways, creating impromptu intersections that cut a gash into the side of the slum, revealing a hellish maze of shattered plywood, mud bricks, stacked tires and dirt mounds, miles of flapping blue roofs diffusing the thin smoke trails from ten thousand cooking fires.

Standing in the dark doorways, in small pockets on the side of the road, hunched down in front of dung-fired ovens, poking at the trash heaps with a short stick, or, backs turned to traffic, pissing down the side of the embankment, the citizens of the community found a way to make it through another day.

Few of the men bothered to look up as the car sped past. Walking, heads down, nowhere to go, going anyway, busy watching the dust rise up as they shuffled along. A group of twenty-year-olds, barefoot, kicked a lopsided soccer ball up and down a back alley, too young and cocksure to know that they were already middle aged. Toothless old men in once-white dhotis and the thin remnants of button-down shirts sat tall in front of their scrap wood homes, the reward for a lifetime of labor.

Against a backdrop of lifeless browns and greasy shades of gray, the washed-out hues of the worn and patched saris glowed. Unlike the cities, where stylish women wore their ornate pallu tossed over their right shoulders, the tail end draping to mid thigh, the women here used the final yard of fabric as an ever-present veil, protection from the sun and the curious stares of strangers. None of the women wore the two-piece *shalwar kamiz*, and Jason remembered Laxmi's sermon, fashion a reflection of tradition and control.

And there were children everywhere, the youngest ones naked, the others dressed in filthy rags, playing inches from the speeding traffic, matted hair and dirty faces offset by model-bright smiles, laughing at everything, the bliss of ignorance making theirs the best life imaginable.

From the moment he had ridden off in the auto-rickshaw with Rachel, Jason had been trying to comprehend the poverty he saw everywhere he looked. From the trendy streets of Mumbai, flush with its Bollywood billions, to the manicured parks in Bangalore, to the tourist-heavy resort beaches on the coast, destitution and despair were always there, the beggars and the squalid shacks just part of the landscape. But here, the slum already two miles long and stretching down the road as far as he could see, the poverty was no longer part of the landscape, it was

317

the landscape, impossible to ignore.

'Why doesn't somebody do something about this?'

'What do you suggest?'

'Tear down these shacks for a start,' Jason said. 'Build them something decent to live in. Get those kids in school, maybe tell the adults to stop having so many kids.'

'My god, we never *thought* of that,' Manny said, slapping his forehead with the base of his palm. 'You are a genius. We shall get this cleaned up in no time now.

'I don't mean to be sarcastic,' Manny continued, 'but if the answers were simple this wouldn't exist.' He waved his flabby arm to take in both sides of the road. 'Not here in India, not anywhere in the world. I know you will find this hard to believe, my friend, but we are trying. India is a young nation with a noble past and, I am certain, a great future. As bad as this is.' He waved his arm a second time. 'As awful as it is, it is better than it was. Give us time.'

They rode on in silence, the densely packed shacks transforming back to a wall of lean-tos, gaps appearing, growing longer until all that was left of the shantytown were isolated camps and lone squatters. And an image that he knew he could never shake. The sun was low on the horizon when the

318

silhouette of the international headquarters of Bangalore World Systems rose into view.

'The land had belonged to an uncle,' Manny said as they unloaded coolers and cooking supplies from the boxy trunk. 'A small parcel, too little to farm, but we had to keep it in the family anyway. It is my name on the lease and now the whole ruinous structure is mine.'

'Couldn't you tear it down, build something new here? Maybe lease it to a small-time local farmer?' Jason paused. 'I know, I know,' he said when Manny stopped to look at him, his eyes rolling up under his thick brow. 'You never thought of it before.'

Manny smiled. 'You are a quick learner. Now let us see how quickly you master Indian cuisine.' He handed Jason an open-topped cardboard box that held a blackened cook stove. 'Careful you do not soil your shirt — that contraption leaks kerosene like a sieve but it makes the finest *iggaru royya* you will ever taste.

'There used to be doors here,' Manny said panting as they stepped through the two-story entranceway. His shirt was already soaked in sweat and by his heavy breathing, Jason knew the walk from the car was more exercise than the fat man was used to. He set down the cooler he was carrying and took a seat on the top, the sturdy plastic sides bowing. He waved his hand indicating that Jason should set down the box and rest before they tried climbing the stairs. 'The building was never finished, we worked out of a few rooms upstairs. Those were done. The rest didn't look much different than it does now. There were windows and doors and railings for the stairs. Plumbing and electricity, of course. All of that was stripped out within days of our closing up shop, no doubt by the residents of the village we passed.'

In the gathering darkness, Jason could make out the places on the wall where missing couplings had held long-gone light switches, recessed channels that had guided now looted pipes and tin air ducts. Scattered about the room, plastic bags and loose sheets of paper collected against interior walls and cement supports, mixed in with the shifting dunes of dust and dirt that edged in through the open doorway. A grand staircase filled the center of the space, the concrete flights connecting the floors, hanging free from the walls, a dark, room-sized shaft that rose four flights, topped with the frame of a missing skylight. Jason looked up at the dangling remnants of the ceiling lights, trying to imagine the floor plan, and didn't notice when the man with the gun entered the room.

It was a shotgun and the old man held it low on his hip, keeping his eyes on Jason as he stepped into the room. He wore khaki shorts and a shirt that was several shades lighter, but his feet were bare. Manny was busy wiping his forehead with a terrycloth rag when he saw the man and his gun.

'*Chacaji*,' Manny said, struggling to his feet. The old man lowered the gun and his head, stepping down to touch the tops of Manny's feet. Manny held out his hand, trying to prevent the gesture of respect, speaking to the man in Hindi, his voice kind and soft, his eyes and smile wide. 'This is Mr Chaudhrythe, the security guard. He has been with my family since before I was born.' Jason shook the bony hand, the man's calloused skin leather-tough. 'He is more like family than some of my family,' Manny said and turned to speak to the guard. By their tones Jason knew that it was not a relationship based on employment.

'I told him we were having a gathering and invited him up. He says no thank you, but I'll be sure to bring him down a plate later.'

The two men shook hands again, Manny insisting that he could carry the cooler without help, and they mounted the first flight of stairs as Mr Chaudhrythe took his place back in the shadows.

# 28

'That was Attar's office over there by the open window. Mine was near that empty Thumbs Up bottle,' Manny said, bent low over the kerosene lamp, pointing backwards with the tip of a screwdriver. 'Sriram's office was down the hall.' He gestured with the flat of his hand to indicate where a passageway once ran. 'And across from Sriram was Narvin. Ketan had that window that looked out over the road and right about here would have been where old Piyush sat.' With an airy hiss and a puff of inky smoke, the kerosene lamp came to life, casting hard-edged shadows around the open space. Other than a dozen support columns and mounds of trash, the floor was empty.

'What about Amrish Sharma?' Jason asked. 'Taco?'

Manny looked back over the room. 'There. Near the stairs.'

'It was crowded up here.'

'It was the only floor that was done. But, oh, did we have grand plans for this building.'

Jason helped Manny lift the soot-covered stove out of the cardboard box, setting it on the cement floor, moving the lamp far to the side when he saw how much kerosene they had already spilled. After prying the caps off a pair of Kingfishers with the ancient bottle opener built into the side of the cooler, Jason unloaded the small, covered aluminum pots and knock-off Tupperware containers that held the evening's feast, Manny arranging his supplies to both sides of the stove, thinking through the meal before lighting the stove.

'You may not have guessed it by looking at me,' Manny said, his back to Jason as he opened a box of kitchen matches, his cell phone dropping out of his shirt pocket to clatter on top of the stove, 'but I am fond of eating. Regrettably my wife is not a good cook. Since the day we were married I have had to fend for myself lest I waste away.'

'How about your mother, was she a good cook?'

'Oh wonderful, truly wonderful. And that is not just a son's boasts. Everyone who ate at my home said as much. Hold this for me please?' he said, handing Jason his cell phone over his shoulder. 'My amma's *pakki biryani* was so delicious the brass statue of Ganesh would get up from the kitchen shrine and join us at the table, shoveling in great mouthfuls with his trunk. This is the truth, so help me.' He placed a hand on his sloping chest and rolled his eyes heavenward.

'Speaking of mothers,' Jason said, pocketing the cell phone, pausing to pull down a long swig of beer, sure now that Manny was listening, 'Piyush came to see me at the hotel this morning.' He paused again, watching Manny's back as he struggled to light the stove, snapping the matchsticks with his jerky movement. 'He says Sriram's mother doesn't live in Ooty.'

'Its proper name is Uthagamanadalam.'

'She's dead, Manny. She died when you were just kids and you knew it.'

Manny rolled the matchstick between his fingers for a moment before striking it alongside of the box, sparking a small flame. He cupped his hand around the match head, lowering it down to the stove's burner, a ring of blue flame springing up. He tossed the box of matches down near the cooler, then pushed his hands down on his thighs as he stood, grunting, letting his round shoulders sag as he turned to face Jason. 'I suppose I should explain.'

Sharp clapping erupted from the floor below them, falling in sync, beating out a fast rhythm. 'We are the men of Tappa Tappa Kega,' a pair of voices boomed off key. 'We want a beer so shake-a leg-a leg-a!' Their heavy footfalls timed with their claps, Attar Singh and Ravi Mutry bounded up the open stairwell, two steps at a time, dropping down on one knee, arms out-stretched for a big 'Ta-da!' finish, Ravi's leather shoulder bag swinging as they held their pose.

'Watch that stairwell, you lunatics,' Manny shouted, laughing, breaking into rapid applause, nudging Jason's elbow until he joined in, saying out of the side of his mouth, 'Remember, this was a surprise.'

Attar and Ravi helped each other to their feet, Attar laughing, wiping away tears, Ravi's laugh hesitant and embarrassed. Both men had seemed so formal when he first met them, making their frat-house entrance all the more unexpected. Tall and thin, Attar seemed less imposing than Jason remembered, a heartbeat later remembering also Attar's fiery outburst on the road to the Amber Palace. Dressed in a ubiquitous button-down white shirt, synthetic khakis and sandals, he looked like a hundred million other Indian men his age.

The last time Jason had seen Ravi had been at Sriram's memorial service in one of the meeting rooms at Raj-Tech. Now, instead of his designer suit, Ravi wore a crisp pair of dress pants and an expensive logo-less polo shirt, a gold-trimmed shoulder bag serving as a casual attaché case. He looked younger, less corporate, yet still uncomfortable with Manny's bear hug embrace and two-cheek kiss greeting.

'I bet you thought you had seen the last of me,' Attar said, patting Jason on the back.

'You don't know how surprised I am. I'm learning that Manny here is good at keeping secrets.'

'I'm just glad I was able to get away from the office,' Ravi said, shaking Jason's hand. 'It's good to see you again. You're a bit thinner and it's hard to tell in this light but you look tanned. I guess you're surviving India all right.'

'Thanks for setting Rachel and me up in the hotel. I didn't know what we were going to do,' Jason said, kicking himself as the words came out, knowing what was coming next.

'Hey, speaking of Rachel, where is that lovely bride of yours?' Attar said, taking the open beers Manny held out for them, handing one to Ravi.

'I didn't know you two were married,' Ravi said.

'Oh yes. Quite an attractive woman, totally dotty over this fellow.' Attar gave Jason a playful punch in the arm.

Jason ran his thumbnail through the flimsy beer label, hoping the moment would pass.

'He has not mentioned a *thing* about a wife,' Manny said. 'Is she here in Bangalore? You should have said something, we have plenty of food.'

Jason puffed out his cheeks and sighed. 'There's something I ought to clear up about Rachel. It's kind of hard to explain, but, well, Rachel's . . . she's . . . she's sorta . . . '

'Always freakin' late,' Rachel said, jogging up the last few steps of the dark stairwell.

Jason spun around, his mouth open, his heart stopping as he watched her approach. She had on the same baggy pair of cargo pants she had worn most of the trip, the ones that rode low on her narrow hips and dipped far below her navel. The oversized tee shirt — pulled tight and knotted to the side — was new, the silkscreen outline of an old-style train still shiny, the short sleeves rolled up past a faint tan line just below her shoulders. She carried an empty beer bottle and with her free hand she brushed her hair out of her face, revealing her sparkling eyes and contagious smile. It was only then that he noticed Narvin a few steps behind, carrying the backpack.

'I found this bum on the side of the road,' she said, jerking a thumb back at the Bollywood executive. 'He claims he knows you guys.'

A cheer went up and Manny pushed past Jason to join Ravi and Attar, bear hugging their old friend, dangerously close to the black hole in the floor that plunged four stories down past the concrete steps. The shouts and hugs turned to backslaps and calls for more beer, the yellow-white light of the kerosene lamp giving the whole scene a waxy pallor.

Jason's head was still spinning when Rachel walked over and slid her arm around his, kissing him on the cheek, the others too excited to notice.

'You look surprised,' she said, clicking his beer with her empty. 'I told you I'd be here.' Jason closed his mouth, opening it again to speak, trying again, nothing coming out.

'Don't tell me you lost your tongue,' Rachel said, stepping towards the cooler. 'That's one of the main reasons I came back.' She felt around the ice-less cooler for the coldest beers, pulling out two with one hand, popping the tops with a couple of quick wrist flicks. Twenty feet away the reunion was going well, a rush of speedy questions and short answers as they recapped the past ten years of their lives, interspaced with loud laughs, do-you-remember-whens and what-ever-happened-tos, Manny and Attar doing most of the talking, Narvin and Ravi sidestepping comments about fame and success.

'I thought I'd never see you again,' Jason said, not sure yet how to feel.

'Don't be silly. I left you a note.'

'All it said was that Narvin had made you an offer that you couldn't resist.'

Rachel shook her head. 'No, I'm sure I told you I was coming back. I wouldn't be that rude.'

Jason sipped his beer, tempted to pull out his wallet and show her the note he had kept, instead letting the feeling pass. He watched as she chugged a third of the Kingfisher lager, stopping in mid swallow when he asked her about Narvin's offer.

'Oh my god, you can't *believe* what we did.'

'Do I want to hear this?'

'There's a train that runs near here — a *steam* train, Jason, an honest to god, coal-fired, whistle-blowing steam train.' She grabbed at his arm as she spoke, her grip tight and her nails sharp. 'One of these Indian Heritage things — narrow gauge, four six two carriage with a bogie tender. I *swear* it's a mid-20s Stoke-on-Trent engine, but the cars are new, Indian made, probably up in Calcutta. Narvin — he's freakin' amazing — he arranged it so I could ride up in the engine — I mean, that's *definitely* against the rules. There were butterfly doors on the firebox and they let me stoke the coals. Oh my god it was better than sex.'

Jason watched her as she spoke, one hand

gesturing as if to pull the words out faster, the other waving the beer till white foam oozed down the long glass neck. The way her eyes lit up, how her cheeks seemed ready to burst, unable to hold in her smile, her passion electric, his skin tingling when she touched his arm.

'And then — you won't believe this. Guess who I had dinner with?'

'Narvin?'

'Noooo,' she said, frustration at his stupidity dragging the word out, making her hand shake. 'V. F. *Mulla.*' She waited, wide-eyed, for Jason's reaction, her frustration building as his shoulders rose in a gentle shrug. '*Steam Trains of the Twentieth Century? The History of the Chittaranjan Locomotive Works?*'

'Sorry. I'm more of a Stephen King kind of guy.'

'The man wrote the book on the ES Class. And the work he did with S.V. Joshi . . . ' Her words trailed off, hinting at greatness.

'Must have been a long dinner.'

'The dinner was just a couple hours,' she said, his sarcasm bouncing off. 'The parties . . . Speaking of which, if I don't eat soon I'm going to have a killer hangover.' She turned to the four men by the stairs. 'Hey, who's the cook in the crowd?' she shouted loud enough to be heard over their chatter. 'And none of this 'woman's work' nonsense. Trust me, you don't want me anywhere near the stove.'

★  ★  ★

'I'll take my coffee like we used to make it for the headmaster,' Narvin said, leaning back on the cinder blocks he used as a seat.

'Then hot, black and bitter it shall be,' Manny said, turning the flame up under the large brass kettle. 'Just like that man's soul. Remember how upset he would get if your tie did not exactly touch the top of your belt buckle? *Mister* Kumar,' Manny shouted, dropping his voice to an authoritative bass, 'kindly bring that *embarrassment* of a tie *and* your straight edge to my office *post haste.*'

'I thought my knuckles would never recover.' Narvin flexed his hands, cringing at the memory.

'Indian public schools are rather strict,' Attar said, footnoting the conversation for the others. 'And there was always an exam to sit. Math, science, geography, history, English . . . and not that American English. *Proper* English.'

'I'll have you know I aced my SATs,' Ravi said, rising to the schoolyard challenge.

'It's American English,' Jason said, the

words coming out slowly as he remembered the downloaded monologue on language and the dozens of words in the emails he had circled early that morning in his hotel room. 'If you grew up in the States that's how you learned to spell.'

'That King's English crap, with those extra letters stuck in there?' Ravi said to Rachel.

'I'm Canadian. Sounds right to me.'

'That's because you don't know how to spell, either,' Ravi said, adding a slight smile as he leaned toward Jason. 'I guess we're the only two who got a good education.'

'That's a wafty crank of a coincidence,' Jason said, looking out into a dark corner, the monotone words trailing off as he spoke.

'Remember the time the headmaster caught you cribbing for that exam?' Manny's shoulders shook as Narvin buried his face in his hands.

'God, that was awful. He called my parents, you know. Oh, I paid for that one. And the man was quite unfair. I was blamed for everything but the Fall of Rome but he would let Sriram get away with murder.' He started to laugh, stopping when he realized his mistake. Huddled around the cook stove, its circular flame standing in for a campfire, they were quiet for the first time since they arrived.

'Good dinner, Manny,' Rachel said after a long minute, the others jumping in, quick to agree.

With a rumbling cough, Manny cleared his throat. 'It was my first day at the new school. Third grade. Miss Pandya's class. I was scared so badly my knees were shaking. Me in my short pants, my hair pasted down with a handful of palm oil. Sriram was the first one in that class to speak with me.'

'That's sweet that you remember,' Rachel said.

'How could I forget? He said give me your lunch tiffin or I shall throttle you.' Manny laughed loudly as he spoke. 'Oh that man. From that moment on we were fast friends.'

'We used to try to sneak into the theater for the Saturday matinee,' Narvin said. 'They caught us every damn week.'

'I met Sriram when we were working towards our Masters in Bangalore, but the boy was still evident in the man.' Attar's smile grew as he spoke. 'He was mad over cricket and I never knew anyone who enjoyed sweets as much.'

Manny gave Attar a comic double take, looking down at his protruding stomach then back up at Attar, drawing howls of beer-heightened laughter.

'He was a hard worker and eager to learn.

One of my most diligent employees at Raj-Tech.'

'Remember how he got my mother up to dance at our wedding reception? And that cowboy hat he wore the whole day?' Rachel said, chuckling at her imagined memories.

'But the man had his faults,' Narvin said, letting the others finish the thought in their heads, the room growing still.

Jason leaned forward. 'I didn't know Sriram that long. I probably didn't know him that well either. The man I knew — the one I'm going to remember — he was kind and funny — a good friend — a guy who liked what he did and who loved his wife.' Jason looked around the circle, the others, nodding, staring at the blue flame of the cook stove, Narvin, meeting his gaze, holding it till Jason shifted his eyes back to the warm beer in his hands.

Rachel placed her hand on Jason's back, rubbing it up and down as she spoke. 'And he never forgot to call his mom on her birthday.' Jason watched as Manny, Attar, and Narvin exchanged shrugs. 'A girl remembers a guy that's nice to his mom. Did Jason show you guys the sari Sriram bought for her?'

The four men's heads snapped up.

'No. I hadn't planned on telling anyone about it,' Jason said, standing up and looking about the dark recesses of the fourth floor. 'Anyone of you remember where the men's room was?'

'It was there,' Manny said, pointing to a hacked-off stand of pipes that ran along one edge of the open stairwell, 'but to be safe I suggest you try one of the windows. The night sky is amazing.'

His back to the light of the stove, Jason eased his way toward a dark corner, stopping to stand behind one of the concrete pillars. 'Great, Narvin,' Jason could hear Rachel say, 'you dropped my backpack in a freakin' puddle.'

'Now *whom* did you say this sari was for?' Attar asked Rachel as she set the pack on her cinderblock seat.

'Sriram's mom,' Rachel said, clicking open the plastic snaps. She pulled the balled-up sari from the bag, the four men leaning in for a better look. 'It's kinda roughed up — I told Jason I should carry it but no, he's always right. That funny smell is Jason's cologne.'

Manny shook his head. 'It smells like kerosene to me.'

'Here,' she said, handing Attar one of the corners. 'Stretch this out. Watch it, it's real long. Don't trip over anything.'

From where he was standing, Jason could see them all, the flash of recognition in one man's face when he saw the sari, his eyes widening, then, with a blink, assuming the same curious stare the others wore.

'I don't know *how* he got these in there,' Rachel said, holding the corner up, pointing out the holes left from the passing bullet. 'I was going to have Narvin stop by a sari shop and get a new one, give her that instead, but we were running late as it was.'

'That won't be necessary,' Manny said. 'This one will be just fine. In fact just before you arrived I was telling Jason about a trip I am about to take.'

'This is a good sari,' Narvin said, more to himself than to the others, rubbing the thin material between his fingers. 'The kind you'd want to give someone special. Your mother, an aunt maybe. Or your fiancée.'

'Red was my mother's favorite color,' Attar said, holding the corner up over his head to better see the pattern. 'I always bought her red saris.'

Ravi sighed. 'Rachel, I hate to be the one to tell you this, but Sriram's mother died some years ago.'

Rachel looked up at Ravi, her mouth dropping open. She looked to the others, Attar nodding, Manny and Narvin continuing to stare at the sari. 'He never said she was dead.' Her voice was just loud enough to be heard over the hiss of the cook stove. She looked down the length of the sari and back at Ravi. 'Why would he ask Jason to give this to his mother if she were dead?'

'It's not that hard to explain,' Ravi said. 'Sriram never got over the loss of his mother and I could tell that it was really starting to get to him. It affected his work, his home life . . . ' he said, pausing, letting the silence tell part of the story. 'I urged him to take some time off, go home to India. In the end I thought we'd agreed. He'd take a few weeks, make a pilgrimage to a local shrine, present the sari there in honor of his mother and then . . . oh, what now,' he said, pulling a cell phone out of his pocket.

'If it is my fiancée, tell her I'm not here,' Narvin said, winking at Rachel.

Ravi flipped open the cell phone, his thumb hitting the illuminated buttons. 'Sorry to be so rude, but this may be important.' He made a quarter turn and cupped his free hand against his ear. 'Yes?'

'Tell me, Ravi,' Jason said, stepping from behind the concrete pillar, snapping Manny's cell phone shut, his voice filling the room. 'How do you spell honor?'

Attar laughed. 'Considering he went to school in the States, no doubt incorrectly.'

Jason moved out of the shadows towards

the light of the cook stove. 'It's funny, Ravi. Getting that one piece in place — everything else just came together.'

'Are you still going on about English classes?' Manny said, lifting the brass kettle from the stove with a thick pot holder, filling the row of Styrofoam cups lined up on his makeshift counter.

'This is about email messages,' Jason said, waiting as Ravi turned.

'Curious that one sent out from India offering a reward spelled honor in the American way.'

Ravi closed his cell phone, slipping it back into his pocket. 'I was just trying to look out for you. Make sure nothing bad happened to you.'

'What's this all about, Jason?' Narvin said, taking a step back, letting the sari fall from his hands, waiting for Manny to fill his cup.

Jason took another step towards the group, keeping his eyes locked on Ravi. 'Ravi was the one who posted my picture on that website, the one with the phone number and the reward.'

'Really?' Manny said, chuckling as he poured, his thumb and little finger of his left hand forming an invisible phone. 'Hello, Ravi. I have found Jason for you. I believe you owe me five hundred dollars.'

'It's true,' Ravi said, his hands open, his eyes sparkling as he smiled. 'Forgive me for trying to help.'

'I still want my five hundred dollars,' Manny said, Attar laughing as he handed Rachel the corner of the sari, reaching for a steaming coffee.

Jason stood opposite Ravi, the cook stove hissing between them. 'You're the one that broke into the Bangalore World Systems computers. You're the one that stole the program, and you're the one that created the virus that shut them down.'

Feet shuffling, Manny and Attar looked away from Jason and into their Styrofoam cups. 'That was uncalled for, Jason,' Narvin said. 'I know you feel obliged to clear Sriram's name, but accusing Ravi just because he's successful . . . '

'Narvin, you're the one who told me the only one who could get through Sriram's security system was the man who created it.'

'That's right. And that was Sriram.'

'But Ravi was the one who designed it.'

Ravi blew out an impatient breath. 'That's ridiculous. Sriram was a genius, he didn't need my help.'

'Even geniuses need a mentor, somebody to get them started. That was you, Ravi. You taught Sriram how to build an impregnable security system. One that you would know how to get around.'

'Jason, stop,' Ravi said. 'You're embarrassing yourself and nothing you say can change what Sriram did.'

'What Sriram did was figure you out. He knew something was happening — you all said that,' Jason said, looking one by one at Attar, Manny, and Narvin. 'But by the time he solved it, it was too late. He realized there was nothing he could do to stop Ravi from ruining BWS.'

'You're forgetting that I was the one who gave Sriram a job. Why would I hire a man I just ripped off?' Ravi closed his eyes as he spoke, dismissing the whole idea.

'And why would he get him a green card,' Attar said.

'For Vidya too,' Narvin said, his voice low.

'That would not be a wise business practice,' Manny said.

'You're not giving yourselves enough credit. That program was beyond anything Ravi could figure out on his own.' Jason turned back to Ravi. 'Sriram knew you needed him and he used that against you. The problem is, Ravi, you thought he was just like you, that he would steal from his friends. He told you just what you wanted to hear and you fell for it. You couldn't imagine someone wanting to live in India, but he was always planning to come back. After he got what he wanted from you.' Jason pointed at the folds of bright red fabric that spilled out of Rachel's hands, the silver and gold threads of the embroidered pattern shimmering in the flickering light.

'*This*?' Rachel said, raising the sari as she spoke, shafts of light poking through the bullet holes to dance across the far wall. 'Jason, hon, I don't know . . . '

'I told you what this sari is for. Sriram was going to make a pilgrimage to an area temple. That sari was to be donated in honor of his mother. Tell him,' Ravi said, turning to the others. 'People do this stuff all the time.'

Manny tilted his head. 'I suppose it is possible.'

Ravi gave a quick nod. 'Thank you. And now with Sriram dead, what I would like to do is deliver the sari and make a donation in his name.' Ravi lifted the end of the sari off the floor: 'Let's fold this up before Jason lets anything else happen to it,' he said to Rachel.

'It's not a sari,' Jason said. 'It's a computer program. And you're not taking it anywhere.'

Ravi stopped folding and stared at Jason, part of the fabric slipping from his grip to float to the floor. 'A *computer program*? Jason, you are really too much. And, yes, I am

341

taking it. Someone has to honor Sriram's request.'

'Sriram wanted these guys to have it,' Jason said. 'The ones you ripped off. And I'm not going to let you rip them off again.'

'Enough of this bullshit,' Ravi said, throwing the fabric down at his feet, stepping over to his leather shoulder bag that sat by the open stairwell. 'I have the vacation request form Sriram filled out — in his own handwriting. It'll confirm everything I'm saying and shut your ass up.' He undid the gold clasp and started rummaging around, pulling a few papers out of his way. 'Here it is,' he said, pulling a pistol from his bag as he stood.

'What the hell is this?' Narvin said, backing into Attar and Manny as Jason took a step forward.

'It's proof I was right,' Jason said.

Arm straight out, Ravi pointed the gun at Jason. 'I don't want to hurt anybody. I'm only taking back what's mine.'

Jason took a half step forward, stopping when he saw Ravi tighten his grip. 'Sriram was patient,' Jason said. 'It took him years but he was finally going to get even. But you found out that he was planning to steal Raj-Tech's big breakthrough, bring it here to India, maybe start a new computer company, maybe bring this one back.' He waved an arm around the empty space, Ravi's eyes staying fixed on his chest.

'You went to their apartment. Maybe he saw it coming, maybe he fought back, I don't know. But you shot them — both of them — then made it look like Sriram did it. That was the easy part — the police just about let you write the report. The hard part was figuring out how Sriram was getting it out of the country. You didn't find out that it was in the sari until I was already in India. You tried to have the bag stolen — you even had Taco try to kill me.'

'The man was insane,' Ravi said, his eyes softer as he spoke. 'He should have done it the way I told him. He wasn't supposed to get hurt.'

'Like your man on the train?' Jason said, holding his arms far out to his sides, sliding a foot forward. 'So now what? You going to shoot us too?'

'Jesus, Jason,' Narvin said. 'Don't give him any ideas.'

'Stay back,' Ravi said, reaching down, picking up the tail end of the sari, gripping it in his left hand, twirling his arm in a tight circle, winding the sari around his forearm as he spoke. 'No one has to get hurt. I just want to take this and leave.' With every turn the silky red fabric moved towards him across the concrete floor.

'Excuse me,' Rachel said. 'Isn't this where someone points out that he'll never get away with it and that the minute he leaves we'll call the police?'

Manny sighed, watching as Ravi wound more and more of the sari around his arm, the gun steady despite his jerky movement. 'This is India. The truth is he will get away with it. If he has not yet bought off the police he will most assuredly do so later.'

Rachel turned to Jason. 'After all you went through? The monkey, that guy shooting at you? Your arm? You almost got killed for this thing. And that's it, you're just going to give it to him?'

'That's it,' Jason said without emotion. 'It's over.'

With a final sweep of his arm, the last of the fabric jumped from the floor. Rachel held tight to the top corner, a yard of red silk and a yard of embroidered pallu suspended between them. Ravi gave the fabric a sharp tug but Rachel refused to let go.

'Give it to him, Rachel,' Jason said. 'It's not worth it.'

Rachel looked down the fabric at the end of the gun. 'No.'

'Please, miss,' Manny said. 'Let it go.'

'Rachel, don't be stupid,' Narvin said. 'Let go.'

She shifted her feet, widening her stance.

Ravi gave the sari another tug, Rachel tugging back, both hands on the sari now, leaning back, Ravi telling her to let go, his teeth clenched, the gun, still trained on Jason, swinging over to point at Rachel, the others shouting, waving their arms, Jason stepping in front of Rachel, grabbing the sari, pulling it from her grip, the sound of ripping fabric as she fell backwards, kicking the cook stove forward as Jason dropped the fabric, the room darkening as the end of the sari draped down over the open flame, then brighter as the sari caught fire.

With a snap of his arm, Ravi yanked the sari free of the stove, the blazing fabric arching high in the air, flying back at him, a wooshing sound as the flames raced up the sari, still damp with kerosene. Ravi, stumbling backwards now, the gun still held out, his left arm turning, fighting to unravel the wad of silk, loops of fabric dancing beside him, fanning the rushing flames, sooty embers filling the air. Ravi screamed as the others shouted, telling him to stop, warning him, moving towards him, backing off when the first shot sent chips of concrete flying from the floor, the second scraping the ceiling,

their heads ducked, no one seeing Ravi topple
backwards into the open stairwell, his frantic
struggle to regain his balance, the flaming
sari following him down past four flights of
unfinished steps to the dark entrance hall
of Bangalore World Systems.

# 29

As the elevator doors opened at the hotel lobby, Jason realized — for the second time in two days — that he should have taken the stairs.

He half expected a squad of khaki-shirted police officers, guns drawn, grabbing him by the collar and tossing him down hard on the polished floor, shouting a thousand things at once as they put the iron shackles on him, leading him away, never to be seen again. Instead, as he stepped out into the lobby, a squad of hotel maids ducked behind him into the waiting elevator, each one mumbling a mispronounced good morning as the doors eased closed. The lone strap of his backpack on his shoulder, Jason crossed the lobby to where Manny, Attar, and Narvin sat waiting.

'I hope you're not as tired as you look,' Jason said as he swung his backpack on to the floor, dropping into an overstuffed chair, and rolling up the sleeves on his last semi-clean button-down shirt. 'What time did you finish up last night?'

Manny held up one hand as he used the other to cover a gaping yawn. 'I started back shortly after sunrise. It must have been early — I even beat the rush hour traffic into the city.'

'And you're certain everything is ... ' Jason let his words trail off, not sure what to say.

'Everything is taken care of. The security guard — Mr Chaudhrythe — he saw to most of it.'

'You're sure you can trust this guy?'

Manny lifted his head, his barrel chest rising with a noisy intake of air. 'I trust him more than I trust you.'

'I'm sorry,' Jason said. 'I don't mean to be rude, it's just that it's all kind of strange to me.'

'You think we do this *every* weekend?' Narvin said, getting them all to smile for the first time in hours.

Manny leaned forward, his thick forearms resting on his even thicker thighs. 'Mr Chaudhrythe has many connections in the shantytown, the one we drove through. I am not sure why, but I wanted to make sure that Ravi received the proper rites and prayers.'

'So it's already done? The funeral, or, uh, whatever?'

'Yes, the funeral was this morning, just after sun up. Another naked, nameless beggar has left this mortal coil.'

Jason felt a shiver race up his sweating back, not sure if the others had seen him shake. 'Is there any chance the police will find the grave . . . dig him up . . . ID him from his dental records?'

'This is India, Jason,' Attar said. 'We cremate the dead.'

'You're forgetting the Muslims,' Narvin said. 'And the Parsees. And the Jews. And most of the Christians.'

Manny looked past Attar to Narvin. 'In this case the poor beggar was a Hindu.'

Jason nodded. 'What about you guys? Any problems?'

Attar smirked, flicking his fingers at the suggestion. 'Raj-Tech should really update their security. We used a computer at an all-night Internet café. There were a few firewalls to get around, a tricky little back-trace feature that was a bit stubborn — but nothing too complex.'

'They have a keypad system. Punch in your code to access certain floors, specialized rooms, that sort of thing.' Narvin poked at the air with a stiff index finger as he spoke, hitting imaginary buttons. 'According to Raj-Tech's records — well, according to their records *now* — Ravi was working alone in a secure section of the building yesterday afternoon and, lo and behold, he's still in the building as we speak.'

'Between Manny's Mr Chaudhrythe and our efforts at the computer,' Attar said, looking at his friends, 'Ravi Murty just disappeared.'

'Ten years too late,' Manny said. 'But I will take it nonetheless.'

Jason leaned back in the chair, rubbing the stubble on his chin as he thought, the others swapping yawns and stretches. 'Well, I guess that's it.'

Manny slapped his hands on his knees and stood. 'We best be going. The road to the airport will be crowded already. Now, where is your lovely bride? We do not want you to be late.'

'The way she handled herself last night,' Attar said, the admiration clear in his voice. 'The way she stood up to Ravi, told him no even when he was pointing a gun *right* at her . . .'

Narvin smiled. 'You had better be good to her, Jason. She's one in a million.'

Where to start, Jason thought as he reached for his backpack.

Tell them that everything they said was true?

That she *was* the most amazing woman he had ever met and that he knew he'd never meet anyone like her again?

Or should he start at the beginning, tell them how they had only met that first day in India?

That everything she had told them about their life together was a lie?

That there was no farmhouse, no plans for a family, no memories of Sriram dancing at their wedding, no wedding to have memories of at all?

Or should he just skip ahead, tell them how, when he stepped out of the shower an hour ago, she was gone, the lone airplane ticket from Freedom Tours — the one in his name, the one Danny slipped under their door that morning — was propped up on the pillow in the center of their bed?

'Rachel's not going to be joining us,' Jason said as he climbed out of the chair. 'She has some work to do here for the Fashion Institute. Some rare pieces she has to photograph, a lecture over at the university. She's joining me in Delhi, then we're off to Paris for a week or so.'

Manny's smile grew and he set a fat hand on Jason's back. 'I was hoping you were going to tell us that you had something special planned for that woman.'

They stepped out into the humid Bangalore morning, Manny's white Ambassador parked among the auto-rickshaws and air-conditioned

351

cabs. Manny leaned against the fender, catching his breath before attempting to climb in behind the wheel.

'How about you, Manny?' Jason said. 'You still off to Ooty to see Sriram's mother?'

'Oh. That,' Manny said, ignoring Attar's and Narvin's curious looks. 'You must forgive me for that, Jason. When you told me that Sriram wanted you to deliver a sari to his mother, I knew something was not right. Honestly, I did not know what it was, but I assumed it would be valuable.' He chuckled. 'Unfortunately for us all, it was.'

'Actually,' Jason said, swinging open the passenger door to roll down the window, a blast of hot air blowing past him, 'it was worthless.'

The three men looked at each other. 'Worthless?' Attar said. 'But what about the computer program you said was in the embroidery?'

'If Sriram somehow encoded one of Raj-Tech's programs it could have been worth millions,' Narvin said.

'Ravi saw it as well,' Manny said. 'And he died trying to get it back.'

Jason shook his head. 'Sorry, guys. I realized something this morning when I was putting on my shirt. That sari was defective.'

Manny puffed up his cheeks, sighing a fat

sigh. 'That is silly, Jason. How can a sari be defective?'

'No button hole.'

Manny exchanged glances with Narvin and Attar before turning back to Jason.

'So that's why I know this has to be wrong,' Jason said, pulling a small wad of red fabric from his pocket, the large, cloth-covered button resting in the center of his palm, remembering both the ripping sound that came just before Ravi fell to his death and the pile of his things Rachel had left on the nightstand that morning.

'It's got the same fabric as the sari,' Jason said, holding the bit of cloth so the broad button stood up like a flower, turning it from side to side as he spoke. 'But, if there's no button hole, then someone went through a lot of trouble for nothing. Buying an oversized, two-piece button, opening it up, attaching the fabric, closing it back shut with all that space inside — space big enough to fit, oh I don't know, a postage stamp, a couple M&Ms, a microchip — sewing it on a red sari.' Jason shrugged. 'Seems like a waste of time to me.'

They leaned over the roof of the car to get a better look, their eyes fixed on the button, Narvin grinning, Manny wiping sweat off his forehead with his sleeve, Attar wetting his lips before he spoke, his voice just a whisper. 'What do you think is inside?'

Jason smiled. 'Magic.'

★ ★ ★

He was tempted to cut ahead, but Jason waited as his fellow passengers threaded their way through the single open doorway, their passage slowed by armloads of luggage and shuffle-stepping widows in white saris.

Jason glanced up at the illuminated board that listed both arrivals and departures and hoped that things were running late. Overhead, metallic messages blared out of trashcan-sized speakers, the information unintelligible in Hindi, Tamil, Malayalam, Kannada, and English. Jason held up his ticket at the door, the guard too busy buffing the shine on his uniform belt buckle to notice.

Passing through the final gate, Jason scanned the crowd. To his left, those waiting to depart piled their luggage in stacks and counted up family members, a moment of panic as they patted down pockets, searching for the tickets they held in their hands. To his right, those waiting for the next batch of arrivals checked their watches against the arrival board, tapping watch faces and shaking heads, the pacing and the angry inquiries still an hour away.

In front of him, the Madras Express pulled into the station.

Her baggy jeans, the bullet holes lost in the folds, dipped down on her hips, her black tribal tattoo hard to spot against the rich brown of her tan. Her teeshirt hung loose, wrinkled where it was usually knotted, and she held her backpack low so that it brushed against the dusty concrete as she walked. Poking out of a once-white Blue Jays cap, an auburn ponytail swayed with each step.

'Excuse me,' he said, stepping up behind her, smiling when he saw the look in her eyes as she turned. 'Is this the train we take to the Taj Mahal?'

We do hope that you have enjoyed reading this large print book.

Did you know that all of our titles are available for purchase?

We publish a wide range of high quality large print books including:
**Romances, Mysteries, Classics
General Fiction
Non Fiction and Westerns**

Special interest titles available in large print are:
**The Little Oxford Dictionary
Music Book
Song Book
Hymn Book
Service Book**

Also available from us courtesy of Oxford University Press:
**Young Readers' Dictionary
(large print edition)
Young Readers' Thesaurus
(large print edition)**

For further information or a free brochure, please contact us at:
**Ulverscroft Large Print Books Ltd.,
The Green, Bradgate Road, Anstey,
Leicester, LE7 7FU, England.
Tel:** (00 44) 0116 236 4325
**Fax:** (00 44) 0116 234 0205

## RELATIVE DANGER

### Charles Benoit

Picture a hotel room in Singapore, 1948. A dispute is under way between black marketeer Russell Pearce and an associate, which ends up with Pearce's murder. Fast forward to present-day Pennsylvania, where Pearce's nephew, Doug, receives a letter from a friend of his uncle inviting him to Toronto. Doug accepts . . . On arrival, he is enlisted by the wealthy Edna to play detective and solve the murder of his uncle. But Doug soon knows he's made a mistake and that someone else is interested in his quest . . . From Morocco to Egypt to Bahrain to Singapore, Doug stumbles on, facing danger all the way.

# DARTMOUTH CONSPIRACY

## James Stevenson

September 1942: Luftwaffe pilot Karl Deichman must bomb the Royal Naval College in Dartmouth, despite knowing his cousin and childhood friend is resident there. Yet his orders give him no choice — the attack must proceed . . . After the war, Karl returns to England, haunted by the thought: *Did I kill Andrew?* His quest leads him to a former secret agent, a wartime spy, and an ex-RAF Spitfire pilot; but as he uncovers the secret of the Dartmouth Conspiracy, he is drawn into a lethal trap. And it will be more than sixty years before the final jigsaw-piece falls into place . . .